That afternoon, when the bus's hissing air brakes signaled our stop, we leapt from the bottom step onto the dirt shoulder of the road.

I picked the perfect stone from the side of the road. It had to be small and round, with no sharp edges, and light enough to kick all the way home.

Tessa followed on my heels, talking my ear off, and stepping on the heel of one of my tennies. "Gave you a flat!"

"Back off!" I glared at her. Mama said those shoes were like gold, and we were to protect them. I gave the rock a punt and forged ahead.

Oblivious to things going on out there in the desert, we were lulled into a sense of safety and routine. Like Eve, we didn't feel the danger around us until it was too late to escape. Instead, I should have been paying attention to the truck following us slowly.

Down the deserted road.

Yes, this is our story.

My story.

Praise for *GUNNYSACK HELL*

"An evil man stalks the young daughters of a family in California's high desert in 1962. It's scary enough when he follows them in his truck, but when footprints appear near their isolated cabin, the whole family faces peril. Engagingly written using alternating narrators, this book will grip readers from start to finish."

~*Joseph Bentz (A Son Comes Home)*

~*~

"Pure genius! Told through various family members' points of view, this novel takes readers down a tunnel filled with mystery, thrills, and excitement."

~*L. C. Hayden (Harry Bronson Thriller Series)*

~*~

"This debut novel will make you check the windows and doors and look in on your kids before turning out the lights. Is the house just settling? Or is someone out there?"

~*Cathleen Armstrong (A Place to Call Home Series)*

~*~

"*GUNNYSACK HELL* is a keep-you-up-all-night page-turner with vivid language and captivating characters."

~*Carol Alwood (The Good Shadows Series)*

~*~

"*GUNNYSACK HELL* glimpses inside a family up against the threat of a frightening, surreal menace and whose survival depends upon every member finding a moment of heroism."

~*Daniel R. Marvello (The Vaetra Chronicles)*

Gunnysack Hell

by

Nancy Brashear

Gunnysack Hell

Cover Art by *Jennifer Greeff*

The Wild Rose Press, Inc.
PO Box 708
Adams Basin, NY 14410-0708
Visit us at www.thewildrosepress.com

Publishing History
First Vintage Rose Edition, 2021
Trade Paperback ISBN 978-1-5092-3464-6
Digital ISBN 978-1-5092-3465-3

Published in the United States of America

Dedication

In memory of my mother, Peggy Powell,
who encouraged me to approach life as an adventure
and to always keep the faith

Acknowledgments

Thank you to the many people who helped *Gunnysack Hell* become a reality:

My husband, Patrick, for listening to every word I wrote and feeding me well; Serious Scribblers writing group (Cathleen Armstrong, Susan Beatty, Kathleen Robison); mentors (Joseph Bentz, Laura Drake, L.C. Hayden, Janeen Ippolito); beta readers (Carol Alwood, Cathleen Armstrong, Masha Brashear, James Byrd, Kelly Preston, Kathleen Robison); content experts (Patrick Brashear—construction; Toni Cox—childbirth; Suzanne Engelman—psychological profile; Melissa Morley—historical research; John Preston—wrestling moves; Dottie Saville—man-made lakes).

Technical help and social media: Sandy Barela, Chautona Havig, and Denise Barela; Christopher Brashear, first website and photos; Pam Brashear, social media and consultations; Linda Carroll-Bradd, editing course; Abigail DeJong—Instagram images; Joy Hunt—final website designer; Tami Jeffers, first editor; Julie Williams—formatting; Liz Tolsma—historical blogs; Jeff Parker, law enforcement info; encouragers: Thomas Allbaugh, Susan Daffron, Marti Garlett (first short story), Nilsa Thorsos, Becky Zapatka, and others.

Many thanks to The Wild Rose Press for choosing my book: Ally Robertson, editor extraordinaire and encourager; RJ Morris, Release Team, and Marketing; and Jennifer Greeff (beautiful cover art).

Above all, I want to thank my late mother, Peggy Powell, who always believed in my writing (and me!), and, yes, raised us, for a while, in a little homestead cabin in the Mojave Desert.

Chapter 1
Evil Man - Overture

I must follow the voices
in my head
telling me what to do
to be set free…
set me me me…free…
I watch
I wait
it is not complete
soon
I purify
I anoint
I finish
to be free

Chapter 2
Nonni - The Serpent

I read this morning that Donald Fricker was granted parole after serving twenty years in prison. I'd done my best to banish his name from my memory, but once I saw it in print, the decades disappeared in the flick of a newspaper page. My childhood flooded back to eight-year-old me, too scared to identify him and save my family.

I've written down everything that happened during that six-month period of time so I can finally understand that evil man's plans to destroy our family.

It was May of 1962. My family had recently moved to our new home, our grandparents' one-room homestead cabin in the California high desert with tarpaper and chicken-wire lining the walls. It never occurred to me to ask my father why we had moved from our three-bedroom suburban home by the beach to "off the grid."

All I knew was that we used kerosene lanterns, the chemical outhouse under the tall water tank, a wood-burning stove, and an old-fashioned ice-box that our father replenished with a big block of ice from Jolly's Corner on his way home each day.

We had no television, phone, or neighbors, but Daddy brought home the *Sunday Times*. I read the funnies every week. We had a short stack of books that

I loved. *Alice in Wonderland, The Wizard of Oz, Jack and the Beanstalk, Little House on the Prairie* topped the list.

Daddy often pulled *A Dipper Full of Stars*, which contained stories and charts of our favorite constellations, from the shelf so we could locate them in the brilliant heavens above us. His favorite was Orion, the Hunter; mine was Pleiades, the Seven Sisters. And, of course, I kept a diary in my childish scrawl of everything that happened. I was destined to be a writer.

Tessa, my six-year-old sister, and I walked home alone, every day, from the bus stop, a mile and a half down an isolated dirt road.

That's when it happened, the thing that changed our family. I'll never forget that day. I protected Tessa even though I broke all of my promises to Mama I'd made just the night before. To walk directly home from the bus stop, not to talk to strangers, and to stay away from open wells.

Each morning our father drove us at break-neck speed to our bus stop at the corner of the Lone Wolf Colony, a health retreat for retired telephone company employees, and the main highway. A deserted farmhouse sat directly across from it.

"Crazy driving!" He brushed his dark hair back from his shining green eyes.

"Crazy driving!" Our voices vibrated as our always dusty blue truck bounced along the twisty dirt road. Going for a ride in that truck, anywhere, was an adventure we kids looked forward to.

We followed Mama's other rules, too, but sometimes they changed. After Tessa picked up a baby sidewinder and Daddy had to swing her in a circle to shoot it straight out into the brush, Mama struck snakes off her loving list.

"When you hear the sound of rattles, stand statue still and don't bat an eyelash!" In our drills, we listened for the sound of her shaking the frying pan with popcorn kernels in it. Then, we'd freeze in place.

Mama seemed more concerned about rattle snakes than sidewinders, but to be safe, she taught us to fear all snakes. By the time I was in fifth-grade Snake Education, it was too late for me to reverse my responses. I simultaneously hated and feared snakes.

Even now, I firmly believe that the serpent in the Garden of Eden was the real culprit in the fall of man and that Eve got a bad rap. Those loathsome creatures, living in the sagebrush along our path home and occasionally slithering across the ruts in front of us were diabolical in their intentions to trip us up. Literally.

I'd learned about another danger after eavesdropping on Mama and Daddy when they thought we were asleep inside the cabin.

"The Cold War… protect ourselves… " The tip of Daddy's cigarette glowed orange in the dark.

Mama's words carried to my ready ears. "Remember that cloud? A giant mushroom on the horizon early one morning? A bomb. The government was testing a nuclear bomb and not telling us! Good thing we have a shelter out back."

As I was drinking my sun tea the next day, I asked her, "What's a Cold War? It's hot out here!"

She took her thumb and massaged the wrinkle between my eyebrows. "Don't worry, honey. We have the fallout shelter your grandpa built out behind. Just in case."

"But it's down under the ground, and it's locked!"

"I'll unlock it if we need it, but don't worry. We're safe out here. I promise."

Mama rubbed her rounded belly and waited for my response.

"Okay." I nodded. Even though I still didn't understand, I silently vowed to keep my eyes open for this new danger.

Every morning, before I made it out to the outhouse, I searched the sky. And on the way home from the bus, I scanned again for mushroom clouds along the horizon and up high in the wild blue yonder. Pieces of a jigsaw puzzle I was trying to solve. Danger was in the air.

We ate dinner at the picnic table with the sun setting behind Mt. Baldy. Sometimes Mama cooked my favorite meal of my childhood, a macaroni-and-cheese boxed product made with canned milk, which she then packed into our Bundt cake pan.

Afterwards, she gently tapped it onto a plate and poured a can of drained, canned peas into the middle of the noodle ring. When our garden was producing, we'd put sliced zucchini or green beans in it.

When I smelled the delicious cheesy flavor wafting across the picnic table, my mouth watered, and I could hardly wait for her to finish saying grace.

"Thank you, Jesus, for your many blessings." Mama lifted her head and smiled at us. "Time to pass the Kraft Dinner Ring!"

Even to this day, I associate that comfort food with family memories, snapshots etched into my memory.

Daddy dragged our mattresses out of the cabin, onto the dirt. "Lay down here, quiet. You can sleep outside tonight. Maybe other nights if it's not too cold." He brought out his pickaxe and shovel from the outhouse where they were stored.

We were close enough to the ground for snakes to curl up like coasters on our tummies if they found us. Tessa and I lay there, tingling with fear and anticipation, watching Daddy work on the trenches for the foundation of the new house he was building for us. When it was too dark for him to dig any longer, he put away his tools and returned to the cabin.

We snuggled up, hypnotized by the sparkling majesty above until Tessa broke the silence with a giggle.

Mama poked her head out of the cabin. "You girls go to sleep now. Morning'll be here before you know it. Love you a bushel and a peck!"

"And a hug around the neck!" Our words spiraled into the universe.

"Tessie! Look at the Milky Way, high up there!" I flung my arms around in a big arc and bopped her on the face.

"Ouch!" She rubbed her nose.

"Shhhhh." I turned my attention back to the sky. "We're as small as ants. If anyone in the sky looks down at us, we're just like ants!"

The longer I stared upward, the more invisible I felt. Like I was dissolving into the earth.

"My moon!" Tessa giggled and pointed to the glowing orange orb rising above the silhouette of the mountains to the north of us.

"Tessa, I double-dare you not to blink!" Stars shot

down, fizzling before they reached us. The nighttime whirring of the katydids mesmerized us.

We both stared without blinking until our eyes were as dry as the dirt we lay on, and we had to give in. The temperature dropped, sending goose bumps marching along my arms, and the stars danced above us.

We woke to the stillness of a new day, punctuated by the faint yip of coyotes. The desert floor was still carpeted with colorful and exotic wildflowers sprouting next to creosote bushes, Joshua trees, and white-tasseled Yuccas. We lived in an enchanted land.

A budding author, I created a one-page story about sand fairies that lived in the wildflowers. Tessa was a terrific audience of one, and soon she could recite it from memory. Her enthusiasm kept me writing, something I've continued to do daily.

The days passed with me walking home from the bus stop with Tessa, ever on guard for snakes and occasionally glancing at the sky. Sometimes, I heard the faraway rumble of the train.

That afternoon, when the bus's hissing air brakes signaled our stop, we leapt from the bottom step onto the dirt shoulder of the road.

I picked the perfect stone from the side of the road. It had to be small and round, with no sharp edges, and light enough to kick all the way home.

Tessa followed on my heels, talking my ear off, and stepping on the heel of one of my tennies. "Gave you a flat!"

"Back off!" I glared at her. Mama said those shoes were like gold, and we were to protect them. I gave the rock a punt and forged ahead.

Oblivious to things going on out there in the desert, we were lulled into a sense of safety and routine. Like Eve, we didn't feel the danger around us until it was too late to escape. Instead, I should have been paying attention to the truck following us slowly.

Down the deserted road.

Yes, this is our story.

My story.

Chapter 3
Claire - Long Trek Home

Although it's early enough my daughters haven't left yet, the moisture in the morning air already clings to my skin predicting a storm that's building to a grand finale.

I gather the remnants of breakfast from the picnic table and glance up at gray clouds skirting the sky. My eyes drift to the windy road out front that leads to the bus stop, a mile and a half away, where Tessa and Nonni pick up the bus.

"Girls," I call as I stack the cereal bowls. "Time to get into gear!" Something jabs me in the rib, and when I grab my side, I feel a sharp edge, maybe an elbow, rippling against my abdomen from the inside out.

"You, little lassie, will have plenty of time to kick up your heels soon." I rub my hand along the underside of my swollen belly with its new batch of stretch marks. "Just don't do too much of it now."

Rand steps out of the cabin. "What'ja say, hon?"

"Nothing. Just hollering to the girls to get ready to leave. And talking to our soon-to-be acrobat. She's doing some serious jumping today."

"They're putting on their shoes. And how're you so sure it's a girl?" As he strolls by, he pats my shoulder with his free hand. He continues to his truck where he places his lunch box and thermos on the seat.

9

"It's mother's intuition." I'm filled with conviction.

He returns and wraps both his arms around me as far as they can reach, which isn't enough. I don't remember being this large with either of the girls. The nurse told me that each child stretches the muscles a little more, and I've evidently outgrown my body. This will be my third, and last, pregnancy.

I nestle into his chest and smell Old Spice. "Sprucing up for the boss? Or just covering up the lack of long, hot showers?" My little joke brings another squeeze from him and a protest from within.

We both jump, and I yelp. "Another kick!"

He smiles down at me. "Wow! She'll grow up to be a Rockette!" His fingers find their way to my ear lobe and give it an affectionate little rub. I lean into him, and there's a long pause. "Don't forget Ma's coming tomorrow."

His comment jolts me back into reality. I couldn't forget that if I tried. He'd overridden my arguments and called his mother from the pay phone at Jolly's Corner to invite her to help with the girls and baby.

Mother Grace, as she insists I call her, is so critical of my mothering and housekeeping skills that I wish she weren't coming. Even though I'm so exhausted I barely stagger through each blistering day.

The weather has turned from seasonally warm to hot, real hot. This one-room log cabin, which served the O'Brien family as a getaway for more than twenty years, features only a single window and door. I'm suffocating. With one more adult and a new baby in that room, I don't know how we'll survive.

Tessa scrambles out of the cabin onto the dirt.

"Can't catch me!" Her taunt carries through the warm morning air.

Nonni is on her tail. "Told you not to touch my stuff!"

"Come on over here." I motion them to me

Nonni protests. "She took my socks!"

Tessa looks down at the ruffled cuffs, and a small smile steals across her face.

"No time to change now. You, little missy, can wash them when you get home. Both of you, come here." They draw near, and I kiss them on their foreheads, one at a time. I breathe in their fresh morning scent and am surprised when a sense of foreboding settles on me. I give them an extra nuzzle for good measure.

"Get your lunch boxes from the picnic table and head toward the truck. Your daddy's waiting."

There are five weeks of school left. At seven-thirty each morning, Rand drops them where they'll be picked up by the Lone Wolf Colony. A windbreak of Italian Cypress trees protects the cabins and main house. Sometimes there's activity going on there, but mostly it's deserted.

An empty farmhouse is situated on the other side of the road with a scrawny oak tree providing shade for inhabitants who no longer live there. There must be some kind of underground water table sustaining that tree, and those at the Colony, for them to survive in this mostly-parched terrain.

Our acreage is bone dry, without a well, and I'm jealous of all those trees and what they symbolize. After all, this area is called Apple Valley although I've yet to see an apple tree here. One day, I'll plant my own trees in our yard. And with no well, I'll be just fine watering them from our tank on the tower.

The day slides by while I meander through one task at a time. Hand washing a bucket of clothes. Hanging them on the makeshift line to dry before night arrives. Sweeping the dust from the cabin floor. Making a new bottle of sun tea, which we also call Mormon tea and brew from a plant that grows out here in the wild.

My feet ache, so I take a rest in the rocking chair on porch.

Around three o'clock, I stand out front and squint at the yellow bus stopped at the end of the long dirt road. Two tiny figures, so far away I can hardly see them, dismount.

In my mind, I envision them on a map, moving steadily down Chipmunk Trail toward me. Rand and I have only one truck, which he drives to work.

When Mother Grace arrives in her old Studebaker, we'll probably use her car only for priorities or emergencies. Gas is expensive, and the girls are healthy.

They can walk home, and I'm here to watch. I'm thankful we live in one of the safest areas in Southern California, with only snakes and spiders as predators. Unless the Communists shoot missiles or drop bombs on us. But Rand says that's not going to happen. And we're ready if they do.

As peaceful as it is out here in the wilderness, there are things I miss. I miss walking the girls to school around the corner. I miss chatting with their teachers and neighborhood mothers. I miss our former middle-class luxury in our two-bedroom home near the beach with the cheerful flowered wallpaper in the dining room. I miss the amenities of modern living.

And I miss my husband bringing home a regular paycheck, especially with another payment due for the baby's delivery. Rand's gone every day and sometimes into evenings working hard to earn the money we need for this, but his well job is about to run out.

I keep that worry to myself. It wasn't his fault he got fired, and we had to move out here in a hurry.

What I don't miss is his drinking his way up the corporate ladder, and that's a relief after his alcoholic father died from liver failure last year. And I don't miss worrying about the climbing crime rate in the city in which we no longer live.

Our circumstances are primitive, and I'm doing things the old-fashioned, time-intensive way. But when Mother Grace is up to her elbows in soapsuds, things should be a bit easier, and that will be my consolation for her being here.

The sun slowly works its way across the sky. In a couple of hours, the sunset's glow on the tin roofs between our cabin and Mt. Baldy will create the illusion of the desert floor in flames. This terrifies me after last year's fire season, but I have to admit that the effect is stunning.

I move to the line where I touch the skirts and shirts the girls wear to school drying. There's still some dampness in them. I hope they dry before the clouds let loose. I pinch a clothespin to loosen Tessa's sheet and gather it into my arms.

Even though it has wind-dried, small smatterings of dirt from the frolicking breeze stick to it. Tessa's bed wetting is a problem, so I hang the sheet out to dry in the morning and only wash it every couple of days or so. Our cabin has a slight odor of ammonia that we've learned to ignore.

Now that evenings have warmed up, we sometimes lie on mattresses under the stars and breathe in the starlight accompanied with the smell of creosote, the earthy aroma of rain.

Once in a while, when the girls have fallen asleep, Rand and I steal some alone-time. Cuddling is a lot harder, anyway, with a belly the size of a San Francisco cable car, something Rand promised me I'd ride one day.

This is our last night before his mother arrives and we lose all of our privacy.

I glance down the lane. The red of Tessa's dress pulls my focus to her leapfrogging with both feet while Nonni kicks a rock as they traverse their way home.

My eyes water, more than justified by the wind or bright sun, as that fierce mother love raises her head. I feel a throbbing sensation in my womb and push my fist deep into the small of my back.

Not yet, I whisper to myself. *A month to go.*

The girls move faster now, running, and stirring up scuffs of dust. I wipe the back of my arm across my wet cheeks, push my hair back from my sweaty forehead, and shield my eyes to see them more clearly.

Even though my feet are swollen, and my body resists a slow plod in this hot, humid air, my heart leaks gladness as I walk toward them, arms wide open, and raindrops splatter on my face like tears.

Chapter 4
Randall - Corporation to Cabin

"Ma will hafta sleep here." I push the mattress against the wall.

"So close to us? Sheesh! She's only twelve inches away!" Claire shoves it farther away.

There's a small space next to us for the baby. The girls' bunk beds line most of the opposite wall. The icebox, wood-burning stove, and a small table are positioned on the third wall beside the only window. The dresser, snugged in next to the door, is topped with shelves.

No doubt about it. This place is crowded. And with Ma and the baby coming, our quarters are growing closer. One thing's for sure. If we're going to stay here, with or without Ma, we need more space. I've already begun digging the new foundation.

"We're packed in like sardines." She flits around the cabin. "I didn't ask her to come."

I place a hand on her arm and give her a sympathetic look. "Had to do it. You're gonna need some help for a while, and I'm busy working my butt off."

Her eyes brim with tears. We're just too far out here in the boondocks. I have to work. We still owe a final payment to the doctor and maternity home.

"I'm willing to go it alone. We'll be fine." She

straightens her shoulders.

"Can't leave you, the girls, and the new baby out here alone. Without a vehicle. Or help. I'm sorry, hon. It's temporary."

"You owe me big time, mister. She goes when I say." Her eyes challenge me.

"When you say. We okay, then?"

She nods, and I know I've won on this issue.

The squeals of the girls playing out front filter to us. Claire tips her head, listening, and turns back to me. The wrinkle between her eyebrows deepens.

"Something else the matter?" I catch her expression. Unfinished business.

"Just anxious about… things."

"Like…" I immediately kick myself for having opened up this door of discussion. I can guess what she's about to bring up.

"Like…your work. Or, soon, your lack of it."

"I'm bringing home more cash tonight. For the money can."

"Baby's due soon. Doctor says, this being the third, she might even come early."

"Hang in there. Everything will work out." All these years we've jumped over hurdles and come out on the other side of the prickly hedges, further ahead. Even when things like drinking my way up the corporate ladder got in the way. Claire's accusations had made me think, and I didn't like what I saw.

"Watch out. You're turning into a lush like your old man."

We still argue but usually circle back around to making up and healing the gaps. Which don't last long.

After we married, she began her own laundry

business so I could cut back on work hours and finish college. But I didn't end up doing that because the company promoted me to quality control with required overtime. I loved that job, which was all about doing things right in the first place. And faster and cheaper.

I practiced on Claire, following her around the house, coaching her on how to be more time efficient in completing household routines and taking care of our children. That didn't last long.

"Back off, mister." She'd pointed the knife she was drying in my direction. "I'm doing my best. Back off! They're your kids, too. You can lend a hand here."

"I'm trying to help you!"

"I don't want your criticism. I want your help!"

She could be like that sometimes. Over-reacting. Emotional. Dismissing my suggestions.

Or like when I got fired for writing, on my own time, for an organization the corporation thought would hurt the company image. I didn't reckon on what would come down on me at work. Five whole years there, and boom! I'm out on the street.

I'd sold our home to a buddy from work. We couldn't afford the payment without my job, and we hadn't lived there long enough to make much of a profit. I'd traded our almost-new Plymouth station wagon for a 1950 Chevy pickup truck, which the four of us barely squeezed into. I stacked the back with our goods, punched the accelerator, and hurried us to my parents' homestead cabin. Three hours away. In the middle of nowhere.

As we'd turned off the paved road by the Lone Wolf Colony, the final piece of our journey to our new home, Nonni'd burped. Tessa laughed so hard she snorted. We joined in until we hit a bump, all of us bouncing, airborne, in unison.

Claire wrapped her arms around her swollen belly. Her tears of laughter dissolved into a river of sadness. "We left the cradle behind! It was for ALL our babies!"

I flashed back to a mental picture of it sitting in the garage. I'd been planning to tie it last, upside down, on top of our Grapes-of-Wrath heap. We were more than two hours out by this time. No way I was going back.

"I'll build you a new one."

"That one has history. My family history! I slept in it when I was a baby. And so did Nonni and Tessa."

I decided to keep my eyes on the road and my mouth shut until we'd arrived at the cabin.

We'd landed on our feet in a rent-free home. And I'd found a job right away. Even if it's running out in a couple of weeks, I have a lead on another job that might pull me away during the week. One of the reasons I invited Ma here.

Yes, it's a race against time to pay the doctor at the Mojave Maternity Home, but it will work out. I step closer to Claire and rub the furrow between her brows with my calloused thumb.

She sighs. I pull her into my embrace and breathe into her soft hair.

She sniffs. "So much has happened this year. The corporation's unfair treatment of you. I'll never forgive them. Moving here. The baby due. And your work's running out. And now your mother's coming."

I speak in what I hope is a reassuring tone. "We'll get through this and into the future in a snap. A fresh beginning."

She looks up at me and pushes away. "I'm

broiling." She wipes a small line of sweat from her upper lip. Claire's always been willing to sacrifice. Me, too. For the good of our family. And here we are, a month later, rooted into Ma's homestead cabin, the O'Brien family getaway.

I turn to Claire. "Time to focus on my future moneymaker. My brainstorm of raising chickens in the state-of-the art facility I've designed." Contracting with a consortium that supplies poultry to grocery stores throughout California. We have plenty of acreage for this business right here on these five acres. Surrounded by an immense desert dotted with empty 1940s cinderblock, tin, and wood shacks. The cacophony of cackles won't bother neighbors with the closest at least a mile away as the hawk flies. It's a perfect location for this venture.

"I know you can do it." She nods. "We can do it. Even if we didn't expect to try this for at least five years."

This whole sequence of events, with me getting fired and us leaving the city, has pushed us closer, and sooner, to following this dream. Our dream.

"These chicks will be our means to making a living. Hang in there with me, okay?" I make a squawking sound and flap my elbows. She laughs. No matter what, she's my rock. She supports my dreams.

This new business and its income will sustain a more modern style of living. The future brings new opportunities. Claire and I'll begin fresh. The girls are up for the adventure. The new baby is coming. I haven't had a drink in a month. And I'm filled with hope even if Ma's going to be snoring in my ear.

It's time to reinvent myself. Just as soon as the

baby is born.
I have big ideas.
And lots of plans.

Chapter 5
Nonni - Fairy Wings

"Daddy! Daddy! The water tower's buzzing!" I pull him to the back of the cabin and point up. A blanket of red insects with slim fairy wings clings to our tank, atop our wooden outhouse with our rustic toilet, a chemical honey pot, inside.

Above, that huge galvanized steel tank, about thirty feet up, is where we get all of the water we use, five hundred gallons of precious water that has to be refilled from time to time.

"Do they sting?" Hopping from foot to foot, I balance the pros and cons of using the bathroom underneath all the buzzing.

I've already fallen into the toilet once and ended up with a formaldehyde burn on my tender bottom from which it took a week to recover. Ever since, I always check two or three times before sitting down to make sure the aluminum seat is in place.

Or maybe I should try for the shelter of nearby creosote bushes.

I've never seen these flying bugs before and they worry me, but so do the snakes out in the brush. It's a toss up.

"Nope. Just don't rile them up, baby girl." Daddy squints at the sight. "Someday we'll have indoor plumbing, but until then, the old water tank will have to do."

That won't happen for another three years. Water and money rule our parents' lives, but we kids don't know that.

"I'm not a baby!" I jut my chin out. "I'm in the third grade!"

"But you'll always be my *first* baby girl."

I smile, smug in that knowledge. I'm first before Tessa and also before whatever the new baby will be. And I'm hoping for another girl.

Within a couple of days, the flying ants mysteriously disappear. Daddy's digging a well for Mr. Ramirez and is gone every day, all day long. I wish we had a well, too, but according to Mama, there isn't a water table anywhere under our five acres.

"Take this water witch." She holds a forked branch in front of her. "See how I search for water?"

She demonstrates walking with the pointy end in front of her. "It'll dip if there's anything down there." It stays as even as a flapjack flipper. "See. Nothing here. Go on, now."

Tessa and I locate small branches to make our own magic water tools and then we run around the front of the cabin, stopping occasionally, as we hunt for water.

I suspect this is more of an activity to keep us entertained than an expectation that we might actually find something, and that's okay with me.

While Daddy's away working on the well one afternoon, the water deliveryman drives around to the back of the cabin. Mama instructs him to fill the tank up to the quarter mark, and she shoos us into the cabin, so we won't be in the way.

He backs his truck up close to the water tower and

rolls out the hose. The motor thumps as the water is pumped up into the tank.

Tessa and I stand on our bare tiptoes on the table with our heads hanging out of the open casement window.

All we see is the back of the man's neck and the silhouette of his hat, and even though I cup my ears to hear better, I only catch disjointed snippets.

A deep-throated voice says, "…new…this route."

Mama's reply drifts through the window. "Randall…Phelan…next month."

It's boring grown-up talk, not worth my effort, so I give it up and play checkers with Tessa on the floor. The thumping noises stop.

"Crown me!"

Tessa makes a face and places a red tile on mine, and I have a new queen.

"Nah nah ne nah nah!" I do my 1960s victory dance around Tessa who sticks her foot out and trips me. I get up, dust off my scuffed knees, and give her a nasty look.

"Come out." Mama interrupts. "Nonni, take your sister and work on your game some more. No arguing."

She often refers to us as wild children who live to drive her crazy. Somedays maybe we do. Today she rubs her round belly and sighs. "Just try to get along. Lordy. Lordy."

We bump up next to her and take off in a game of tag. I race in a big circle eight, with Tessa screeching behind, by the cabin and around the water tank.

When we ring around to the front, I keep a watchful eye on the truck, which has reached our bus stop by the main road, until its dusty trail disappears into the sky like smoke.

After our run, I retrieve the rake from its resting place on the front porch of the cabin and continue designing my latest rendition of Zig Zag, which I'd barely begun the day before.

Really, it was a precursor to Pac Man, which wouldn't come along for another two decades. I didn't know that then or maybe I could have made a bundle on it later.

I created my legendary game on the hard, barren dirt out front where there's a long enough stretch of lane to land a small Cessna, which is what my parents' friend, Nick, who worked with Daddy at the factory, did last weekend. Daddy knows how to fly it, too.

This quiet time, an hour or so before twilight, is ideal for working on my game. The heat has died down, and it's unlikely my ridged designs will be disturbed.

The sun slowly shifts downward toward the crest of Mount Baldy, and golden streaks from heaven scratch themselves into the horizon.

The deliveryman had already been here, and Daddy knows not to run over my track.

I drag the rake precisely in the shape of a large oval to create the outside boundary. Next, I'll build trails that twist back and forth on each other, but only a few of them will connect to the safe zone.

The rest will dead-end in tidy swirls I've perfected by anchoring the rake in one spot and marching the flat, metal tines in a circle.

"Tessa. Get us some rocks." She scampers off into the brush. "And watch out for snakes!"

"Sammy Snake!" She shakes her rear end at me and takes off giggling.

I study my design with its round safe zone, just big enough for one person, in the very heart of the game. In the rules I invented, whoever's "it" counts to ten with covered eyes.

The hunted has enough time to burrow into the interior of the game on one of the paths before the chase begins. Often, we find ourselves on different tracks near each other, but my rules clearly state you have to be directly behind someone, on the same path, to tag her out.

Then, the game begins again with roles reversed. But if the hunted makes it to the middle, the safe zone, she can pop out the other side—and the pursuer can't get her.

I'm focused on the design when Daddy turns the corner, home from his busy day. He waves at me and maneuvers his truck past my artistic designs, gives the tires a playful spin, and brakes to a stop.

Mama steps from the cabin, wiping her hands on her apron, and motions him out back to the water tank. Tessa and I trail behind.

Daddy climbs up the tall ladder, all the way to the top, unscrews a metal cap, and drops in some chlorine from a little bottle he pulls from the pocket of his khaki work pants. Finished, he hops down from the bottom rung.

"Nothing better than a tank of water to hold you over for a few weeks." He rubs his hands together. "And only a few wings left from our pesky friends."

Looking back, I realize that those flying ants represented the instinct to survive in a parched land with the only water tower for miles around directly behind our cabin.

When they took flight, they must have looked like a warning from the Bible. A dark shadow in the sky. We didn't see them arrive or leave.

How simple life was then with our family encapsulated in our little cabin on its wide stretch of open land below the expansive sky.

I believed our parents had created an invisible safe zone. They believed it, too.

I guess the challenge is that sometimes the track blows away, and you can find yourself running blind in the dust. Sometimes it's not even a game anymore.

Sometimes there's no place to run to at all.

Chapter 6
Tessa - Special Gift

For art today, I choose the brightest crayons from the big box on Mrs. Williams' desk and draw thick stripes of color onto a pink sheet of construction paper.

After I've done that, I peel the paper off a black crayon, lay it on its side, and rub it all over the paper until everything is black.

Now for the best part. I scratch a design through the black crayon with one of the pennies Mrs. Williams gave each of us.

Magic! I've made a beautiful rainbow in red, yellow, purple, blue, and orange.

"Tessa, that's a creative design." Even Mrs. Williams smiles at me for five seconds when she sees it.

Colors make me happy, and they show things about people.

Mama knows this. "Shhhhhhhh. Let's keep this a secret, just for our family, because others might not understand. You have a special thing going on here!"

I see colors around people and things, and then I guess what they're like and how they feel. Or if they're happy. Or mad.

No one else except Mama knows I can do this.

Nice people have fuzzy lines around them in soft Easter-egg colors like pink or yellow or blue or green.

Mean or angry people have dark colored fuzzy lines around them in red or dark brown.

My last teacher, Mrs. Lighthouse, twinkled light blue, a happy color.

My new teacher, Mrs. Williams, has medium green—not exactly dark, but not bright or happy either.

I only saw the color red one time and that was around a man leaving Jolly's Corner. That's where we buy ice for our cabin.

I didn't see his face, just the back of him as he left the store. The outline of the backside of him was red. I felt danger, and it smelled like vinegar.

Mama said, "God gave you a special gift, so he may ask you to use it one day."

I hope I don't see that color again. It makes me feel creepy, and people don't want to hear a little kid like me talking about creepy things.

Lots of times, people don't listen to me anyway. They think I don't know things, but I know lots of stuff!

I wish Mrs. Williams liked me more, but she doesn't because I can't read yet and I'm new in class. I'm only in the first grade, and I'm trying.

But at least she liked my picture today.

I need to learn to read right away. Mama's belly is big, and I want to read to the baby when she is born.

And Mama says she's coming soon!

Chapter 7
Gracie - Legacy

I'm kick-me-in-the-heart surprised Claire agreed for me to come to the homestead, actually *my* homestead, since we don't see eye-to-eye on hardly nothing. With that baby coming any time and the two youngsters in school, she must be desperate.

Of course, it was Sonny that called so mebbe I'm giving her credit where none's due.

They need my help, and I can work hard. I ain't no goldbricker. My daddy was a sharecropper in Louisiana, so from the time I could bend over to pick cotton, I worked the fields alongside my family. Until I got married at seventeen and finally moved out to California.

I reckon I can take nothing and make it into something. Disappointment don't set me back. No. It don't.

I can bake honey wheat bread from scratch. Sew a dress without a pattern. Grow tomatoes, plums, and beans in a cup of dirt. Can them for winter. Make quilts from scraps of my life with my eyes shut.

But I could not make my husband stop drinking, and Pops drank until it killed him. But not before they amputated his leg.

That's another darn thing. Randall was drinking, too, when he worked for that automobile-making company. Getting fired was the best thing that could have happened to him.

He's here living in our cabin in Apple Valley and has big plans to raise chickens once he can earn the money after the baby comes.

Pops and I hadn't been out to the cabin in the last year, with him sick and all, so I'm fine with them all living here.

But nobody better forget that old man and me built this log cabin in the middle of nowhere on free land we grabbed as recreational homesteaders on this land cattle ranchers used to lease from the federal gov'ment.

My aunt, who died a few years back, was out there one night when a bear came and knocked the old outhouse right over, splintering it to toothpicks. Auntie Louella hollered so loud that she would a woken the neighbors if we'd had any.

We'd had absolutely no luck in finding a well on this dry chunk of land. After we built a big wooden structure, we put a big metal water tank on top for drinking and washing stuff.

I don't care what they say. You cain't wash a pan all the way clean with dirt.

Before Pops' liver gave out, we had a fallout shelter, which I call a bomb shelter, delivered out to the property.

A big old truck hauled it in, the long way around, under the power poles from the east side of the valley, because it would not have made it over the bumps and ruts of our dirt road. And it made an unusual sight along the way, that's for sure.

After the last big war and how the world is now, it just makes plain old-fashioned sense to have somewhere safe to hide if everything goes to hades in a hand basket. Especially out in the middle of nowhere. Who knows what those Communists might do next?

It took us most of a year to dig the space deep enough for it out back in our five acres, hidden in sagebrush. We welded it together to make a hidey-hole beneath the desert floor.

After attaching the roof with the metal door in it that I hafta swing back flat against the dirt to get inside, we worked below.

I've climbed many-a-time down the attached metal ladder, about eight feet to the floor, to add more of my canned goods and other supplies to the shelves we placed along the walls.

Mostly it's acting like a storage room, but if'n someone drops the big bomb on us, we have a place to hide away.

If truth be told, since Pops died last year, it's been lonely even though he was a cantankerous old coot. Doing my best, keeping busy with my garden and canning.

One night, out of the blue, Randall calls to ask where I buried the key to the cabin. And now, a month later, he asks me to come out to help Claire.

You could have knocked me over with a feather, and her baby is coming any time.

My next-door neighbors here by my home at the beach have promised to water my tomatoes, bell peppers, and squash in exchange for some of the produce so I could go out there.

If I can get home before the growing season is done, I'll do me some more canning for next year.

I put a couple of full-grown plants, mostly

zucchini, tomatoes, and green beans from my garden, on the front passenger seat with the intention of getting them rooted in the desert dirt before it's too hot.

I've stuffed Sally, my old Studebaker, with supplies and started out at noon, planning to arrive in the daylight.

I cain't admit it out loud, but I'm a mite sad as I turn off the main highway where the Lone Wolf Colony sits near rusty mailboxes and feel a bit like I'm coming home from a long trip away.

The long line of cypress trees that the Wolf planted two decades back are swaying and whistling in the wind, a sound you never forget. Situated kitty corner, the deserted farmhouse hunkers down with its sad scorched boards peeling. The old oak tree shows a sparse crown of leaves.

I do a double-take when a truck pulls around the backside. When I look back, there ain't nothing there.

That's the problem since Pops died. My mind wanders and sudden-like I'm seeing things. Sometimes even hearing him speak inside my mind.

It's a miracle I got here though it took me four hours instead of three. I drove past winery after winery, ignoring rows of grape stakes trying to hypnotize me.

I stopped at the fruit stand before the Cajon Pass to pick up some strawberries, something I didn't have in my home garden. Nestled them in the back next to the rice, oatmeal, and my favorite cast-iron fry pan.

Last stop was Jolly's Corner, about five miles back. I hustled in to pick up a fresh block of ice and a package of ground beef.

I would almost kill for one of those frosty cold Coca Colas in a bottle with carbonation so fierce that it scratches the back of your throat. But I got the diabetes now and have to stay away from sugar.

Dagnabbit. I gotta hurry because I see water dripping onto my floorboard from the box holding the ice.

I am a combination of jittery-nerved and trepidatious. Randall and the kids'll be glad to see me. But Claire? I don't know about that girl.

He didn't even tell me he married her until after the fact, and I have placed the blame on that girl ever since for anything bad that happens. Even for them moving out here.

She needs to prove herself to me before I'll give her my confidence.

But I do have some secret forgiveness for her in my heart. She did give me those two beautiful granddaughters, and the baby coming soon could be a boy.

A real O'Brien boy to carry on our legacy!

Chapter 8
Randall - Moonlight Stroll

Ma babysits for us tonight. I drive Claire to meet Annie and Hank Ritchie, our closest neighbors, about two miles away. Ma says she's only staying until the baby is born and a couple of weeks old, so tonight's a good time for Claire to meet them.

Without a phone out here, we're dropping in. They're the folks who hooked me up with their friend, Mr. Ramirez, who hired me to help dig his well for his compound. The Ritchies have a small cabin with an old bus parked alongside it.

We're about halfway there when the truck lurches. Then stops. Outta gas. Outta luck. I can't believe I didn't check the gauge earlier, but I was in a hurry to get home to see Ma.

Claire glares at me with those dagger eyes she reserves for times like this. A look with a thousand sharp unspoken words.

"Honey." I soften my voice. "We're almost there. I'm sure they'll have extra gas we can bum off them."

Claire looks at the thin strapped, gold sandals she put on for this special occasion. She sighs. "I don't know how far I can walk in these."

I open her door and hold her hand as she awkwardly slides her swollen feet to the ground.

Maybe there's a way to retrieve this warm evening.

I look up and feel the magic of Venus twinkling brightly in the violet, star-studded sky. It's breath taking.

I can tell, however, that Claire isn't enjoying it the way I am. She sighs again, pulls away, and walks unsteadily on the uneven dirt road.

I stride ahead, on the lookout for holes and bumps. The weak beam of my flashlight plays on the dirt road in front of us. "Be careful!" I call out.

"Big rock poking out there." I flash the beam down at it so Claire will see it.

"*You* be careful," she snipes. I whip around to look at her, the beam from the flashlight fanning in a circle. The light flickers out. I shake the flashlight, trying to infuse life into it.

Nothing happens.

Any peace I had flees. I am seized with an impulse to heave the damn cylinder as far as I can into the brush that surrounds us. The flashlight is as dark as the car is non-moving.

Another item to put on my to-do list for when I have two nickels to rub together. Which will only happen after I pay for the Maternity Home. That birthing payment is on the absolute top of the list.

We're running out of time, so I've just kept working harder. And faster.

The minute I think I'm ahead, something else happens. Sometimes big and sometimes small. And I'm supposed to be the efficiency expert. Case in point.

Two strikes against me in the last five minutes. But, hey. Who's keeping score? It's best to keep these observations to myself.

"Sorry, babe," I call out. I swivel around to look at

our destination.

"It's okay," she replies in a small, resigned tone. "These things happen. I guess."

We continue in silence, the only sounds dirt and gravel crunching underfoot. I concentrate on moving my feet, something I can control.

Looking ahead, I notice the light-colored sandy desert floor with the dark silhouettes of Joshua trees rising up from it.

I walk, sloughing my worries as we near the glowing cabin ahead.

Out here, distances are deceiving. The air magnifies objects, making them appear closer than they are. Just when you think you're almost there, they ripple out of range.

I mull my thoughts over about the day while plodding forward, careful to stay near Claire. Mr. Ramirez paid me in cash, which I'll add to the can when we get back to the cabin. This job's almost finished.

He recommended me to an investor, Mr. Henderson, who is short-handed in the final phase of building a private ski-boat resort lake.

The project's located about two hours away, roughly a four-hour drive each day. If he hires me, I'll pitch a sleeping bag for a couple of nights between trips home.

I feel a little guilty I won't be around to help with the family. I'll talk Ma into staying longer even if Claire won't be happy with this idea.

I hear whirring overhead in the dark and see the flashing lights of a small plane flying over. A smile plays across my lips in the dark as I remember co-piloting Nick's Cessna out near out near Joshua Tree, a place called Giant Rock.

The smile fades as I realize that writing a few articles for *Flashes from the Rock* for that private community out there led to Chrysler firing me.

Nick sent me a letter telling me he also got fired by Chrysler, and I bet it was for hanging out with me although he was the one who took me out there first.

He's rented a home in a neighborhood development and parked his plane at the Victorville Airport. And he's going to drop by the cabin this weekend to talk about employment opportunities.

Maybe if Mr. Henderson hires me, they'll hire him, too. Maybe Nick'd be interested in the chicken project, too.

I feel buoyed by the possibilities.

It sounds like a crazy idea but if I get this lake resort job, it'll bring in the last of the cash we need for the doctor. It'll keep water and food coming in. I can work more on the addition to the cabin.

Maybe there'll be enough to begin my chicken empire soon after the baby is born. But I shouldn't count my chickens before they hatch, eh?

I look back over my shoulder at Claire, who's come to a dead stop. "You okay?"

"It's these darn shoes." She lifts her feet in her sandals, one at a time, and shakes sand from them. She rubs her lower back. "I'm not feeling so good. Maybe this wasn't such a good idea."

"This what? Walking? Visiting?" I turn around to take a closer look at her. In the moonlight, her face is paler than a bowl of milk.

She trembles, and I reach out to steady her. "You

okay?"

"No. I need to lay…down." She teeters to the ground.

"Hang on!" I scoop her up close to me. "We're almost there."

"Help!" I clutch Claire tightly in my arms. With my arm supporting her, I move as quickly as I can, careful not to trip in the dark.

The door of the cabin opens. A woman stands in the doorway with light streaming out around her like an angel of mercy.

"Hey!" she shouts. "What's going on out there?"

"We need help!"

She calls over her shoulder. "Hank! We got visitors! And they're in trouble!"

Chapter 9
Claire - The Jesus Bus

I hear a woman calling in the distance. The sky spins around and swirls faster and faster.

As Rand reaches for me, I remember a long ago moonlight stroll, when he picked me up and hustled directly into the waves.

I wish he could carry me now since each step is torture, and my feet refuse to take another step.

Another wave of dizziness hits me, and I'm down on the ground with his arms cradling me. How did that happen?

For the first time in my life, which includes the birth of two healthy baby girls, I see cartoon stars circling my head.

And I can barely make out the features of his face, lined with concern.

I hear the woman's words echo like they're funneled through a tunnel. "Aaaaaare youuuu okaaaaay?" I struggle to break Rand's firm grasp on me, but he's not letting go.

A tall woman hovers over me, her long, black hair brushing my neck. She flags Rand and me into the tiny cabin and motions me to the chair next a kerosene lantern.

I hear a low growl as he gently drops me into it.

"Hush, Delaware!" Annie claps twice at the large,

dark form shifting about on the double bed pushed up against the not-too-faraway wall.

The creature's gleaming eyes size me up. An elongated tongue hangs out of the dog's mouth as it pants. After a cursory look at me, it resumes licking a giant paw.

The bed it occupies looks so inviting that all I crave is to lie prone, eyes closed, on it. Even if I'm relatively sure the dog might eat me for dessert.

"Don't mind my manners, honey. So glad to finally meet you in person." Annie hands me a cup of water.

As I take it, her face, with its beautiful bronze skin, wrinkles with concern.

"You're tuckered out. When's that baby due?"

"Soon. Three weeks or so." The stars cease spinning. "Really could be any time. My last girl was ten days late, and so I just don't know when…and actually, my last doctor wasn't sure about the heartbeat."

I babble, hardly making sense to myself.

Rand gazes at me from across the room with sympathetic eyes. As if reading my mind, he nonchalantly sweeps his attention to the crowded quarters with the table, two chairs, and the behemoth on the bed.

"Is there somewhere Claire can rest for a few minutes?"

Her husband, Hank, is shorter than Annie, and his long, white hair is pulled into a tight braid at the base of his neck.

He leans against his cane and cocks his head. "She can rest out back in the bus." His kind brown eyes look at me for a response.

"Yes." I have just enough energy to give him an answer with a wan smile. At this point, I'd take lying down on the floor as an option.

Annie pats me on the arm. "And then we'll work out how to get y'all back home." Rand must have filled her in about our running out of gas.

She turns to me, her face crinkled with concern. "You okay to walk a few steps outside, and up into the bus?"

"Yes." My voice sounds to me like I'm answering from underwater.

She takes my hand, leads me around the cabin to the bus with its paisley patterns on the side. "Our Jesus Bus!" She points above the windshield to the painted face of a bearded man with eyes that glow in the dark.

"We were missionaries for a long time before we settled out here. We drove all over, bringing our Sunday School on Wheels to folks in their homes, before the engine broke."

We walk in front of it, and the Jesus eyes follow me.

Annie climbs the steps, tugs down two stubborn windows to let in the scant night breeze, and motions me to follow.

The stairs are steep, and I wrap my hands firmly around the handrails to pull myself up into the bus.

She points me to a mattress on the floor near the back.

By this time, I don't care about dust or spiders, although I hope there aren't scorpions anywhere, remembering the one I found in my shoe yesterday.

All I want is to lie down, close my eyes, and rest up for what might turn out to be a long walk home if things don't work out with the gas.

With as much grace as I can manage, I lower my body across the long bench seat instead, at the back of the bus deciding I probably can't make it down onto the mattress or get back up again.

It's been a long, hot day, and an even longer evening. My back still aches, but not like it did earlier.

Annie starts down the stairs of the bus. "I'll bring you that glass of water."

A few minutes later, she's back in the bus with me. "Here, dear. Sip."

I inhale the dusty air, and my throat itches as I struggle to sit up, the call of water drawing me toward it like one of those deadly singing sirens.

"Thanks." I take a swallow and set the glass on the floor.

"Shout out if you need anything. I'll hear you through the open windows."

"I'll be okay. Thanks."

Annie hurries down the stairs and back to the cabin, and I stretch out, closing my eyes.

Murmuring sounds mingle with serious tones and float through air to the bus. I wonder what they're talking about. I hear the word "gunnysack," but that doesn't make sense.

Then, in that disconnected state-of-mind when you're on the edge of consciousness, feeling almost like a ghost that's returning from the dead, I drift into a dream. Or is it a memory?

It's 1940, and I'm ten years old and back in the Victorian mansion in Santa Ana with my mother, Irene, who ran it as a boarding home.

She was a singer in the all-girl Honey Tones,

which performed at private and public events around Southern California on weekends.

Raising me alone and working three jobs, she hadn't fully embraced motherhood, and my childhood was a roller coaster of emotions. I never could figure out the mood she'd be in until we'd been up and together for a few minutes.

As a child, I'd vowed that one day I'd have a family of my own with a husband and a couple of kids, and that they would be the loves of my life.

That's always been my plan.

We lived on the second floor of an old mansion, which consisted of a converted ballroom, library, and coat closet, with a fancy bathroom with a turn-of-the century bathtub standing on little lion paws.

We ate evening meals, always preceded by tiny trimmed vegetables on a fancy crystal Fostoria relish tray, with other residents in the dining room on the bottom floor.

That's where I met the Colonel, who taught me to play poker, told me war stories, and talked about his travels. Because of him, I long to visit San Francisco with its trolley cars, Ghirardelli Square's famous chocolate shop, and the harbor built on sunken ships during the Gold Rush. One day.

My eyes flutter open. Where is that child who used to be me? Here I am, a city girl, through and through.

I love electricity and modern appliances, and I miss my modern kitchen. I love the hustle and bustle of traffic. I love the crowds shopping at Christmas. I loved my washer and dryer and television set and telephone.

Yes, here I am. Living in a primitive cabin in the desert with a mother-in-law who despises me.

I'm sacked out on a dusty bus seat going nowhere and thinking about how I once yearned to see the world the Colonel had described to me.

Nowadays, I travel only as far the general store for blocks of ice.

I love my family, but I sometimes feel claustrophobic in this land of open spaces.

In the distance, I hear a strange braying sound and wonder if there are wild donkeys out there along with the coyotes and rattlesnakes.

My eyes drift shut.

Five more minutes, and I'll get up.

Just five more minutes.

Chapter 10
Nonni - Abandoned

Tessa and I have a routine.

We wake up early, before the sun pops its head over the horizon.

I love the morning air caressing my face. So crisp, clear, and cool. The sky, a palette of robin's egg blue, swept clean for whatever the day might bring.

This morning, Grandma Grace feeds us breakfast, oatmeal with raisins and honey, at the picnic table out front.

She tells us Mama doesn't feel well after her night with Daddy visiting the neighbors and is still resting inside the cabin.

We hop into Daddy's truck, and he drops us off at the corner at the main highway to catch the bus to school.

"Nonni. You're in charge. Take care of your sister, you hear?"

"Daddy. I hear." I flash a dimple at him, and Tessa kicks a foot high in the air.

He touches his forehead in a mock salute before blowing a kiss at us.

We stand still watching his truck shrink into the distance. We play the waiting game, peering down that same stripe of asphalt, for the big, yellow bus.

Time slows to the crawl of a tortoise.

Some parents drive their children to school, and other classmates live close enough to walk or ride their bikes.

Richer kids live above the railroad tracks, in the foothills, in modern homes with garages.

Trina's in my third-grade class, and she lives there, and her mother drives her to school.

Most of us catch the bus from our stops scattered throughout the district.

We carry our peanut butter and jelly sandwiches on white bread, cut into tea-party triangles and wrapped in wax paper, in our metal lunch boxes.

Mine looks like a yellow school bus with Disney characters in it, and Tessa's has a farm theme.

At lunch, Barry will probably pull his uncut bologna sandwich on white Wonder bread from his metal Popeye lunch box and gobble it in four mouth-stuffing bites.

He sits next to me in class and, sometimes, at lunch.

Now that Daddy's added a coop of six hens and a rooster, Mama includes a hardboiled egg for a snack.

For a treat, Grandma Grace tucks in one of her special "no bake" oatmeal cookies. We eat a lot of oatmeal.

"Best thing 'bout that recipe is we don't need no oven at all."

I've quickly grown to consider Grandma Grace's love language that cookie. While we wait for the bus, Tessa reaches into her bag and rips off a chunk.

"No. Save it for later, or you'll be sorry!" I watch out for her even when she taunts me like she's a little devil child.

Tessa stuffs the bite in and talks with her mouth full, shaking her head at me. "Too r-r-ate!"

I give her my best evil eye and hear the rumble of an engine. A truck pulls out from behind the farmhouse.

Didn't Daddy say it's abandoned? We'd consulted our family Webster Dictionary and read the definition: *abandoned*. "Deserted, vacant, empty."

Already an avid collector of words, I'd dated the page, so I'd always remember when I learned that word.

Is there a law that says people can't drive around abandoned houses? I don't think so, but I wonder what anyone's doing at a house that's empty.

It would be nice if a family moved in there with a girl my age who could come to my house, so I'd have someone other than Tessa to play with.

The desert's filled with bone yards of broken and empty places.

We have our own bone yard at the back of the cabin, behind where the new addition will be. Cinder blocks, shovels, a bathtub waiting to be installed, wood for our stove, rolled chicken wire, and rebar—a dangerous metal bar that goes inside the cinder blocks to make them strong—and other nameless things are stacked hodge-podge out there.

And we're not allowed near it because it's dangerous.

Just like we're not allowed near the bomb shelter out in the brush past the water tower and outhouse.

I pull my attention back to the road in front of us. Tessie and I count cars and trucks as they pass.

We call out, "White!" "Silver!" "Green!" at a car with two children in the back seat, a cement truck driven by a dark-haired man, and the truck from the farmhouse.

Far down the road, we spot the bus, a yellow dot chugging toward us to take us to school.

On the way home, after a busy day at school, I wander out of our invisible safe zone. "Let's play Sammy Snake!"

Tessa loves this new game I've invented.

And even though I despise snakes, at the same time I want my eight-year-old life back. I yearn to stride into the dirt without fear.

"Dare you to follow me out to that brush!"

"We'll get into trouble!"

She's worried about that now? I stretch my arms wide and stare into the enormous wild desert on the other side of the lane.

"Double dare you!" I lunge toward the nearest creosote bush, and Tessa follows on my tail.

"Come out, come out, Sammy Snake! Give yourself a shake, shake, shake!"

We spin around, shaking our bottoms like rattles as we raise our fists skyward.

I challenge the enemy. "Sammy, Sammy, go away! Sammy, we don't want to play!"

I scamper farther into enemy territory with Tessa close behind.

Out a few paces, I spy a cement foundation that looks like the one Daddy is building for our new addition. Only this one is old and cracked with part of the fireplace standing. There are no walls or roof.

Fascinated, we creep close, circling it several times.

Tessa wanders off to one side. "Lookee what I

found!"

She leans over it. "Hi, hole!" Her echo bounces back to us like a boomerang. "Hole, hole, hole!"

I scoot close to her, leaning over the hole to peer into the deep, dark shaft.

My hand slips, and my thumbnail rips on the ragged cement edge leaving an edge of blood.

The unexpected pain brings me back to reality, and the word *danger* suddenly sounds in my mind.

I don't feel safe. What if Tessa falls in? What if I tumble in after her? No one knows where we are, so who will find us?

I stick my thumb in my mouth to lick off the tangy blood. We are a fair amount away from the road, the road we're never to leave on our way home.

How have I forgotten this, just in the space of getting from the bus to this dangerous spot?

The rules? I must have broken a couple of them by now. Have we ever been told not to shout into a hole?

I hear the low growl of a truck. Turning, I see it on the road near us, stirring up dust.

It looks vaguely familiar, but most trucks look alike to me. And there are a lot of trucks in the desert, more than when we lived in the city where people mostly drove cars.

I can't see the face of the man driving it, just the outline of his hat, and it looks like his head is turned away from us, looking for something.

Not only have we disobeyed, but we're about to be caught in the act by a stranger, who might tell our parents what we've done.

I spring into action.

"Stay down! Hide and seek!" I pull Tessa to the

ground. "Snake drill!"

Tessa tries to jerk her arm away from me, but I tighten my grasp.

"New game?" she asks.

"No. Yes! Stay down, Tessie."

She must have heard my serious tone because she obeys instead of arguing with me like she usually does.

She freezes, still, and I let go of her to squat back on my heels, keeping my eyes on the truck.

The truck continues down the road and turns left at the deserted crossroads where we always continue walking straight ahead to get home.

I peer through the brush until it's out of sight and then turn back as Tessie tugs on my skirt.

"I peeked around you and saw him, just a little bit." She speaks in a whisper, and her big, round freckles stand out against her flushed face. "He's a bad man."

I sigh and look up at the sky, which seemed so bright a minute before. A breeze trails its fingers down my arm, giving me goose bumps.

"Let's go home."

Chapter 11
Claire - City Girl

Thanks to the Ritchies, who drove us to our car with a small can of gas, we arrived home last night around eleven.

When I finally slipped into bed in our stuffy cabin, I fell into a dreamless state, and suddenly it was morning.

Rand told me to stay in bed a little longer. That he and Mother Grace would get the kids ready and to the bus stop.

I've been a nervous wreck since Rand and the girls left this morning, a little earlier than usual so he could buy ten dollars' worth of gas for the nearly empty tank.

During breakfast, I spilled my coffee on my blouse and dropped the crust of my bread on the ground underneath the picnic table.

I jumped at random noises and movements: sagebrush scratching up against the stoop, a diaper flying from the clothesline, a lizard scooting under my foot, a katydid chirping.

"You're as nervous as a cat in a rowboat!" Mother Grace scolded me at lunch when a bucket skittered across the porch and sent me leaping to my feet in a panic.

She backed off when I gave her a "don't-mess-with-me" look.

She and I had spent the morning scrubbing dirty clothes against a washboard with water I awkwardly toted from the tank and heated on the wood-burning stove.

After we rinsed them out with clean, cold water and twisted the water from them, we hung them on the line to flap. Hopefully, they'll be dry by dinner.

We do the wash only one or two times a week.

Afterwards we pour the rinse water onto our newly planted garden, begun with plants she brought here. They've doubled in size.

I leave her to finish hanging the wash and go to my position in front of the cabin to peer toward the main highway. My back aches.

It seems like a million years ago I had my own washing machine in Santa Monica. Before we moved out here. We'd bought it with every spare penny we had and a small loan from the appliance company, and I'd paid off our debt by doing laundry for neighbors.

Every time I pulled out a delicious armload of damp clothes from it, I'd felt a sense of independence that made me stand taller than my height of five feet and four inches.

I loved that washer. And the dryer. I washed clothes at night and folded them, dry before I climbed into bed with a satisfied feeling inside.

Saddened to sell my appliances to a friend before moving out here, I'd kept the little nest egg for myself.

A woman's got to have some of her own money to survive, one of the sparse lessons I'd learned from my mother.

Now, I'd almost kill to have those appliances back. But we're out here in the boondocks without electricity, so it doesn't matter anyway.

Standing out front of the cabin under that tiny sliver of shade, I rub the small of my back and squint into the sun, knowing by its afternoon position that it's about time for the bus to arrive.

I watch it stop, and the girls hop out, tiny colorful dots in the distance.

A low-flying red-tailed hawk stretches its wings wide, floating lazily in an air current above our acreage, and my eyes follow its graceful circles.

When I turn my attention back to the road, I no longer see the girls. I scan the landscape, searching frantically for their tiny shapes.

A truck drives slowly down the road before turning east at the intersection, toward Dead Man's Corner.

Usually, Rand has the only vehicle on that long stretch of lane, and that's at the beginning and end of the day. Who was that?

My eyes search the terrain, frantic. Where are the girls?

My heart speeds up, and I feel the baby roll over inside me. Whoomph! I cradle my belly with both hands and squint again, and there they are, walking along like they've been there the whole time.

My pulse continues to pound, and I wonder if I'm losing my mind.

A shadow falls on me, and, looking up, I see a cloud loitering in front of the sun.

My breath catches on a hiccup.

Mother Grace pokes her head around the corner of the cabin, and I feel her staring at me.

"I ain't finished hanging that last load. Going out back. You all right?"

A shiver jolts my body. "I can feel it. A storm is coming."

Chapter 12
Gracie - Spooked

Out here the weather can change in the snap of a sheet on the line. You suffer from heat stroke during the day and beg for a sleeping bag to warm you up at night.

One minute it's dry and clear, and the next, gusting winds rustle in with a herd of clouds, dropping the temperature just like that.

Sudden rains might just tamp down the dirt like tobacco in a pipe.

Except when they turn into gully-washers that cut deep ribbons into the ground, like the ones on the other side of our property.

I dump the rinse water on the garden and return to the front of the cabin to check on the girls' progress where I notice that Claire's getting herself worked up about something.

"The bus stopped. It's been a spell since they began walking. Now I can't see them." She brushes her hair back from her face, shades her eyes with her hand against the sun's glare, and peers down the road for them.

Her jaw's clinched, partially shadowed by a cloud blocking the sun.

"'Course they're on their way. Where else would they be?"

"I saw them, and now I can't. You see them?"

I squint at the road. "I cain't see them neither, but that don't mean they're not there."

They must be hidden on the curlicue part of the lane, maybe by a creosote bush or something like that.

I refuse to get all riled up just cuz she is.

Claire paces in circles, stirring up dust, her face pinched like she's about to cry.

"Claire! Take a breath! Stop fretting!" I sigh and traipse into the cabin to get her a drink just to get away from her twitchy ways.

She's beginning to make *me* nervous, especially since she sometimes has a sense of things happening that I don't.

But I don't tell her this.

By the time I come back out with the glass of sun tea to calm her down, she's smiling, a bit of embarrassment plastered on her face.

"Mother Grace." She rubs her hands together, over and over. "They must have been there the whole time!"

She jabs with her pointer finger, straight at the road, to where we see their small shapes moving slow-like toward the house.

They're about a cotton field away, if we was near my family's sharecropper farm in Louisiana.

I reckon, parents nowadays get too excited, too fast, not like when my kids was young, or when I was a child myself, and we was outside either working in the fields or playing until the cows come home.

Sometimes we didn't even see a grownup until we showed up to eat.

No one wondered where we was or what we was doing because that was just the way it was then.

They was glad to have us work, or when that was

over, to have us out from under their feet, and I have to tell you—we was mighty glad to oblige them.

I reckon this. Claire's ready to birth any time now. It's scorching hot, and it's time for that baby boy to be born.

A shadow falls across me, and I look up at a dark cloud hunkered overhead.

A gust of wind catches my hat, and I chase it to a tumbleweed where it gets stuck.

Claire looks up at the sky and mutters something about a storm, and I get shivers down both arms and have to shake them off.

I'm definitely gonna talk to Sonny boy about her nerves because she's getting on mine.

I tell you, she's creeping me out with that look on her face, like she knows something for a fact that I do not.

Chapter 13
Randall - Making Progress

"Rest up a little." I hand Claire her morning cup of tea in bed. "I'll get gas on the way in after I drop the girls off. You need anything from Jolly's on my way home?"

She screws up her forehead, and I can tell she's thinking.

"Maybe a regular carton of milk and a loaf of Wonder Bread." She rubs her eyes. "I really should get up and make sure the girls have everything packed."

"Nope. Ma and I will do that today. Take a while. Heck, spend the whole day in bed!"

She laughs. "That'll be the day. I'll just rest for a few minutes. Thanks." She sips her tea.

I head out with the girls, and my day passes quickly.

Tomorrow the well project will be finished, and that will be the end of the predictable paycheck until I secure something else.

I also got more information on that resort water-ski lake project. I leave a message at the post office for Mr. Henderson, who's looking for more workers.

Mr. Ramirez already gave me a plug. I'm feeling good about the job I did with the well.

I'm also feeling satisfied with the progress I've made so far on our home. I've finished staking the forms for the concrete slabs, which Nick and I will pour this weekend.

The addition will have a great room with a kitchen tucked into it, two bedrooms for the children, and an indoor bathroom.

The cabin can be whatever we want it to be. And I've added another starter coop with more chickens.

I arrive home before dinner. The sky's alight with swirls of gold clouds above Mount Baldy.

The girls run out to greet me like I am a king or something.

Ma looks up from where she's jabbing around the plants with a stick. I wave at her before I poke my head into the cabin.

Claire's pushing something around in Ma's cast iron frying pan on the stove. It's hot in there.

She glances at me and swipes damp hair from her forehead while she continues to stir.

"I'm home," I say. "Obviously."

In earlier days, she'd have laughed about this word choice. Tonight, she doesn't make a comment.

I'll share my good news about the lake after dinner, and that should lighten the mood a bit.

I walk over to her, put my arm around her, and give her a little squeeze. Her shoulders relax, and she returns a faint smile. There's a light bead of sweat on her upper lip.

"Dinner'll be ready in a few minutes." She turns back to the pan and pokes at the contents.

The girls bound into the small room. After they wrestle with me for about five minutes on the tiny floor and we almost trip Claire, I shoo them outside.

"Take a run around the outside of the house," I

instruct. "Three times, all the way around. We'll call you when dinner's ready."

The girls take off, giggling.

I return and place my hands on my tired wife's shoulders and nudge her gently so I can look into her eyes.

"Hey," I say. "How're you feeling today?"

She knows I'm referring to her fainting spell last night. But damn. Running out of gas and having the flashlight bite the dust was pure bad planning on my part. I'm better than that.

These incidences probably contributed to her fainting. I'm sure they did.

I comfort myself with the thought that at least we were in front of the Ritchies' cabin when it happened. And they helped us.

But here we are, almost a day later, and I'm worried about her.

"Claire. Babe." I move my hand to her rounded belly, and she brushes it off.

"Please. Don't. Too hot."

"You okay?"

"Don't know," she says. "Just don't know."

I push my luck and give her a quick hug, in spite of the signals she's sending me.

"Sorry. Exhausted. My back hurts. Can't wait to get this baby out." She reaches over and squeezes my hand.

I smile at her before heading out to look at the progress I'm making on the house.

Ma trails behind me, her chin squared.

"Okay, Ma," I say. "Out with it. What's bugging you?"

"It's Claire." She paces in a small circle with her hands clasped behind her.

"You know I don't butt my way into people's stuff, but she's too skittish. Likes to have driven me nuts today."

I just can't take dealing with any more conflict today. "Give her some space, Ma."

When things get emotional, I get busy with my hands. I've already cleared and leveled the dirt—and almost finished staking it.

I'm a firm believer of checking my measurements twice and, sometimes, three times.

I pull the chalk string taut and snap it.

I'm borrowing a cement mixer this weekend. That way I can mix the mud myself and pour it, one slab at a time, in case Nick can't help. Smaller sections have a better chance of drying without cracks.

With our limited water supply, I'm not gonna be able to cure the concrete under plastic sheets like I did with the patio in Santa Monica.

"She acted strange when the girls was walking home today."

"I know, Ma. She told me she was worried she couldn't see them part of the way."

"They was fine…they got here just fine."

"Back off a little, Ma. She's hot, tired, and, frankly, a little pissy." I look up as the wind whips the plastic sheeting into a snarl above my head, and I leap to catch it.

She narrows her eyes at me. "Well. Don't say I didn't tell you. And I'll tell you again, Sonny."

I point to the sky. "A storm's coming."

Dark clouds billow overhead, and the air is heavy

with the metallic taste that precedes a thundershower.

"That's just what she said." Ma frowns. "And I don't think she was necessarily speaking about the weather."

Chapter 14
Tessa - I'm Sorry

"I beat you! I beat you!"

I do my special dance of happiness. Three twirls, a high jump, and fairy fingers. I finally beat Bobby at tetherball.

We started this new school about month ago after moving from the beach.

In the beginning, I didn't have any friends except for my sister, so I decided to learn to play tetherball at recess to have something to do.

I don't like standing around doing nothing. And Nonni doesn't want me hanging on her all the time.

I worry about that hard ball on the rope. It might fly around the metal pole and smack me right in my face. Again.

I don't want to get hit again. I want to hit it instead.

Yesterday when I stuck my fist out, I hit the hard, yellow ball by accident.

After a few games, I got better at socking it and then whacked Bobby smack in the face with it.

"I'm sorry! It was an accident!" I knew it hurt and felt bad.

Bobby rubbed at a pink spot on his cheek. "You beat me, this time. But you're just a pee wee!"

He teases me. "You're just a teeny, weeny pee wee!"

It's a day later, and I feel like a champion. "Hey! I'm small, but I'm mighty!"

I *am* the shortest person in our class, but that doesn't bother me at all.

I can wrap my arms around Nonni's knees and swing her around like I'm some kind of weightlifter or something.

So I'm not going to worry about being a pee wee.

But today I hit the ball so hard the rope wrapped all the way around the pole.

Winner! Bobby is surprised. You should have seen his face when I picked *him* up and swung him around!

Our desks are next to each other. Yesterday, he poked me with his pencil and made faces at me.

This morning, he whispered words to me, words I'm supposed to know, and I'm learning to read!

At lunch, I reach into my lunchbox for the oatmeal cookie I began chewing on this morning at the bus stop.

Bobby looks at me with big eyes and rubs his nose. "It's still sore." He fake whines like a dog.

I break off a tiny piece and pop it into his open mouth.

After lunch, I work on my art project. I rub my fist back and forth in the middle of the big, slippery glob of green finger paint. The design looks like a big, burning bush.

When I get it just the way I like it, I take a pinch of sawdust from the jar and sprinkle it onto the picture.

Then, I pin my beautiful picture on the string in front of the window to dry.

Mrs. Williams smiles at me. The color around her is light blue.

I'm still happy when school is out, and we're back

on the bus. I love the bouncy, squeaky ride home.

Every day, the bus stops at the railroad tracks.

We always do three things before the bus crosses over them. We lift up our feet. We cross our ankles. We make a wish.

I think it's some kind of a law that children on buses have to do.

Nonni scratches her pale eyebrow. "Whad'ya wish for?"

"It's a secret." I tell her that every time.

If you tell, you don't get your wish even though we all get two secret wishes each day.

One on the way to school. Another one on the way back. And one plus one is two.

This wish is always about learning to read so I can help with the baby when she comes.

I change the other one around depending on what I want.

The bus reaches our stop. The big air brakes make a loud whoooooosh sound.

We bunch up near the door to leave, and the driver stops us. "You girls have everything?"

"Yes, Mrs. Ross," we say together as we head down the steep steps.

We hop off, and Nonni looks for a round rock to kick down the road as we walk home.

We've only walked for about ten minutes when she tells me we're leaving the road.

To walk into the desert.

To have an adventure.

Which is against Mama's rules. We could get into big trouble.

There are snakes out there. And tarantulas. And

coyotes.

And what Mama calls the dreaded Teddy Bear cholla cactus that throws stickers that stab themselves into you like needles.

And other dangerous things.

But wherever Nonni goes, I go.

Then, we run home as quick as our legs can carry us.

We're almost there when the wind begins to push us around. It makes little dust devils in the air.

Nonni picks up her rock and sticks it in her pocket. We race each other down the lane.

The air turns cold, and we get home as the raindrops spit down on us.

Mama and Grandma Grace stand outside by the cabin, waiting for us.

Mama crosses her arms against her chest. That means she's not happy.

Did she see us go off the road? I have a bad, bad feeling we're in trouble.

We rush to her, and she searches our faces with her eyes. Usually she grabs us up into her arms, next to her big belly and gives us a long hug.

Today she does this, but then pushes us back fast and stares, again, into Nonni's eyes. Then mine.

Her voice shakes. "Where were you?"

The wrinkles between her eyebrows look like little railroad tracks.

"We came straight home from the bus." Nonni whispers this lie.

I know this isn't true and that we walked in a crooked line from the bus to the brush.

To the hole in the ground.

To the road.

And then to our home.

"I was watching you."

I knew she was!

"You were not on the road the whole time." She gives each of us a stink-eye stare.

I crack, not able to keep my mouth shut. I need to tell her the *whole* truth.

I brighten my tone. "Mama. We stepped into the bushes. Just for a minute."

I try to make it sound interesting. "We found a deep hole."

I want her to forget she told us to walk only on the road. "We could take you there to see it. You would like it!"

Nonni follows my example and uses her hand to demonstrate.

"It didn't have a top on it. We dropped rocks into it. We had to count to three before we heard them hit the bottom. It was an adventure, and we were only there for a few minutes!"

She bobs her head a couple of times and smiles at Mama. "You like adventures!"

Mama's face turns white, and she rubs her belly. "Not that kind of adventure."

Nonni sucks on her bottom lip. "It looked like it belonged to a ghost cabin that burned down a long time ago. We were on our way back to the road when a truck came down it."

I add this important information. "The man in the truck had a dark red ring around him—"

Nonni interrupts. "He stopped, and we hid."

My words rush out, and I'm anxious to tell Mama

everything I know.

"Then we played hide-and-seek like Nonni told me to do."

Nonni gives me dagger eyes.

Mama turns to her. "You were out there playing in the desert? You know you're not allowed to do that."

She steps closer to her and squints into her eyes. "What truck?"

"I think we saw it this morning when we were at the bus stop. I'm not sure."

I burst in with my memory. "It was green. Just like the truck this morning. I remember that."

I'm eager to add this information, and I'm sure I'm right about the color.

Grandma Grace puts her hands on her hips. "There's lots of green trucks out there."

Nonni replies, "It was brown. I'm sure."

Mama moves close to peer into our eyes. Again. She inhales deeply before she speaks slowly like she thinks we can't hear her.

"Girls, remember this. Always walk on the road where we can see you. Never go near a well. Or look down one. And don't ever, ever speak to strangers. Do. You. Understand?"

Her face is pale white, like the moon on a clear night.

Tears spill down my cheeks. "Yes, Mama. I'm sorry!"

Nonni shrugs her shoulders and drops her chin, mumbling. "Sorry."

"Do you both promise?"

We chant together, "We promise."

In our family, "sorries" are followed by what

Mama calls "love-ees." We gather in a group hug, and the sad feeling leaves me.

Right then, the raindrops gather into big splatters.

We hustle into the cabin. Nonni and I play Candy Land on the floor while we wait for the storm to end.

Mama makes a lot of noise, banging things around. She stirs up a storm of a tuna casserole dinner, the spoon smashing against the inside of the pan. The creamy noodle smell makes my tummy rumble.

Grandma sews a rip in my shorts. It's cozy inside, and I don't want to be anywhere else in the world.

I look beyond the open door at the rain. It pounds down so hard mud splashes up on the patio.

I hear Mama set down the spoon with a "thud."

She gazes out the door, too, with a frightened look on her face like she's seeing something scary.

I follow her eyes, and all I see is a lot of rain. Falling down hard.

I move my blue gingerbread boy past Nonni's yellow one to enter Lollypop Woods.

Nonni snarls at me when I stand up and do my little victory dance.

Three twirls, a high jump, and fairy fingers.

Chapter 15
Nonni - Danger All Around

My bold move doesn't seem like an act of defiance at the time but a way to show that I am braver and older than Tessie.

After all, I'm the first-born child and am supposed to know more than my sister. Right? How can I do that if I never stretch my boundaries?

But that isn't the way it works. When Mama turns us over to Daddy, I know we are in a bad situation for breaking the rules—for going into the wild and finding that well.

Not to mention the fact that I'd lied.

We'd already had to swear to Mama that we would only walk home on the road. She also threw in a couple of other things.

I wonder if those promises mean forever, no matter what.

"Daddy, why's Mama so mad at us for finding the well? We didn't get hurt or anything."

He grinds his cigarette butt into the dirt under his heel. "It's dangerous. You could have gotten hurt. Kathy Fiscus, a girl your age, fell into an abandoned well when she was chasing her sister and cousin."

There's that word again. "An *abandoned* well?" I still don't understand what the problem is.

"The well was not in use anymore. No cover on it.

She fell in and drowned before they could get her out."

"Drowned?" A wave of horror floods through me. "Kathy died?"

"Yes. You and Tessa must stick to the road. No side trips."

"B-b-b-but it didn't even have water in it." Maybe this excuse would dampen the extent of our disobedience.

"You or Tessa could have fallen in. Got stuck. Or…"

Daddy runs the back of his hand across his eyes. "It wasn't a good decision. I'm very disappointed in you."

I hang my head, too mortified to meet his eyes. He's never said that to me before.

I had disappointed him.

"Look at me. Nonni."

I force my gaze to his.

"I couldn't stand losing you. Or Tessa. Understand?"

I don't want to think about that girl, Kathy, falling into the well and dying.

And I don't want to think about Tessa or me falling in, either.

Stuck in a dark pit.

What if we died, too? It would be the worst thing that could happen to a kid.

Or, I guess, their parents. Our parents. And my grandmother. I bite my lip until I taste copper, and a mewl escapes from me.

He opens his arms, and I scamper into them. "I know you didn't think you were doing anything bad. But danger can be invisible until it's too late to get away."

I burrow my face into his khaki shirt, damp with sweat. "I'll try. I'll obey." He's right.

There *is* danger all around—in the sky from missiles and bombs that can fall on us any time to snakes waiting to strike us and now those nasty holes in the ground that can suck us in and make us disappear forever.

I am overwhelmed considering these things, but I make myself promise to watch for danger everywhere I go.

I'll try, try, try to follow all of those silly rules even if I don't understand them.

Tessa pushes her way in between us. "Me, too."

That night, Mama sets out our tin washtubs in the yard right before the storm hits.

Lightning strikes in the hills behind the railroad tracks, and thunder rattles our cabin.

Rain floods gullies, big enough to cut new trails, but the next morning arrives with a clear blue sky.

The air is still, and our footsteps don't stir up even a puff of dust. The thirsty desert has been momentarily quenched.

There's fresh rainwater in the tubs. Tessa and I will get to take private baths for a luxurious change.

When I wake up the next morning, I feel hopeful with a brand new day stretching ahead, a day in which I *can* do better.

I *will* do better.

"These here squash'll be blooming soon. They'll perk back up." Grandma Grace points at tightly fisted blossoms in the garden that had been battered down a bit by the rain.

"They have tripled in size. The bean plants are

hunkered down and'll be all right. That rain was a long time coming."

Daddy grins. "Yep, and it'll be a lot easier to finish the well with the ground softened from the downpour."

"Then you'll need to find something new to do for money." Mama rubs small circles on her belly, wrinkles forming between her eyes. "The doctor needs his money soon."

"It'll work out, hon. It always does. He's almost paid off." Daddy gives her a peck on the cheek and tries to whirl her around, but she pushes him away.

"I'm too bulky and tired for shenanigans. Couldn't sleep a wink last night with all the racket going on out there."

Daddy pulls her into his embrace. "It's going to be fine, Claire. Wait and see."

Her shoulders slump as he massages them. We crowd around them, gently patting Mama.

"Break up this lovefest, girls. It's time for breakfast." Grandma Grace points us to the table.

She steps into the cabin and reappears with bowls in one hand and canned milk in the other.

Tessa and I hurry to finish our cereal before Daddy honks the horn. It's time to leave.

He drops us off, as usual, at the bus stop.

We shout each other down calling out the colors.

"Silver!"

"Black!"

"Tan!"

One big gasoline truck, one small car with a grandpa-looking man driving it, and a grocery truck with its symbol on its side.

Tessa points out that two of these *vehicles*, another

word I've marked off and dated in the dictionary, are different colors than yesterday.

For a six-year-old, she has a good memory and remembers things like this, especially if they involve color.

It's a memorable day in a lot of ways.

With only a month of school left, Mrs. Blankenship decides to do something special. She teaches us to square dance.

Barry's my partner even though he makes a big deal of wiping his hands off after each round.

I have a good time kicking up my heels. I like dances with patterns in them, and there're definite steps and movements involved in what we're doing.

No guessing about what's supposed to happen next. No making bad decisions that disappoint people.

During the last fifteen minutes of the day, Trina's mother arrives.

She jumps up from her desk. "Mom! Did you remember to bring nine candles?"

Trina's celebrating her birthday with homemade cupcakes. They're decorated with bright yellow icing and sprinkled with confetti candy in the colors of the rainbow.

There's one for each of us.

After Trina delivers one to each student in our class, her mother approaches me with two muslin bags. Cloth diapers poke out of the top of one.

"Honey, take these bags of supplies and baby bottles for your mom. Tell her I'm packing up a couple more to send home with you tomorrow."

Mama had mentioned that Tessa and I would be bringing them home. We'll each carry one of them home today.

"Thank you, Mrs. Anderson."

"Tell your mom I'll be sending more things later." She smiles at me.

Mrs. Blankenship motions for me to park the bags beside her desk.

Trina and I munch in unison, and I narrow my eyes at her. "Can you spell *abandoned*?"

This word will move me ahead in our private competition, and I'm proud that I know it.

Nevertheless, I'm surprised when she spells it with confidence.

"Even Steven." She laughs. "It's my birthday, so I should win anyway!"

I do a quick mental calculation.

Yes, we have the same amount of wins in the spelling category, but I'm down in the home category after the birthday treat today.

That's when I realize there're two basic types of folks in the world.

Those who *have*, and those who *don't*.

Those who have ovens, and those who don't.

Those who can bake their own fancy desserts, and those who can't.

The cupcakes are mouth-wateringly delicious.

At the end of the school day, Tessa and I scuffle off to the bus, each of us with a bag in our arms.

"Nah, nah-nah, nah nah!" Tessa taunts me as she bumps me out of the way to spring up the steps.

Mrs. Ross turns her head toward us, her red-polished fingernails tapping against the steering wheel. "Take your turns, little missies."

We rush to claim our favorite seats at the back.

When we get to the railroad tracks, the brakes hiss, we pick up our feet, cross our ankles, and make wishes.

Like birthday wishes, even Trina's birthday wishes, they don't count if you say them out loud.

Mine is that the baby will be born soon, something that is going to happen whether I wish on it or not.

Chapter 16
Gracie - Taffy

We, meaning Claire and me, always stash the ceramic thunder mug under the bunk bed for the girls, and then everyone chants, "Put de pot under de bed and turn out de light!"

About two in the morning, I ran out to the outhouse in the midst of the gully washer, and, I swear, it was like walking on water with Jesus to get there and back.

We woke up to a blue sky so clear and flat it fit like a smooth, fresh sheet with its corners tucked into the horizon.

The bushes, Joshua trees, even the dirt, look spanking clean.

The air smells of mesquite with a touch of cinnamon, though I cain't say where that comes from.

Tessa slept through it all without stirring but it musta been like putting her hand into a bucket of water because her sheet was damp again this morning.

I'll hang it out on the line to dry in the sunshine today. Oh, that girl.

By the time everyone's bustling about, most of the storm's soaked right straight into the thirsty earth, down to the useless water table way below, wherever that is.

Even though it's not our rainy season, Heaven dumped a lake on us last night.

It's been a wetter year than usual, that's for sure.

But except for a few puddles, I cain't even tell cuz the ground sucked the water right down.

When Pops and I got hold of this land for what they called recreational homesteading, we tried to use the divining rod, that stick that looks like a big old wishbone from a turkey at Thanksgiving, to locate water so's we might dig our own well, but it didn't work for us.

Some folks out here have wells, but some of us cain't cuz the land ain't right for it.

We are, of course, part of those folks waiting for others to move out here, so we can pitch in for the real water lines from the city water.

First unexpected thing that happens is a yeller dog shows up here out of nowhere, driven to us by the storm.

None of us ever seen it before.

When I open the door, it almost rolls in. Pitiful smelling with its wet, scraggly fur, it squints its small eyes at me.

I shout, "Shhoooo!" and clap my hands at it, but it does not move.

Right away, Tessa runs over to it, not the least bit afraid it might bite her, leans over, wraps her arms around its neck, and declares, "Mine! All mine!!"

Then, that darn dog licks her right on the nose, staggers to its muddy paws, and begins to follow *her* around, I mean three inches from the back of her heels, wherever she treads.

"Keep that dirty dog outta the cabin!" I make my opinion known.

Sonny stands still, taking in his measure of the intruder.

"She might work out as a chicken dog, guarding for us, when we get the big coop in."

After he and the girls retrieve their lunches from the icebox, Tessa snuggles up to the dog, again, and looks directly into those amber eyes. "Taffy, stay here, and I'll see you after school."

She turns to us and says with that O'Brien glint of determination, "I am calling that dog Taffy because that's her color. Like butterscotch taffy. My favorite! She's mine now!"

That dog trots after the truck down the road for a short while until she finally tuckers out and comes back, her tail between her legs.

By this time, I'm ready to pitch a fit. "Shoooo!"

I shout and stamp my foot, but she ignores me and walks in circles, making herself at home on the small porch out front next to the rocking chair.

Then, she points her nose toward bus stop, far away.

It looks that she's settling in to wait for Tessa to return.

After a couple of hours, I break down and give her a cup of our precious water. That's probably a huge mistake, and now she'll likely never leave.

The second thing is that Claire shows me a soggy pack of cigarettes on the ground near the garden.

Sonny smokes a little when he has spare change, mostly behind our backs, but I've never seen this brand.

We wonder where it came from.

Mebbe the rain washed it in from a neighbor way upstream, on the other side of the tracks?

Mebbe he bought another brand?

It's a mysterious thing since we are the only folks

out here.

But one thing I know is that it did not walk here on its own two feet!

I'm going to ask him about it when he comes home tonight.

And if he did buy it, I'm going to tell him not to spend money foolhardy like that when he needs to pay the doctor for the baby. And for the water and ice and small things we buy at Jolly's.

He knows that I always say work comes before comfort.

I hoped Claire would wake up calmer today, but I did not realize how much she hates storms.

She says the racket of the thunder kept her awake all night. That she just lay there praying for it to pass over, which it finally did.

Sonny slept like he was dead, and she didn't want to wake him up.

We're all getting ready for the baby.

The other day Sonny brought us a hunkin' drawer he found somewhere to make into a cradle.

I figger it's big enough to last until the baby's 'bout six months old. Or more.

I sanded off rough patches.

Claire washed it out and padded it with a couple of baby blankets I'd made for the baby.

If I'd known how little they had, I would have brought the treadle sewing machine I'd inherited from my own ma so I could make some more blankets and diapers.

The mom of one of Nonni's friends, Trina, had sent a note to Claire a couple of days ago asking if she wanted some of her one-year-old boy's clothes and supplies. She even offered to drive them over.

Claire's too proud and embarrassed of living in this humble-pie one-room cabin to allow her to do that.

So this Alyssa woman is bringing everything to school for Nonni and Tessa to bring home, maybe today.

I surely hope there's some baby bottles in them. We'll boil them in a pan of water on the wood-burning stove and let them air dry.

It's a darn shame Claire gave all her baby stuff away when Tessa turned three because she doesn't have squat.

I do not approve of charity, but it's called for now.

If I didn't know better, I would think that Claire was nesting, like those striped chipmunks poking their heads up and chittering at us from their holes in the ground.

She did not eat a lick of food today, either.

She's been pacing and cleaning, and she keeps looking out at the road, waiting for them girls to get off the bus.

Yesterday it took the girls an extra fifteen minutes to get here from the bus stop since they took their unauthorized trip into the bush.

After the trouble they got into, I don't think they'll be doing that again.

Ifn's they know what's good for them.

Chapter 17
Claire - Teetering on a Ledge

I'm pacing circle eights this afternoon.

I use my internal clock and the position of the sun to judge it's about time for the kids to board the bus at school.

Shortly after, they'll be dropped off at the end of the lane to begin their walk home.

While I wait, I use my frenetic energy to check the "cradle," make a space for the hand-me-down baby supplies coming home with the girls today, and count the money in the coffee can.

I shake the shelter lock, making sure the kids can't accidentally get into it.

After yesterday, I'm not too sure of Nonni's judgment.

I do everything I can to derail my uneasy state of mind. I'm usually a take-charge type of woman, especially when it comes to my family.

But today I feel out of sorts and at a disadvantage, physically and emotionally, especially since Gracie watches my every move.

With the baby due any time, the primitive conditions of the cabin, and general lack of resources, I can't help myself and my family the way I want.

I hate, hate, hate, hate feeling helpless.

Even though Mother Grace assists with chores and

the girls, I feel judged by her—that I'm not good enough as a daughter-in-law, mother, wife, or homemaker.

And I especially failed with the timing of this soon-to-be-born baby, who has been unusually still on this blistering day.

I force myself to think of something positive and imagine Nonni kicking a small rock and Tessa skipping hop-step until they arrive home. A beginning of a small smile tugs at the corner of my mouth.

Then, a premonition I can't quite put my finger on, swirling with feelings of the girls, hovers over me, ramping up to a high-pitched whine.

"Look there." I point to their small shapes slowly trudging down the road, not yet far from the bus stop. "Ahhhhhh."

Gracie looks up from the picnic table where she's folding sheets. "Too bad they weren't walking when Sonny got home early today or…"

I abruptly swing toward her and interrupt in an irritated whine while hearing Rand hammer out back. "Or he could have picked the girls up."

What's this? I'm finishing Gracie's sentences now?

I should have asked him to go back and get the girls, but he rarely has daylight hours to work on the house, and he's out back working straightening the forms or mixing concrete.

Or I could go get them myself.

My thoughts inexplicably turn to shoes. Something's not right.

I force myself to concentrate on how the girls must see the road leading to the cabin, tiny at the end of the wild squiggle that marks the end of the trail, our home growing larger with each step.

Today is different.

I can't see the cabin through their eyes. A blanket of unrest covers me. No. More than unrest. More like un-ease. Or dis-ease. Or disease.

That's it. Some kind of a sickness of spirit has touched them, us, and we don't know it.

That serpent in the Garden of Eden is out there somewhere.

Even though it's over one hundred degrees in the shade, I shiver.

"What's the matter with you?" Gracie peers into my face.

"Thinking about that darn well the girls found yesterday."

"They promised to stay on the road. If they don't, I'll tan their fannies myself."

"Mmmmmmmm." I keep vigil, moving out front of the cabin, searching the road for them.

"There's a truck," I report.

I'm surprised to see one on this road at this time of the day and am even more surprised to note that it is stopped.

When did that happen? It's like the hands of the clock have stopped, too.

I push my fist into the small of my throbbing lower back and squint, my eyes scanning for the girls. "Where are they?"

My heart flutters.

"What's happening?" Gracie peers down the road, but her eyes aren't as sharp as mine.

"Cain't see them neither. What's that truck up to?"

I bend over. "Mother Grace. Get Randall. I need

him."

She gives me a hard look and scurries off.

I take a deep breath.

Claire, back off from that ledge. You're teetering.

It's my nerves.

Nothing more.

But I need for Rand to check it out. Even if he's upset at the interruption.

I try to anticipate my relief when the three of them arrive back here, laughing, and everything fine.

Chapter 18
Tessa - The Encounter

Nonni and I lug the lumpy cloth bags onto the bus. Mama will be really happy.

It will be like opening a birthday present with fun things in it. But for the baby.

I can't wait for my baby sister to arrive!

Peter stands halfway down the aisle of the bus. He blocks us from reaching our favorite seats across the back where we usually sit.

He's bigger than we are, and he stares at us without blinking.

Peter smacks my knee with his lunch box. "Move it! Or you'll be sorry!"

His sister Genean pokes her head from around him. "Yeah. Move."

Mrs. Ross sits behind the big steering wheel, but she doesn't notice 'cuz she's busy talking to another kid.

She doesn't hear what they said to us, or she would make them apologize.

And give the seats back to us.

But she's busy.

"Don't tell, or I'll kick you in the butt!" Peter sticks his face close to mine, and his breath smells like tuna.

I turn my head.

He makes a rude gesture like he's punching us, and I do believe he'll hit us if we don't obey him.

We slowly shuffle backward, with our arms full, to sit in empty seats across from Cristina and Alonzo.

"They made us move, too!" Cristina points at Peter and Genean, who are stretched across the bench seat in front of the emergency exit.

We stuff everything under our feet.

When it's time to leave, our feet hit the ground before we hear Mrs. Ross calling, "Your bags!"

Cristina staggers down the stairs with both bags in her arms. Laughing, she almost falls out of the bus when she bends over to hand them to us.

We begin our walk home.

Our home looks tiny as my pinkie nail at the end of a long and crooked finger.

Nonni picks out a rock and scoots it to the middle of the empty road.

Her right shoe is already covered with dust. Mama worries about our shoes.

"You can't go to school without them, girls, so take care of them."

I worry about them, too.

When I look at my feet, I curl my toes under.

I can't help it that my feet grow a little bit every night when I'm asleep.

"Shoes cost money we don't have."

I don't mind that by the time I fit into Nonni's shoes they'll already have holes in them.

Like the pair she's wearing now.

It's a regular old day with a few fluffy clouds marching above us as we set out.

"Lookee!" I point up. "There's a line of elephants.

See that one? His trunk?"

Nonni stops. "I see the little one, like Dumbo with his big, floppy ears. He's at the end trying to catch up."

I admire the cartoon scene in the sky, and chicken hawks sail overhead stretching their reddish-brown wings wide.

She calls out. "Look at the pretty blue, white, and orange wildflowers."

I hurry to the side of the road where she's pointing.

I love their bright colors!

The orange ones are poppies, the special flower for our state. California poppies.

I am happy that I recognize them.

I think Mrs. Williams would be proud of me too.

The white flowers have little spots of yellow in the middle. The blue ones have curly petals.

We set down our bags, and Nonni and I make little bouquets in different colors.

"Mine is for Mama!"

She replies with a giggle, "This one is for Grandma Grace."

I return to the bag and wrap my arm around it. I hold the flowers tight in my other hand.

I have to pay extra attention as I walk. I can hardly see the road with all of the stuff I'm carrying.

Nonni does the same. But she keeps kicking her rock 'til we get to the spot in the road where we left for the well yesterday. Where we got into trouble.

We stop and then stick our chins in the air.

"Keep your face turned away from it!" Nonni directs.

That's when I hear growl of a truck coming down the road behind us.

Nonni leaves the rock in the middle of the road.

We move over for it to pass, but it stops beside us.

"Hey, girls. I need help!" A man with a cowboy hat is driving, and he smiles at us.

He waves like he knows us.

Then he reaches over from behind the steering wheel.

He rolls the window down on the passenger side. Next to us.

She and I look at each other. My sister's eyes widen with worry.

She shoves me behind her, and I twist to see around her. But she's mostly in the way, and I can only see a little bit of the man's ear and hat.

She swivels her head toward me. "Don't look, Tessie. Don't talk! He's a stranger. Remember yesterday? We promised Mama and Daddy we wouldn't talk to strangers."

Just yesterday!

His voice is low and rattles like gravel in a bucket. "Hello, girls. I'm lost! Can you help me?" He waits.

We don't reply. I look down at the ground. I close my eyes and hope, hope, hope that when I open them, he'll be gone.

"Walk. Don't talk. We promised." Nonni touches my elbow.

We begin walking.

Slowly, clutching our bags, and staring straight ahead down at the road.

Pretending like he isn't there.

We don't want to get in trouble. Again.

Why doesn't he go away? He must know little kids like us aren't allowed to talk to strangers.

We hear the truck crunching on the dirt, and it catches up with us.

"It's okay," he says through the open window.

The truck slowly inches forward with our steps.

"Here. Look at this picture. Jack's wife. I'm looking for Jack's wife."

We still don't look up, but we do have a neighbor named Jack.

"You don't have to talk. Just look at it. Point which way I should drive. Do you know her? Look!" His voice is loud and stern. "Look now!"

I peek around Nonni. He's holding a photograph in his hand, waving it in our direction.

I can clearly see it from where we're standing, statue still. Just like Mama told us to do with dangerous snakes when it's too late to run.

I can't help it.

I follow his directions and look at the picture.

It's a naked lady. I've never seen her before.

What I do see is a dark shadow, a dark red shadow, all around him, and I smell vinegar.

In my six-year-old heart, I know we're in trouble.

And that something bad, real bad, is about to happen to us.

A voice deep down inside me screams, "Run! Run! Run!"

It's like my feet are stuck in mud. But no matter what, I will keep our promise. We will keep our promises.

We don't say a word to the stranger.

Chapter 19
Randall - Gun It!

"Really? You need me? Right now?" I squint to see what Claire's pointing at. "I was about to mix cement for the patio while there's daylight. This better be good."

She straightens up and puts her hands on her hips. She frowns as she stares at the road, shading her eyes with her right hand.

The color in her face drains. "Where are they? Something's the matter! I know it!"

"It's okay." I attempt to placate her without taking my eyes from the road.

I'm feeling creeped out myself. I want to brush off her panic, but sometimes she has a sixth sense that shouldn't be ignored.

"There!" She points down the road. "Two trucks now."

We squint at the dust lines drifting in different directions.

She's right. One vehicle continues toward us before turning east at the crossroad. Another dust cloud beelines toward the Lone Wolf Colony.

As the air clears, we strain to catch sight of the girls.

A sob escapes from her. "Just like yesterday. It feels just like it did yesterday."

Ma puts her hand on Claire's elbow. She touches her in a way she usually doesn't and that Claire wouldn't normally tolerate.

I check my watch. "It'll be okay. They're out there, probably under all that dust. Or maybe they're late."

They should've gotten off the bus about fifteen minutes ago.

I can't stand here doing nothing. I spring into action and grab my keys from the picnic table.

Suddenly things don't feel right to me, either.

"I'll get the girls! We'll be back in a jiffy."

Claire melts onto the picnic bench. She leans back, tipping her face toward the glaring sun with her eyes closed. "Sweet Jesus! Protect my babies!"

Ma's gaze bores into me.

"Better gun it, Sonny."

Chapter 20
Nonni - Breaking Promises

I can't believe it.

By the end of the day, we've broken every promise we made to Mama, Daddy, and Grandma Grace.

To walk straight home on the road.

Not to speak to strangers.

And to never, ever go near that well.

But I have a deep, dark feeling that bad man is in even bigger trouble than Tessa or me even if we live to be one hundred years old.

Which we might not, after this afternoon.

Later, we couldn't agree on the color of the truck although Tessa's recollection of green proved true.

But I remembered everything the man said and did.

It wasn't until about a decade later that I understood what he was asking for and what it meant— and then I almost had a nervous breakdown—but that's another story.

However, at age eight, confronted by this stranger forcing himself into our lives, my feet refuse to move.

"Do something. Anything." I command my feet. "Run!"

They stay rooted to the ground.

"Well. You know her? Where she lives?" The man waves the photo at us through the open passenger window.

His piercing blue eyes command me. "You. Girl. Come on over here. Now."

Again, I will my feet to run down the road toward our cabin.

If I do that, if we do that, I hope he'll go away.

He must know he shouldn't be talking to us.

What? What's he asking?

I've never seen a picture of a naked lady before. Mama doesn't run around naked though Tessa and I take baths together.

We sometimes run around without clothes to dry off.

This photo seems like a different type of naked.

He says, "Answer me. Point to where she lives."

We aren't allowed to talk to strangers unless we're with our parents. But we've never had a stranger talk to us before when we were alone.

We haven't talked to *him,* so we haven't done anything wrong.

Why, oh why, oh why, won't he go away?

I can't get that picture out of my mind.

How do I tell him I didn't know the woman in the photo without talking to him?

Do I have to answer him?

How can I make him go away?

If I had a magic wish, it would be for Tessa and me to disappear, pouf, right in front of him.

Run!

Before I can move, or get Tessa, who's standing behind me, to move, he says, "I will pay you a quarter."

That gets my attention for a split second.

Now, a quarter is a lot of money. Tessa and I don't get an allowance, so we don't have any money.

With a quarter, I can buy twenty-five pieces of root beer flavored penny candy at the market, and I love candy.

Mama doesn't care much for sweets, except for angel food cake or chocolate pudding with sliced bananas on top, so we hardly ever have any at home.

And usually not candy. She says they'll rot our teeth.

Maybe I can still get the quarter without talking to him.

I sneak a peek, but he's looking down at something in the truck.

"I'll pay you a quarter," he repeats, "to…"

Quick as one of those snakes we'd been warned about, he uncoils across the passenger seat and flips the handle so that the door swings open toward us, almost smacking us.

He points down.

Again, I don't know what he's talking about, but everything happening feels wrong.

Totally wrong.

"Come here!"

His voice cuts through the air like a knife straight into my heart.

I peek up at his face and can tell he's used to ordering people about.

There's something slightly familiar about him. I notice the scar across his eyebrow.

My heart pumps so hard I'm afraid he hears it *chug chug chugging*.

What should I do?

Tessa whimpers. "Red. Bad man."

Hearing her breaks me out of my trance. "Run! Out

there!" I wave my hand toward the wilderness.

We let go of our scrunched flowers.

Tessie trips, drops her bag, and twists around to pick it up.

"Leave it!" I tremble. "Run!"

Still clutching my bag, I dart into the desert with her behind me.

"Damn you, kids! Come back! Your mama needs you!"

His voice sounds deeper than before. And louder.

Kind of like Daddy's, only Daddy's is kind and doesn't strike fear in my heart.

Have I heard it somewhere before?

I stop for no more than, as Grandma Grace would say, a split second when he says this, and then my instincts urge me forward.

"Run toward the well!" I stretch my fingers out and push her ahead of me. "Faster!"

"Come back! Or I'm gonna follow you home. You'll be sorry!"

I push Tessa ahead of me, a sob escaping from my clenched lips.

"Stop! Or your family will suffer, and it will be your fault!"

I crane my head to take a quick look at the man, who is now standing at the back of his truck zipping up his pants.

He reaches into the truck bed and pulls out a couple of big, brown cloth bags and a coil of rope.

Tessa trips, and I fall against her. "Up, Tessie," I demand. She scrambles to her feet.

This is not a game of tag where we chase each other around the cabin. Or a game of Zig Zag where we take turns being "it."

He is "it," and *he* is scary. And we need our safe zone now.

"I said. Come back! Right. Here!"

I stumble through the heat waves rippling off the bright dirt.

Twisting around, I take another quick peek.

He moves slowly while we scamper through uneven gullies and around bushes.

Am I stuck in a bad dream, the kind where I'm running but my feet are caught in that rubber cement we use in school for art projects?

Because that's exactly what this reminds me of. Only it isn't a nightmare.

I'm wide awake, and the pounding in my heart is real.

The man finishes gathering his supplies, or whatever they are, and stares out toward us like he can see us.

"Mama needs you!"

While his face looks a little like Daddy's when he hasn't shaved over the weekend, the strange look on his face prickles pins and needles down my spine.

No, this isn't a game.

He takes another leisurely step toward us, like he has all the time in the world, which he probably does.

This road is almost always empty when we walk home. Except for today.

"Faster!" I drop my bag and hear the clinking sound of glass baby bottles.

I scoop up a couple of them up as I dart ahead.

"I. Am. Going. To. Get. You!"

He steps off the road into the wild but suddenly

pivots as a truck barrels down the road toward him spewing dust.

We throw ourselves under the closest bush and lay flat on our tummies, praying no snakes are napping under it.

I squint through a break near the bottom of the creosote branches.

The driver of that second truck might be Jack, but I'm not sure. I've only seen him once, and that was on the day he helped Daddy with the cement foundation.

I stare at the man with the cowboy hat who's dropped his supplies down on the ground behind the truck.

It looks like the Jack-man is probably asking him if he needs help.

I wonder if he's showing him the picture. The man shakes his head *no* and shrugs his shoulders with a laugh before the Jack-man gets back into his truck and drives away.

"Look, Tessie."

I maneuver up onto my knees so I can see better, careful to keep my head down. "He's putting his stuff into his truck. He's turning around and driving to the main highway."

I can't believe it, but it's true. When I crane my neck the other way, I see the dust following Jack east of the crossroads.

Why didn't I call out to him for help?

Tessa whines, "Can we go home now? I wanna go home."

"Wait. I have to think!"

"He said he's gonna get us."

How does he know where we live? He says we'll

be sorry. What does that mean?

The more I think about it, the more confused I am.

Should we go home now or not?

Will he come after us and hurt Mama and Grandma Grace?

Tessa hiccups. "He said Mama needs us."

"We're almost to the well. Quick." I say. "We'll be safe there."

"But we promised we'd never go there again!"

"Mama wouldn't send that man to get us."

"He's a bad man. With a big dark red cloud around him."

I agree. I hadn't seen the cloud, but I also know in my heart that he's a bad man.

I straighten my back a little, my knees still bent, and peer down the road toward the Lone Wolf Colony.

The man's truck sits there. Right at the corner of the big highway but not moving. Stopped.

Is he going to turn around to come back and get us like he said he would?

Tessa crawls forward a little on her hands and knees.

I have a bad feeling about all of this, and I need to protect Tessa.

After all, every day when Daddy lets us out at the bus stop, he says, "I'm counting on you, Nonni. Take care of your baby sister."

I take my job seriously. "Yes, sir, Daddy sir!"

That's our private joke about Daddy's time in the Army and how he had to address his bosses, but without the "Daddy" part.

I had agreed again this morning, and I need to keep this promise even if I've broken a few of the others today.

What should I do? Wait out here?

What if he comes back to get us? This feels safer than being on the road.

Then I hear a noise.

"Tessa, run!"

Chapter 21
Tessa - She Saved Me

Nonni saves us. She does. My sister tells me to run into the desert with her.

We hide behind scratchy bushes on our bellies.

We're breaking our promises, and we're also breaking some other kind of law.

I'm not sure which one, but I can feel it.

After a minute or ten, she crawls back to get the bag she dropped.

Mine is by the road, too far away.

This is what happens next.

Nonni whispers, "Stay down. Hide behind the bush."

She squats behind the bush. "He's driving back to our bus stop."

She stands up to take a better look. "Stay flat on your tummy on the ground."

I don't wiggle. Not even a little bit.

"The truck's stopped at that corner. It's not moving."

"I wanna go home now." I hiccup.

Dust fills my mouth.

I cough.

Tears roll from my eyes and drip into the dirt.

"We better stay out here until he's gone. So he doesn't follow us home." She peeks from behind the bush to see if the truck has moved.

This makes sense, but I still want to go home. Right now. Into Mama's arms.

"The truck's not moving!" She points toward the main road.

I don't want him to follow us home.

He might hurt me and Nonni and Mama and Grandma. That's what he told us he would do.

I'm worried, but Nonni's smart. We must wait here until she says it's safe to leave.

"Stay down." She rocks on her knees and peeks around the bush. "He's sitting there in his truck."

"I want to look, too." I begin to stand up.

She pushes me back down.

I grab at her arm. "He's a bad, bad man. The color around him is bad."

She sits back down on the ground and motions me next to her. "I know. He's a scary stranger, and we have to stay away from him. It's time to crawl over there."

She points to the well where we'd been the day before.

There's a crumbled fireplace on the other side of it.

"Go!" She gives me a little tap on my hiney, and I begin crawling over the dirt and rocks.

"Keep going," she whispers as we draw closer to the well.

Dark clouds are grabbing onto each other in the sky above us.

I'm tired. I want to lie down on my belly. To rest for a minute. Or maybe three hours.

But I know we must keep moving.

Nonni will make me do it even if I don't want to.

"Move faster. We can stop in a minute."

I wipe my eyes with the back of my hand. I sniff hard.

I move forward a couple of inches at a time. Finally, we reach the next bush.

From this spot, I see the concrete rim of the well. Right where I looked into it yesterday.

This does not feel right.

We promised!

We're going to get into the biggest trouble of our lives.

But there's nothing we can do about it now.

That big, bad man is out there ready to get us, and he might come back.

"Shhhhhh! Stop here for a minute, and we can rest." Nonni looks into the bag before closing it.

She purses her lips like she's sucking on a sour lemon candy. That's what her face looks like when she's thinking hard about something.

Suddenly I feel a sneeze coming.

I pinch the top of my nose, but I can't stop it.

It feels like ants are marching around inside my nose.

"Aa-a-a-a-a-chooooooo!" I clamp my hand over my mouth.

My ears feel like they're going to explode. I shake my head.

I pinch my nose, hard, and I sneeze again.

She raises her head, startled.

She straightens up a little to look down the road. "It's okay. He's probably too far away to hear you."

"I couldn't help it!" Fear floods me.

"Shhhhhh!" Nonni reaches over.

She pats my arm, like Mama does when I'm sad or

upset. "I have another idea. Pretend we're playing Zig Zag. We'll go to the well. Then, we'll crawl over to that broken fireplace. It will be our Safe Zone. We can hide behind it, and we'll be fine."

That's what Mama always says. "We'll be fine."

She nudges me with her foot.

My sister has a plan, so I stop crying.

I can do this. "Okay. But you go. In front of me."

"Stay low. Follow me." Nonni gets down on her hands and knees.

She begins scuffling toward the well. She drags the bag behind her through the dirt.

I follow her tracks, copying her moves.

I try not to put my hands or knees on pebbles or poky branches that will hurt them.

I crawl forward with my ears listening for the truck to return, but mostly I hear myself breathing hard and my heart pounding.

It feels like Daddy's hammer nailing two pieces of wood together.

Another cloud blocks the sun, and I shiver.

A bad feeling hangs over my head. I know we'll be in trouble.

We are in that dangerous land our parents made us promise never to go into.

That we *promised* them we would stay away from.

I don't want them to be mad at me. But I have to follow Nonni.

There's danger everywhere, and the Safe Zone will save us.

Nonni will save me.

She reaches the well, sits down, and digs into the bag.

She pulls out two glass baby bottles and unscrews the lids.

I scoot down on my bottom next to her.

"Look around, Tessa. Grab some small rocks that will fit into these."

I don't move, but I look around.

I find pebbles I can reach from where I'm sitting. Some are round and some sharp.

I stack them up into a pile.

Nonni drops them, one at a time, into the bottles.

She hands me one. "Here. Fill the rest of this up with dirt. All the way to the top."

She digs her fingers into the ground and shows me how to do this.

Again, I copy everything she does.

She fills the other bottle with dirt. Then, she twists the lid with the nipple back on.

I do the same.

The new baby, when she comes, will not like to drink this dirt milkshake.

This I'm sure of.

"Watch me." She has one of the bottles in her hand. "Aim it at the bad man's head if he gets near us." She's on one knee now.

"Like this." She pulls her arm back behind her head and pretends to throw it at something in front of us.

But she doesn't let go.

I hold the bottle. Just like her. I pretend to throw it, too, but don't let go.

I'm still shaking all over. But I know I can throw the bottle hard if I have to.

I know I can.

My arm is strong from playing tetherball with Bobby each day. I even beat him today.

Mama always says, "Practice makes perfect."

I wish I could throw the bottle right now at that man's head.

If the bad man comes back, I'll throw the bottle at his face.

I'll pretend like I'm whacking his face with the tetherball, just like I did Bobby's that one time.

Nonni motions me to follow her. She pushes the bag under the bush.

Then we begin crawling again.

I don't want to be a crybaby, but I'm shaking again, all over.

I can't stop myself, and I can hardly crawl.

She stands up to check on where the bad man is now.

My foot shakes so hard my shoe flies off. I grab for it, but it slips out of my hand. It flips over my head right into the well.

I grab for it, but it's gone.

Gone!

Mama told me to take care of my shoes so I can wear them to school.

Mama says we don't have money to buy more.

Now, one shoe is down in the well.

I can't believe it.

My heart feels like it is breaking.

I crawl over and peek down into it. I can't see it. I scoot closer and lean against the rough edge of the well to look in.

Crack!

The broken cement crumbles.

I begin to tip in. I grab at the side of the well with my fingernails. I scratch at the cement, but I'm still falling in. Head first.

I can't stop myself.

"Nooooo!"

She grabs my legs and wraps her arms around them.

At school, I hang upside down on the monkey bars all the time.

But this view, upside down into the well, is dark and deep and scary.

Far below, I see my shoe lying in a pool of water.

My tears roll up my forehead and into my hair. Some of them drop into the well.

I think I hear them plunk when they hit the bottom.

All of a sudden, I remember the *Peanuts* comic strip and the funny boy and his dog.

Each week I wait for the Sunday funnies with its rows of colorful pictures.

Last week, Nonni read me the picture story about a man, a prisoner, tied up in a pit with a big pendulum.

She marked *prisoner* and *pendulum* in the dictionary.

In that cartoon, Charlie Brown said, "It sounds like an exciting story."

Well, here I am now hanging upside down in this pit. It is exciting and scary in that same bad way.

I can hardly breathe.

There is no pendulum to slice me up, but I know it's going to hurt a lot if she lets go and I fall on my head.

I hold my breath.

"Don't wiggle!" She squeezes me tighter.

I force myself to hold still.

I barely hear her.

She whispers. "Shhhhhh! I hear something. He's back!"

Chapter 22
Randall - Bouquets

My truck thumps toward the spot where the two trucks had crossed paths. Maybe Claire has spooked me. Or even Ma, whose demeanor usually errs on the side of stoic.

My optimistic frame of mind evaporates.

I punch the accelerator. Clouds cast ominous shadows on the ground. The air tastes of copper.

The road's empty except for a solitary truck moving away toward the Colony. My watch shows 3:30. It's at least fifteen minutes past the girls' usual departure from the bus.

Where are they?

The district must surely check gas tanks and tires each day. With my problem-solving efficiency expert hat on, I visualize a vehicle checklist.

If the bus is late, that driver better have a damn good excuse.

And it's odd—having not one, but two, trucks on our isolated stretch of road. Three trucks, if you count mine.

I slow down, my eyes scanning for any sign of the girls. They promised us they wouldn't leave the road or explore the countryside again.

Have I terrified them enough to keep my daughters on the road after all? Them finding an abandoned well yesterday was an eye-opener for me. For us.

Somebody needs to do something about these hundreds of death traps scattered throughout the desert.

Even with uncapped wells in the vicinity, Claire and I are in full agreement. The desert is a safe place to raise a family, our family.

Especially since we've scared the crap out of the girls about the danger of those viper pits.

There's little or no crime that I know of. I've only met honest, hard-working people trying to do their best. They've all come, like us. To this harsh land with hidden beauty for personal reasons and their own expectations of success.

I'll admit that after our not-so-little foray into living off the grid in the old homestead, I'm looking forward one day to flipping a light switch on the wall and flushing an indoor toilet. I can hardly wait to twist a faucet handle. Or fill a glass of water.

And if I'm getting tired of feeling like we're on a never-ending campout, I can imagine how Claire, a city girl at heart, must feel with the kids and all. Ma can handle roughing it better.

Contrast is good, however. I appreciate the simple, honest life out here with no city crimes or corporate jungle battles. And I still can't believe they'd fired me!

I pull myself back from my thoughts when I see two little bouquets of wilted wildflowers abandoned in the dirt on a berm.

I stomp on the brakes. The back of the truck fishtails in the dirt, and I throw open the driver's door. There are a few bright patches of growth next to the road, so this is where the girls picked the flowers.

I search the soft dirt and identify the imprint of a

small shoe, about Tessa's size. I take another look around and see a print about the size of mine.

My heart does a 360-degree flip. It rained last night, so these shoe prints are from today. Nonni and Tessa are the only children walking down this road from the bus.

So.

Where are they?

The vein pounds in my temple. I follow the small prints in the dirt around the bushes closest to me. I trip over a small bag, tipped over, baby clothes spilling out.

It's like the other ones Claire told me Nonni and Tessa brought home from school.

What's it doing out here on the ground?

Shivers jolt down my arms. My heart thud-thud-thuds hard in my chest. Maybe Claire is right. Something *is* wrong, terribly wrong.

I spot another set of footprints, a little bigger than Tessa's, near the creosote bush. Nonni's?

Both sets lead into the forbidden wild. The forbidden territory. My fear spikes into anger.

If those kids are out there, they'd better have a damn good reason. As far as I'm concerned, they're in deep trouble. Belt-spanking trouble.

But what about those man-sized set of prints on the berm? My mouth goes dry, and I can't swallow.

I peer up the road again toward the bus stop. The truck parked there a few minutes ago has disappeared.

My mind turns back to the scene in front of me, racing for explanations of what's in front of me.

Have the girls really been here, walking into the bushes? Or is the bus late? Maybe, even with the rain, these are their prints from yesterday.

But the fresh flowers point to the girls being here this afternoon, just a few minutes ago.

The big, fat $64,000 question remains, "Where are they?"

I can't come up with a viable scenario that explains everything I see in front of me.

I put my fingers into my mouth. I shriek out our ear-splitting family whistle, which I use to round everyone up for dinner. I know it cuts through the desert air for a long distance, so I whistle again.

A short blast, followed by a longer one that trails down.

I cup my hands to my mouth. "Girls! Girls! Answer me!"

"Help! Daddy! Help!" A scream pierces the air.

I leap through the brush. Down dirt gullies. Over sandy hillocks. Bounding toward her scream.

I scramble into the small clearing. Lose my footing. Land on my hands and knees.

I see Nonni, her arms wrapped around Tessa's legs, the rest of her sister's body out of sight down what must be that well. The one they promised to stay away from for the rest of their lives.

"Help! She's slipping!" Nonni sobs.

I lunge forward and forcibly grab my youngest daughter's hips. And I pull her up and over the edge of the gaping hole.

This death trap.

Her face is purple and sweaty. Tear tracks roll up her dusty forehead as I turn her right side up.

I slam her into my chest and squeeze her tight. Our hearts pound against each other.

I reach out and gather Nonni into our little circle.

We stand still for a minute.

We breathe hard, hang onto each other, and sense the tragedy that was narrowly averted. My momentary relief at finding and rescuing the girls is replaced with red-hot anger.

"What in Sam Hill do you girls think you were—" I sound stern. I *am* stern.

Nonni interrupts me. "Daddy, I thought you were the bad man coming back to get us."

I'm stunned. "What? What? What'ja say, honey?"

"The bad man…" Tessa repeats. "He said Mama needed us. He got mad when we ran away."

"What did the bad man want?" I barely can force myself to stay calm.

Nonni speaks so softly I almost miss what she says. "He asked us where Jack lived. Made us look at a picture of a naked lady. Wanted me to…"

Fury floods through every cell of my body.

I race through the brush toward my truck with Tessa, who's missing one of her shoes, tucked under one of my arms.

I drag Nonni behind me.

I see everything through a fiery lens: the dirt, the sky, the truck.

I'm filled with a terrible, bloody, primeval urge to find this evil man.

To put my bare hands around his neck.

To squeeze the life from him.

Tessa looks at me from her awkward position. Her face is white against her big, splotchy freckles, and her body flaps like a rag doll.

She whimpers. "Sorry, Daddy."

Nonni, at my elbow, is silent.

Tessa raises her voice. "Daddy! I'm sorry! She saved me!"

I throw both of them into the front seat of the truck.

I glance at Nonni's pale, expressionless face as I hurtle our truck back to our cabin.

Rage flows through my veins. I hit a crook in the road so hard I bounce up and bite my tongue.

I swallow the tangy, metallic blood in a single gulp.

I'm so angry I can't speak.

Chapter 23
Claire - High Stakes

"He has them! Praise Jesus!"

Rand's truck barrels down the lane toward us, and I can see the girls sitting next to him.

I look at the swirling clouds above, waiting for peace to fill me. It doesn't.

"I cain't wait to hear what they've been up to. It better be good, or they'll be in for it!" Gracie's chin juts forward, but she's not ready to claim victory yet.

Rand cranks the steering wheel hard to the right, his tires spewing dirt and rocks in a small rooster tail, before slamming on his brakes.

The truck slides another yard before stopping.

He flings open the driver's door and reaches across the seat to pull the girls out, one at a time. They're covered in dirt, sweat, and tears. His jaw is tight and his eyes, narrowed.

Tessa cries, "Bad man, bad man," while Nonni looks like she's in one of her sleepwalking trances.

The yellow dog gets up from the shade where she's resting and pushes against Tessa, who buries her face in its furry neck.

"Watch out for that dirty dog!" Mother Grace waves her hands at the dog. "Shoo!"

Tessa cries out with unusual defiance. "No! Taffy's mine!"

"What bad man?" I shove the dog away from Tessa. "Come to the picnic table."

I drag the girls to the front of the cabin, and the dog follows, undeterred.

"We have a big problem here." Rand's voice vibrates with some emotion I can't quite put my finger on.

Alarmed by his tone, I turn toward him, and a whoosh of warm liquid floods down my legs, drenching my legs and feet.

"Ohhhh. Nooooooo. My water! It broke!"

I balance myself against the table and sit down heavily on the wood plank bench.

With both Nonni and Tessa, once my water had broken, my labor began in earnest. My second delivery was shorter by five hours.

"We have to go to the maternity hospital. Right now." I gasp as a pain deep in my pelvis forces me to bend over.

Rand's eyes flash with alarm, and he rattles his keys. "Ma! Drive Claire to the hospital in Sally. That car have enough gas?"

She nods but a frown crosses her face. "Why ain't you driving her there yourself? What's going on?"

He shakes the keys in his hand. "I'm taking Nonni and Tessa to the sheriff's office."

"Ma's driving me? Where're you going?" I slowly straighten up as the pain subsides.

"Don't worry. Taking care of it. Ma'll get you there. Go!"

I hear him but don't understand what he's saying.

"We'll meet you there. Soon." He takes Nonni's arm and points to the truck.

"Claire, you hang on a dang minute!" Mother Grace hurries into the cabin to retrieve a damp washcloth.

"Girls, lemme clean you up a little. Y'all look like you've been finger painting on your faces and rolling around in the dirt!"

Her actions hold a false note of playfulness, totally out of character for her, and her hand shakes as she dabs at their faces and hands.

"Ma! No time for that!"

The pain strikes again, doubling me in half. As soon as I catch my breath, I let out a series of short "hee hee hee hoos."

Nonni and Tessa stare at me, speechless, with questions in their big eyes.

"Hurry, Ma! Claire needs help! Now! There's a bad man out there, and they better catch him before I do."

Chapter 24
Nonni - I'm Going to Jail

Daddy drives like a crazy man, Tessie cries, and I'm sure I'm going to jail. My words stick deep inside my chest, and I can't get them out. I made this happen.

If. If. If.

If I hadn't stopped walking when the man asked us that question, maybe he would've kept driving.

If I'd yelled to Jack for help, maybe he would've helped us.

If I hadn't headed Tessa and me out to the wilderness, she wouldn't have tipped into the well.

If we hadn't run out there, Daddy wouldn't be mad at us for being out there in the first place.

Now he's angry, very angry. At us, and, I think, at the bad man. We're all in big trouble, and it's all my fault.

Once we arrive at the sheriff's office, I figure we'll be arrested. For being bad children.

Who didn't obey their parents.

Who broke the three promises they'd made the day before.

Who disappointed their father.

Again.

My mouth is so dry, I can't even work up a spit swallow. I'm not sure that I can even speak. Or will ever be able to speak again.

I wonder how long we'll be there. In jail.

We round the corner at the main street by the Lone Wolf Colony, without even slowing down, and Daddy drives extra fast on the paved road where we hardly bounce around at all.

When he skids into the Sheriff's Station, slamming on his brakes at the last minute, an officer runs outside to see what's happened.

This is where it gets interesting. It might have been helpful if Daddy had talked to Tessa and me about why we were going to see the sheriff and what might happen, but maybe he didn't know how.

Instead of our being arrested, as I expected, we are given glasses of cold water and told to wait in a small room with plastic chairs while Daddy speaks to the sheriff in a different room.

If I wasn't so worried, I could have enjoyed the ice cubes more.

After a while, Daddy comes back and sits at the Formica table with us. Finally, the sheriff bustles into the room.

"Hello there, little ladies," he says. "Tell me what happened."

He drills us about what the man looked like and what the truck looked like.

I'm finally able to speak, if only in a whisper, but I can't remember the colors of the truck, or, at least, they change every time I try to name them.

In my mind, it's a two-toned truck, maybe brown on the top and tan on the bottom half—or the other way around.

I don't know what model of truck it is since all trucks look pretty much the same to me.

Tessa, however, is very specific about its color—green, and she doesn't budge on her opinion. Of course, it turns out later she was right.

Her main impression of the man, from where she'd stood behind me, is that he is surrounded by dark red shadow surrounding him.

That description doesn't lend itself to confidence on the part of the sheriff.

"It was dark. It was *this* big!" Tessa waves her arms wide above her head, in a big arch. "Did you write this down?"

She stares at the sheriff who scribbles it into his small brown leather notebook, shaking his head.

He asks me if I've seen the man.

I respond that I don't think I've seen him before, but maybe I've heard him speak somewhere before. At the store or somewhere like that. I'm not sure.

The sheriff asks me the same questions in different ways like he's trying to catch me in a lie.

I may break promises, by accident, but I never lie! Okay, I lied yesterday to Mama about walking straight home, but that was different.

When he asks me to tell him about the picture and the quarter again, I don't have the vocabulary required to talk about this grown-up topic and struggle with retelling this story.

"Thanks for your help, little ladies." The sheriff holds out his giant paw of a hand, and we each shake it.

"We'll investigate this right away."

He shakes Daddy's hand, too, and then we're back in the truck going home.

"Daddy. I'm sorry," I mumble, not sure he can hear me over the sound of the engine. "It's all my fault.

Tessa did what I told her to do."

He isn't driving as fast now on the way home, so the ride isn't as frightening as before.

"Pumpkin." As he glances at me, strands of dark hair fall over his wrinkled forehead.

"I'm the one who's the sorriest of all. That I didn't pick you up at the bus stop when I got off work early. This whole nasty fiasco could have been avoided."

He hits his hand against the steering wheel, and I jump.

"I thought the sheriff was going to arrest us! Or me! For breaking my promises." I rub my eyes with my fist.

"No, Nonni. You and Tessa didn't do anything wrong. Not with the man. Or maybe not even going into the desert to be safe. But that well *was* dangerous."

That last comment leaves me thinking in the silence that elapses between us.

Tessa bunches her lips, not saying a word, and I decide I must still be in trouble about the well even though Daddy didn't let the sheriff arrest us. What's going to happen to me?

Then I notice we're not traveling back on the same highway we'd driven out on.

"Where're we going, Daddy?" I'm suddenly fearful he's taking us somewhere else for our punishment.

Like maybe to the dairy where he left the mother cat and her kittens he'd found in the abandoned homestead cabin, one lot over from our cabin.

"Don't you girls remember? Your mama's having the baby now!"

My mind races ahead, still thinking up punishments, and I wonder if he's going to trade me in

for the new baby.
I certainly deserve it.

Chapter 25
Claire - Split in Two

I've never felt so split into two pieces in my life, never needing, yearning, to do two such totally different and impossible things at the same time, tied to the core of my family.

To my girls, now, or to my new baby girl, about to be born.

But I don't have a choice. Mother Grace is driving me to the hospital, and the labor pains are five minutes apart.

We have to get there quickly if I don't want to have this baby in the dirt.

We leave in such a rush I almost forget to grab the coffee can with the cash in it.

Following Rand down the road, we're literally eating his dust, which enters my nose and mouth and travels to my lungs and even my uterus.

My mental clock counts down, and I'm in a traumatic state of psychic and moral pain, worse than labor, for my children.

All day I've felt something was off. Wrong. In the core of my soul.

And I know from being with the girls for all of five minutes after Rand raced home with them that they are *not* okay.

That they have been traumatized.

Why can't I be with them now where they need me to be?

He feels certain that this evil perpetrator can be caught if he gets the girls to the sheriff in time.

Tessa cried and cried and cried while Nonni hardly uttered a sound.

Will they understand whatever it is that happened to them?

Will they forever wonder why I am not there with them at this horrible crisis in their lives?

If I were with them, I know I could help them mold this experience into something manageable that wouldn't affect their future selves.

But I'm not there, and I can't help them at all with whatever they're up against.

Whatever it is.

Breathe, breathe! Lord, take care of all of my family!

Mother Grace hurtles us along this rippled road that threatens to bounce the baby right out.

My labor pains are cresting one upon another like waves. That's the mental image I switch to.

I'm twelve years old with my head bobbing just above the back row of waves rolling by me.

I'm waiting for the "big one" that has enough momentum to carry me to shore with a smooth landing in the frothy surf, untouched by pebbles churning under the foamy edge.

I want a soft landing after a thrilling body-surfing ride in the Pacific Ocean.

That's not going to happen today with the intensity increasing. I'm tensing up for a metaphorical hard landing on the rocks and hope that I can stagger to my feet and run to the shore.

Mother Grace squishes her face into grumpy lines. "You okay?"

"No. I. Am. Not."

I concentrate on that wave again. The current picks up and threatens to suck me under.

I count backwards from sixty, but it's not enough.

Don't push. Blow, blow, blow!

I hear a grunt and realize it's coming from me.

I counteract it with *hee, hee, hee, hoo, hoooooo.*

This pain is so much stronger than what I went through while birthing Tessa and Nonni, who were delivered under the influence of anesthesia in a hospital near the beach.

I feel pressure build in my pelvic region, and my abdomen tenses hard as a rock.

I have an irresistible impulse to bear down.

"Noooooo!"

Good Lord, let it pass, let the pain pass.

I tug down my sodden panties, and my dress puddles around my hips.

I awkwardly pull my dusty feet up and position them against the dashboard, my knees far apart.

"Hee, hee, hoo, hoo, hoooooo!"

I breathe.

And pray.

And float.

And surf.

"Claire!" Mother Grace's voice cuts sharp as a knife. "You cain't do it in the car. You hear me?"

Cresting on another wave of pain, I don't answer her.

If I could, I'd tell her I'm finished with her.

But for now, she is my salvation.

Her words have given me the resolve to decide for myself—and show her that I am in charge of my body.

And my life.

And my family.

But first, I have to get this little hitchhiker, on loan from God, out as soon as we're at the doctor's.

I clench my teeth and use every bit of will power to fight the urge—no, the instinct—to bear down and push it, her, out.

"Keep those knees together."

I feel the pressure splitting me in half. "Hoo, hoo, hoo, hoo, hoooooo!"

I can't take it!

That damn Randall!

I didn't want to get pregnant, didn't plan on it now.

Wouldn't have picked this time for anything in the world, living in this isolated land with no electricity, no matter what Mother Grace says.

"Don't you dare!" Her screech scrapes my eardrums.

"Shut up!" I shout at her, shocked at my boldness, yet satisfied at the same time.

And then I slump down in the seat and push my shoulder against the door, involuntarily tipping my hips upward, seeking release, just as she pulls into the parking lot.

The next wrenching pain engulfs me.

I am hanging onto the wave as it lifts me up higher and higher, its angelic feathery veins etching the translucent curve, majestic, in the sunlight, which is so bright I must close my eyes.

I taste the salt and pray for a soft landing, and I feel

myself plummeting toward the rocks. Ahhhhhh.

"It's coming."

With one hand, I reach down and feel the slippery head.

Chapter 26
Gracie - Itchin' for a Fight

I cain't believe that woman, the gall of her having that baby now. I grip the wheel tighter.

What happened to the girls was terrible. They're just young innocents, flesh of my flesh.

Sonny didn't say anything before he lunged off with the girls to the sheriff's office right after Claire's water broke, leaking onto the dirt, making a little mud puddle.

I lay on the horn as we barrel into the parking lot.

A nurse, smoking near the entrance of the gray cinder-block building, throws herself outta my way, probably so I don't squish her flat.

I fling the car door open. "She's having the baby!"

Wide-eyed, the nurse runs into the building and returns with a wheelchair.

I hurry to the other side of Sally to see how Claire's doing. My skin goes clammy.

How did she pull that off as we arrived? I told her to wait.

"She had the baby." I point accusingly at Claire and the wet bundle she's cradling in her hands.

And I cain't tell if it's my little boy, just like I prayed for. Dreamt about.

Ever since Randall was born more than thirty years ago. If it is, we'll have someone to carry on the O'Brien name in this new generation, so I can breathe some. Pops, too, from beyond the grave.

The nurse rolls the wheelchair to the passenger door. Some way or another, she gets Claire, who's slouched down in the seat with the baby laying halfway onto her stomach, into it.

I grab the money can and follow them to a room with big bed in the middle, pictures on the wall, and a rocking chair in the corner.

A doctor in blue scrubs comes in, pulling on rubber gloves.

After Claire is situated on the bed and he's done a quick examination, he takes the baby from her, clamps and cuts the cord, and gives it a sharp pat on the back.

I hear a squeal.

"A boy?" I'm anxious to welcome my grandson into the family.

"Hmmmpf." His attention is on Claire.

He hands it to the nurse who shows it to her before hustling it across the room to a plastic box on wheels.

"A boy?" I repeat, and Claire lets out an awful noise and recommences grunting.

"Get ready! Another's coming." The doctor reaches down between Claire's knees.

Another one?

Claire moans loudly. Her voice changes, and she keens like a coyote at the moon on an extra long note.

She grunts loudly, and, plop, the doctor holds up another baby, this one red-faced and squalling.

Together, Claire's and the baby's voices meld like they're singing some kind of strange, wordless duet.

The baby turns toward me, and we lock gazes. I swear, it's like he recognizes me.

129

"Two boys?" I ask.

The doctor turns toward me. "Can't talk now." He directs the nurse, "Take the grandmother out."

The nurse shoos me toward a couch in the waiting room.

Another one? This family cain't handle one new mouth to feed, and now they have two?

But if'n they're boys…

My heart's already busting with greed.

The sights and smells bring me back to my seventeen-year-old self like it was yesterday.

I'm birthing my own child, three weeks early, in Louisiana, alone in our room by the barn, while the rest of the family's working the cotton farm on that humid summer day.

My lower back has ached all day, and there I am, squatting to expel the babe onto a blanket on the floor.

My new husband is older than me by a good ten years, and he's the only electrician in town. We'd gotten married one afternoon, and I was in the family way right quicker than you could shake a stick at me.

That l'il baby on the floor whimpers, turns blue, and then lies real still.

"Lord, help me!" I bleed on the blanket, and the room grows dark. But I don't allow myself to cry.

We bury the babe in a small wooden box, lined in burlap sacking, and I beg our swaddled firstborn not to notice.

I lost three more babies before one finally stuck. Randall. Finally. My first to survive, later followed by Jolee, his sister.

Birthing babies surely ain't for the weak of heart.

I push away the sadness that's turned me into my

tough old self.

My stoic husband and I always suffered separate like. That's the way it's meant to be between men and women, and I never saw it different with anyone else.

I don't understand why Randall spends so much time catering to Claire. Why does he talk to her so much? They act like a team of mules under the same yoke.

Maybe if she suffered more, she would grow up, like me.

It ain't fair. And he wants me to take care of her even with my hardened heart.

But she knows what she did. She took him away from me.

The door to the waiting room opens, and the doctor walks toward me. "Congratulations! For the baby girl! And you also have a grandson!"

The nurse pops her head out. "Doc. We have a problem here."

He swirls around and hurries back through the door behind her.

I sit upright. Speechless. Twins!

Claire just birthed twins, but most important of all, she has given me a grandson.

A grandson!

I'm not so excited about that new baby girl that butted her way out first since Randall already has two of those.

But that boy, he was itchin' for a fight.

That's my little Thomas Patrick.

An O'Brien to the core!

Chapter 27
Randall - The Watcher

I fill the tub behind the water tower partway and dump it over my head. My skin finally cools. That hundred-degree plus sun takes its due.

I'm back with the family for a whole twenty-four hours.

I've worked six days straight, from dawn to dusk. I've bunked down with some guys in a stuffy trailer. I hate to be away so much, but we need that money.

Despite their early arrival, the twins, five and six pounds respectively, have been home almost a month. Claire's birthing complications kept her in the maternity home an additional two days.

Though I'd been slated to begin that new job, Mr. Henderson, my lake resort project boss, let me stay home two days after Claire's return home. Then I'd hustled back to the site.

With deadlines and penalties looming, all us guys are working overtime.

Needless to say, Ma has stayed on even though Claire's not too happy about it.

Everyone's sleep deprived, except maybe Tessa, who's always been able to snooze through most anything. While she sleeps with one thumb in her mouth and the other wrapped around a bunch of sweaty curls, we're all up and working hard. Even Nonni changes diapers and burps the twins.

When one baby wakes up, the other wakes up. One cries, two cry. Then, they're both hungry. It's a never-ending cycle.

Claire's determined to build up her milk supply, but she doesn't have enough for both babies. The doc recommended goat's milk as a supplement, and either Ma or I pick it up at the dairy a couple times a week.

Claire's implemented what she calls "equal opportunity" nursing for the babies. Personally, I think they're both going on the bottle soon, full time. That'll make it easier for us to lend a hand.

I circle back around the cabin after leaving my dirty shirt in the laundry tub by the tank. Looking out, I see headlights bouncing along the washboard road, up and down, past the crossroads and continuing toward us.

The car pulls up out front. A man with a husky build and red face steps out. He wipes the back of his hand across his forehead.

"Detective Franklin Hunter."

We're standing out front to greet him when he arrives.

He shows his badge to Claire and Ma. "As you know, I've been working this case."

He looks at me. "Hello, again, Mr. O'Brien."

"Updates?" I ask. I've been squelching the small whisper in the back of my head.

What if this maniac comes back?

I've been assured, and reassured that patrols are in place. How can only four local officers cover more than one hundred square miles of desert?

The sheriff that day told me it was "unlikely that

lightning would strike twice."

My objection to that trite phrase is that while lightning is a random, storm-related phenomenon, stopping two little girls with a prepared spiel, a pornographic photo, and a lewd request is premeditated. And lightning does sometimes strike twice.

There's news. Hunter asks us to send the girls out of hearing range.

Nonni's happy to work on her Zig Zag game in the twilight. She sets Tessa to gathering little rocks that have migrated to the flat area outside our cabin where she's designed her previous two games.

While Tessa piles the stones off to the side, Nonni carefully drags the rake to mark a large oval perimeter.

Hunter tugs on his tie like it's choking him.

Hurry up, man. Time's a ticking.

"There's some news, but I need to ask a couple of questions." His eyes hold a knowing look, and I'm anxious to hear what he has to say. If only he'd hurry up.

A baby cries. Both Claire and Ma jump up, bumping into each other.

Ma gets to the door by a hair. "It's fine. I'll get him."

Claire responds, "Must be Fee."

"No, it isn't." Ma hurries inside, returning with Thomas in her arms and a bottle of goat milk.

"Fiona Grace is still sleeping." She glints at Claire who ignores her but raises an eyebrow at me.

I swear sometimes Claire acts like more of an adult than Ma, or even me. I should be more supportive of Claire, but Ma's a force to reckon with. I don't want to rock the boat until she puts the homestead in our name, like she promised.

We have bigger fish to fry right now. Like what's right in front of us.

I turn to Hunter. "What's up?"

"Did you or the girls see anything suspicious before the event? Or within the last two months?"

"Nope. Don't think so. Nothing out of the ordinary." I scratch my head. I've shuffled through my memories looking for the tiniest of clues and haven't identified one yet.

"Anything before or after school?"

"Not that I know of."

Hunter pivots to look at Claire. She hesitates before she replies.

"I had a strange feeling for a couple of days ahead of that... event, but nothing I could put my finger on." She glances over at the girls who are kicking a tumbleweed out of their way.

"She was as jumpy as a cat. Made us all jumpy!" Ma looks sheepish.

"Any specific type of thing that caused you to be nervous that day?" Hunter turns back to Claire.

She dips her head. Once again, she pauses. "Well, I'm always aware of when the girls are on their way home, and I was worried. Something felt off."

"Any reason?"

"No. I was about to go into labor. It was just a feeling, a strong feeling."

"Anything else?"

She bites her lip. "I felt like someone was watching us."

He asks, "Where? When?"

"Here. At home. At night. Before and *after* the..."

135

"What do you mean?"

Her brow furrows. She hesitates. "I haven't told anyone this, but while Randall's been away working for a week at a stretch, I think we're being watched. At night. But I've kept it to myself because he and Mother Grace already think I over-react about everything. Nobody can do anything about it anyway."

I look at her, startled. I feel the hair rise on the back of my neck. "What?"

She refuses to look at me. "Everyone has tip-toed around me since I had the babies. Like they think I'm a china doll that might break or something."

She finally locks her gaze on me before turning back to Hunter. "Yes, I'm sure someone's watching us. Taffy began barking at night, and it got me to thinking. And worrying. So, I came up with a plan. Before I go to bed, I lay two rows of thread in the dirt close to the window and weigh them down with small pebbles."

Ma arches her eyebrows and stares at her.

"A couple of times the thread's been all tangled up with a man's footprint beside it in the dirt. A little larger than yours, Rand. I know because I took your dress shoe and measured against it."

I'm speechless.

"I wondered what you was doin' with that shoe." Ma's eyes fix on Claire's.

"So, I knew it wasn't just me. Someone's been out here after dark at least twice. And…"

I interrupt, pulling her around to look at me, "Twice? And when were you going to tell me this?"

"This weekend." She lowers her eyes and rubs her arm.

Hunter takes notes. Then he drops a bombshell on

us.

"I don't want to alarm you, but we have reason to believe the perpetrator parked at the abandoned farmhouse near the bus stop for several days before he struck."

I scratch my neck. "I don't think I'm following you."

Hunter looks at us. "We've made casts of the truck tracks and hope to find the tires that match them."

"Ahhh…" Claire's breath comes out ragged as she turns her wide-eyed gaze to me.

Hunter asks me, "Did you notice any vehicles there when you dropped the girls off in the morning?"

I search my memory, checking for something new to pop up. "No, but did you talk to the bus driver? Maybe she saw something."

Hunter rummages in his pocket. "We've been conducting interviews with many people including Mrs. Ross. Nothing new there."

"Who else? Jack? He was there that afternoon."

"We're still trying to reach him. But there's another disturbing element."

Jack had told me his mother was ill. Maybe he was visiting her.

Hunter fishes a package of cigarettes from his jacket. "Okay if I smoke?"

I nod. I take the cigarette he shakes out of the pack for me. He pulls a packet of matches from his other pocket, strikes it, and offers it to me before lighting his own. The act of lighting up feels like a build-up to this new information. A way for the detective to gather his thoughts before speaking them out loud.

"There was an abduction out near Dead Man's

Point yesterday." He expels a stream of smoke.

I don't know what to say. My mind spins, trying to figure out what this means. What it means to us. "What the hell?"

"A pregnant woman was taken from the side of the road, after she had a flat tire. Her husband reported her missing. We found her automobile, abandoned. Later, she was left in an oversized burlap sack, actually, a gunnysack, off the main road. Somehow, she managed to push her way out of it. A passing driver picked her up."

Both Claire and Ma gasp.

"What's this have to do with our case?" My stomach cramps. I rise to my feet and pace around the table. I've already guessed the answer.

"Well, the descriptions of his truck and his face are similar to what your children reported."

My heart skips a beat. Who is this animal? Why's he still out there? Obviously still on the prowl, searching for more victims. Who else has he targeted?

My skin burns. Did he come back here for a second try at nabbing the kids or Claire? Or Ma? Why haven't I pursued this man myself? How could I leave my wife, mother, and children out here alone to work on the new job when evil is roaming through the desert?

Are we safe? Is anyone safe?

My mind floods with questions for which I have no answers.

"It's unusual for a perpetrator to target both children and adults, but we believe it's the same guy. The girls might have been a trial run for his later activity."

"He needs to be put out of commission." The girls

hear my raised voice and look at me. "You should have caught him by now before he comes back. What are you guys, a bunch of amateurs?"

I'm relieved school's out. Ma had driven the girls to and from the bus stop for the last three weeks. Everyone can stay put now. Maybe it's a false sense of security, but it makes me feel like I have some kind of long-range control to know where everyone's supposed to be.

"We've upped surveillance and alerted residents, widespread as they are, to band together for their own patrols."

I hate being away. This resort job won't be over in another three months. Until then, I'm often away from home for a week at a time.

If I were here, I'd sleep with the shotgun under the bed instead of in Ma's trunk. Maybe I can talk Ma into hiding it in the cabin somewhere, but I know Claire will worry about the kids getting into it.

In the meantime, we'll just have to be extra cautious. I'll check with Jack, if he's back, to make sure he checks on my family while I'm away. And I'll ask Annie and Hank, too. And I'll come home as often as I can.

All this time, I've been thinking the guy who did this to my girls had high-tailed it out of town so he wouldn't be caught. How stupid could I be? And now this? I want to take action, but there's nothing I can do.

The detective assures me that patrols are in place. He'll let us know if there are any changes. Several neighbors are on the alert. Things are under observation. And safe. Can I believe him?

Unless there're two of these maniacs, he's still out

here on the loose. Doing his evil deeds. One thing's for sure.

Whoever's doing this mayhem needs to be caught and throttled.

I want to be the one who does that.

Chapter 28
Tessa - The Water Truck

Tommy cries when he's hungry or wet.
Or if he wants to be picked up.
Or if he needs to be burped.
I can quiet him down better than anyone else.
Fiona doesn't cry too much. I don't want her to feel lonely, so I spend extra time playing with her.
I'm allowed to feed my baby sister her bottle if I sit on my mattress. But Mama makes me scoot back against the wall with her against my heart.
I love our hearts beating together.
Grandma Grace says it takes a while for the babies to recognize us. "I ain't lying. Their smiles are from gas."
She sounds sure. "They see mostly shapes, colors, and movements."
I think Grandma's wrong.
The babies know who I am. They know what I look like and what I smell like.
They know what I taste like, too, because sometimes they grizzle on my finger like they think it's a bone.
The babies are six weeks old. Mama lets me help give them sponge baths with a wet washcloth. I have to be careful to keep my hand behind their heads.
I pat their backs when they're ready to nap, and I

show them books and tell them stories from the pictures. I read them a few words, too.

I do lots for them. When they're older, I'll do even more for them.

Tomorrow is the Fourth of July. Daddy said if he gets to come home from the lake in time, he's taking us to the drive-in movie parking lot to see fireworks.

I hope we get to see them! It's hot today with clouds high above. It might rain tonight, but I hope it doesn't.

Sometimes we have thunder and lightning and no rain.

But sometimes we have thunder, lightning, and rain. If that happens, we have the washtubs in the yard to catch the water.

But I don't mind if it rains tonight as long as we get to see beautiful firework flowers up high in the sky tomorrow night like we did last year at the beach. Before we moved here.

Our neighbors, the Ritchies, and their dog, Delaware, sometimes visit us. Taffy and Delaware are friends and sniff each other. They chase each other while the grownups talk.

I heard Daddy tell Mr. Ritchie to "keep an eye on the place" and "watch out for strangers."

Uncle Nick visits us, too. Mama gives him some of her "world famous" sun tea that cooks in a jar on top our roof under the sun.

Nonni gets to climb up the ladder to get it, and I can hardly wait until they let me go up there after it.

Nonni tells me there are crystal doorknobs lying up there on the roof, too. The picture I get of them in my head, dark purple and sparkling, gives me a delicious shiver.

We don't have many visitors, but today I recognize the water truck when it comes to fill our tank.

Tommy cries, and Mama hurries to the cabin to feed him his bottle.

"You girls scoot in there, too, and stay out from underfoot, you hear?"

The look on Grandma's face means business so we straggle into the cabin even though we'd rather stay outside. The generator thumps, thumps, thumps.

I climb onto the small table to look out the window. I know water is being pushed up through the fat hose into the tank above the outhouse.

Mama turns toward me with tired eyes. "Tessa. Get down from the table and help Nonni with Fee."

"Mama, I want to see more!" I reluctantly climb down.

Nonni kneels next to the baby, who squeezes her finger. Mama finishes feeding Tommy and pats him on the back to make him burp.

All I hear are loud pumping sounds coming from the water truck.

She peels Fiona's fingers from her hand. "Here, Tessie. You play with Fee now. It's my turn to look."

I squat next to the baby and give her *my* finger to grizzle on. She smiles.

"No, it's not gas." I croon at her, and she dribbles milky slobber from the corner of her mouth.

Nonni climbs onto the table and peers out the window. With a sudden movement, she whips her face toward me, her braids snapping around her head.

Her eyes and mouth are wide open, and her face is pale like she's seen a ghost.

"Mama," she says. "I need to go to potty. Now!"

Mama looks up. "Honey, can't you wait?"

"Please, Mama. Hafta go!" She sounds like she's choking on something.

"If you can't wait, at least stay out of the way of the truck. And come right back. No fooling around out there."

Mama reaches down to undo the safety pin on Tommy's wet diaper, and Nonni runs out of the door before Mama changes her mind.

I see a dark orange line around her and wonder why she's scared.

Chapter 29
Nonni - We Meet Again

I slip outside and creep toward the water tower with the outhouse underneath.

In the distance, Grandma Grace waters the last of our half-burnt squash plants, and the beans look shriveled, too.

With her back to the cabin, she can't see me. Good. For sure, she'd wave me down, her hand pointing me toward the cabin.

Tessa and I understand her hand signals close up, or from a distance, as she directs us like the drum major at marching band at the Fourth of July parade.

Before we moved here.

The man turns toward the truck to fiddle with the shut-off valve.

A shiver creeps through my body like Mama says she sometimes gets when she paces around the outside of the cabin before sunset and early in the morning.

Or when she sometimes paces around inside the cabin before we go to bed.

Or sometimes late at night, when I peek through slitted eyes and see her pacing from one place to another and moving things around.

My true intention is to sneak a look at the man with the cowboy hat without him seeing me. That is, if Grandma Grace doesn't catch me.

If she'd been vigilant before, she has us on lockdown now that Daddy isn't here. There's no fooling around with her even if there's daylight. I'll be in trouble if I get caught.

Just to be on the safe side, I'll run to the potty while out I'm out here so I'm not adding lying to sneaking around.

I scooch close to the outside corner of the cabin. The man places his boot on the bottom rung of the ladder, ready to climb up to check the water level.

When he's finished, he'll climb back down, shut down the pump, and unscrew the heavy hose from its fitting. That's what I've seen happen before.

I flatten myself against the wall.

I poke my head around the corner, still hearing the pump chugging away.

Suddenly, I'm face-to-face with him.

How'd he get here when he was supposed to be up there?

Small bursts of light circle my head like fireworks. I force myself to breathe in and out.

I can't believe it. It's *him*!

Different hat, different truck, same face.

He speaks so low I almost can't hear him. "Little girl. You talk. Your family gets hurt. You hear?"

I swallow the sawdust lump in my throat and nod my head.

"Look at me." Slowly I look up. "Look into my eyes."

The last time I heard his voice was when he said, "Look at this picture."

Yes. It's *him*. A movement twitches one corner of his mouth, not reaching his pale cold-as-ice blue eyes.

I recognize the small scar in his eyebrow. I must remember all of these details, I tell myself.

"Say anything, your family will suffer. It will be your fault. Understand?"

I mumble, "Yes."

"I'll be back. Now, git!" He turns and continues to the truck where he turns a valve here, a switch there. Within a minute the loud thump, thump, thumping stops.

Grandma Grace catches me by the tank. This day is getting steadily worse by the minute.

She wipes her hands on her apron. "Nonni, back inside now. Don't think you're getting away with this."

The man turns toward me and mouths my name, "Nonni."

He tips his hat at me, and his smile doesn't reach his eyes.

He turns to Grandma Grace, who is at the water tank looking at him with suspicion. "I'll be back in a month, or whenever you need me. I'm not far away, and I'll keep my eyes out for you."

He side-eyes me with a quick, sly look as he says this.

"You sure you tightened the connectors? Don't want any water dripping." Grandma squints at him before hurrying over to check for herself.

I stand rooted to the ground as he opens the door of his truck. A red and black blanket falls onto the dirt. He grabs it and quickly shoves it onto the front seat before climbing back in.

The spell broken, I scoot into the cabin with silence and screams warring within me. I'll burst if I can't talk, and I'm terrified to make a sound. Whatever happens will be on my head. He's warned me twice. Then and now.

I drag myself back into the cabin where Mama's changing Tommy's diaper. Tessa looks at me with a question in her eyes, and Fiona clutches her finger.

"Your shadow's scared," Tessa says.

How did she know?

Chapter 30
Gracie - On the Loose

Detective Hunter stops by today, unexpected like, and I send the girls out to run their Zig Zag track. Sonny's still out of town working on the job.

Claire pops out of the cabin, wiping her hands on a dishcloth. It's just us womenfolk and youngsters here.

"He's on the loose." He strikes a match and lights his cigarette. "Attacked another woman and left her in a gunnysack near the train tracks about ten miles away."

He walks in a circle, blowing out another stream of smoke. "She's in the hospital, seriously injured."

"What are you doing about it?" Claire enunciates each word with a sharp edge that could cut through cured concrete.

One fist is clenched, and her other arm clutches Fiona. Thomas still naps inside the cabin.

"We've stepped up patrols but don't have enough officers to go around. We'll send someone out when folks call."

"Just how're we supposed to do that without a phone?" Claire smacks the picnic table hard.

The detective takes another long drag, drops his cigarette butt onto the dirt, and grinds it under his heel.

He faces her. "Well, ma'am. You do have a problem, but so do the folks in the rest of these wide-open spaces under our jurisdiction. We'll double the patrols when we can. Visibility is our best weapon now."

I cain't believe the patrols are so measly and that we females, youngins and grown, are still in danger. It appears to me that it's up to us to defend ourselves.

We're for sure in a fine mess of nerves without this news. I'm glad the girls cain't hear this new development.

I've held my tongue long enough. "Why cain't you catch that crazy man?"

I glare up at him, but he just shakes his head.

"My advice. Keep your eyes on things, and keep the girls close to you. Let me know if you see anything out of the ordinary." He tips his hat at us and walks toward his vehicle.

"I'll get the dang shotgun out. That's how we plan to defend ourselves!" I shout at his retreating back, but he keeps walking.

Claire grabs my arm. "No, you won't. If the kids got into it by accident, we'd have another big, fat disaster in our lives. That's not an option."

"Okay." I ain't liking this idea. "It'll stay loaded in Sally's trunk. And I just hope to Jesus we don't need it."

Claire considers this and nods.

I know my son don't like being away, 'specially at night. Now we have this new, even bigger, worry.

He don't know the worst of it even if he'd asked the Ritchies to drop by to keep an extra set of eyes on things. Every time they bring their big, black, hairy dog that prances around with that yeller dog Taffy that won't leave us alone.

And I know it was their dog that snuck out back

and dug holes in the garden. That last time, I'd whispered to Claire, "The minute Taffy copies those shenanigans, I'm gonna use the shotgun on her," but she'd just shook her head and turned away.

Hank had said, "You know, this crazy man is going after all kinds of women. He could even go after my Annie."

He's worried about his own wife even though the patrol goes by their cabin, and he's there, too. That causes me worry, but I work hard at not showing it.

That perpetrator could go after me and Claire, too. Or come back for the girls.

It's a miracle, a true miracle, he didn't get the girls on the way home that day.

I think about the new victim. My breath catches in the back of my throat like a tumbleweed. My nerves cain't take much more of this type of bad news.

Finally, the twins sleep almost six hours at a crack during the night, but Nonni's skittish as a cat walking on a railroad track.

I know for a fact she hardly sleeps at all. I hear her whimper in the dark. She ain't the same eight-year-old from when I arrived.

I hope she don't start sleepwalking and wandering around in the dark like she's done before.

Her disposition is turning to be like her mother's, and her crying jag after the water delivery is just one example.

But I have to admit that experience made me a mite uneasy, too. Something about it felt plum wrong.

The other night, that Taffy dog barks and wakes us all up, even the babies. Mebbe a coyote or some other critter was roaming out there.

Claire's still layin' her thread traps in the bushes. She swears that the threads have been moved, but maybe the dog walked through them. Or chipmunks. Or rattlesnakes. Or a breeze moved them.

She keeps her traps from the girls, so's to not alarm them. I have to say Claire has me fairly spooked as of late.

I can hardly wait till Sonny gets back so's he can walk the patrol at night and talk some sense into that woman.

I pray to God someone catches that deranged man soon. The girls are getting cabin fever, or at least they're sick of staying close to us all the time.

Today they play tag in circles around the cabin as the sun is setting, and a little breeze swoops through.

Right as Nonni races around the corner, laughing for the first time in weeks, chasing Tessa who's screaming, that measly Taffy lunges out and snaps at her.

"Mama!" Nonni screams. She collapses onto the picnic bench holding onto her leg. That infernal dog's tooth broke the skin but did not puncture her muscle. We don't have money to take her to the doctor's office. I just pray that she don't get the rabies.

Sonny won't keep a dog that bites his daughter and also ate a chicken that escaped from the coop last week. That's been the main reason he lets Tessa keep Taffy. To guard the chickens that lay eggs for us.

But it don't take a prophet from the Old Testament to know that dog has about worn out its days here.

Claire cleans up Nonni's leg and puts iodine on the wound.

I add my two cents worth. "What good is that dog

now? It's just a darn old biting goldbricker. And a menace."

As usual, Claire ignores my comments and adds her own. "Taffy was protecting Tessa."

I push her reassurance aside because I am for sure gonna talk to him about her. He listens to me.

In fact, I would take the shotgun and shoot that yella dog now, but I am afraid Tessa would suffer too much. She claims it as some new, weird sister dog.

I took Tessa with me to get the ice yesterday, just a quick run to Jolly's in Sally. On the way, we traded a dozen of our fresh eggs for goat milk from the local dairy.

When we got to the store, I told her to pick a penny candy for herself and Nonni, but she got spooked by something.

She murmured, "Dark cloud" over and over, and ran out the store without it.

Though that girl has a mighty sweet tooth, try as I might, I could not get more information out of her. Sometimes, she don't make sense. Mebbe Nonni's rubbing off on her.

When I got to the register, I grabbed penny candies for the girls and one for myself. Sometimes I just gotta have a bite of something sweet.

This whole thing's gotten out of control. Claire's so focused on little ones she does not say much. Her twitchy ways are affecting me.

All's I want is for things to run according to schedule without any fuss. Instead, I feel like crying a little, too, something I swore I'd never do in front of any of them. I did not even cry at Pops' funeral.

Lordy, what's happening to us?

Some supplies are running low. I better check the preserves and other canned goods Sonny stacked in the shelter for me. We've been eating them up, bit at a time.

Mebbe it's about time I take another trip back home to bring more of my special canned goods. I know for sure my garden there is producing lots more than our overheated, under-watered patch here.

At the same time, I'm worried about leaving Claire and the kids alone with Randall gone so much. And if'n I go, she might tell me to stay gone and not come back. I have a purpose now, and it's this little baby boy.

And with that crazy lunatic on the loose, I don't wanna admit it out loud. I'm afraid of what might happen next.

Chapter 31
Claire - The Waiting Game

It's the following weekend when Rand's at home that Detective Hunter returns, this time with better news.

"We're waiting to confirm we got him." He sets down his glass of sun tea on the picnic table, picks up his notebook, and walks toward his car with Randall at his side.

I hear him say, "Bring Nonni to the station this afternoon so she can identify him. Then I'll move ahead with charges. We'll have a lineup ready."

He looks over his shoulder at me and gives me a thumbs up.

I glance at Nonni, who shakes her head, and then at Rand, loping back from the car with a definite, determined look on his face.

I allow myself a glimpse of anticipated relief at living a fear-free life.

Rand says, "Don't worry. I'll get her there. We'll all be relieved to get this nasty business behind us."

He shakes Hunter's hand before returning to Nonni and me.

I draw my first-born into my embrace, sad she must do something that brings her so much pain. We have no choice.

"Honey. The babies are too young for me to leave

with your grandmother, so your daddy'll take you this time. I'll be there, in your pocket." I gently touch her jumper. "Right there."

Rand reaches for her hand. "Honey, all you have to do is point at the man. Easy as marshmallow pie."

The light dusting of freckles across her nose stands out against her pale face. She looks from her father to me. "Is Tessa going, too?"

"No, honey. She didn't really see him, and she's practically a baby." He squeezes her hand. "Since you're the one who saw him and heard him speak, you're the best witness. And you're the oldest."

Nonni rubs her over her damp eyes and looks at Tessa, who's showing Fiona pictures in a book.

"I want to go, too!" Tessa slaps the book on the table. "I'm not a baby. I know lots of things."

I step into this fray. "Tessa, you'll be a bigger help here with the babies. With Grandma Grace and me."

I give her a hug. "You can help best by reading your book to them. Tommy'll want to hear it, too. I need you here, sweetie."

The wrinkles on her forehead are pronounced. "B-b-but…"

I lightly touch a finger to her lips, and she quiets. Tommy's asleep in the cabin where Gracie's getting a head start fixing our celebration dinner with a special casserole and homemade applesauce. She'll add the hamburger to it when Rand brings it back when he returns.

I turn back to Nonni, who stares at the ground, shoulders slumped. "Honey, it'll be okay. Do you hear me?"

Nonni refuses to look me in the eye, and I am

unexpectedly out of patience. Why can't this normally compliant child cooperate? She's been extra jumpy lately, but I suspect this ordeal is wearing away at her, as it is at all of us. Like sandpaper.

And I've caught her lying to me a couple of times recently. That's why we need to end it today. She juts her chin just like Mother Grace's when she's steeling herself for something unpleasant—or just being stubborn.

I take a breath to calm myself. Randall will use his gentle ways on Nonni, the way he sometimes does with me. And I pray my child will identify the man.

Evidently, several witnesses to other crimes have also been called to the lineup to identify him. All she has to do is point out the perpetrator for *our* case to move ahead.

And we need to get this evil man off the streets permanently before he targets other children or women or anyone else.

My dear, brave child finally looks up at me, straightens her shoulders, and whispers. "Yes, Mama."

"You can do this, honey." I wrap my arms around her. "I know you can."

Tessa comes over and tugs on my blouse. "Mama. Can I go? I could help. Ple-e-e-ease?"

"No, honey. We already talked about it. Just Nonni."

I'm not surprised Tessa's trying to get me to change my mind. She's a determined child. But I'm not changing my mind. She's not going with them.

I unstrap Fiona from the chair where she's slumped against the corner and pat her padded backside to check her diaper, which is remarkably still dry.

After swaddling her, I lay her down in the sleeping box with her brother in the cabin. She sticks her fist in her mouth and sucks on it, her eyelids sagging.

Thank you, Jesus, I think as I tiptoe out, *that Tommy didn't wake up.*

Tessa follows on my heels like a pit bull with something in her teeth she doesn't want to let go of. I steer her by her elbow away from the cabin and look into her pleading eyes.

"No, honey. I know you want to help, but it's up to Nonni to do this. Go say goodbye to her. Daddy's about to leave with her."

Tessa's shoulders drop. She sighs loudly before stomping off to the truck to wrap her arms around her sister's knees and twirl her around in a circle.

I don't know where she gets this unexpected Samson-like physical strength for being so small. But I do know where she gets that stubborn streak.

"There," she says. "Tell them I saw him, too."

I follow and rub cheeks with Nonni before she climbs into the truck. "Sweetie, do what's right. I have faith in you!"

Rand plants a kiss on my forehead. "We'll be back soon with good news."

"Don't forget to pick up ice on the way back. And hamburger meat for the celebration dinner your mother's fixing."

My prayers begin before his key is in the ignition. Gracie walks over with a basket of wilted zucchini from the garden and waves goodbye to them.

Shading my eyes, I stand there long enough to watch the truck pick its way through the bumpy turns to the Colony and turn left onto the paved road.

Restless, I check on the napping babies. I touch the damp sheets on the line. I reset my thread traps, which I hope I won't have to ever use again. I examine the remaining vegetables and note scorched leaves on the plants.

I walk part of the Zig Zag maze but can't ferret out the path to the Safe Zone in the middle. I circle the cabin. Three times.

Clouds overhead freeze in place against the blue sky. Time stands still, but I keep moving.

"Claire!" Mother Grace yells at me. "Stop it! You're making me nuts!" She swoops Tessa inside to help with the babies.

I glower at Gracie's back and move to the front of the cabin where I continue my pacing. I peer down the road for the twentieth time. Nothing there. No dust trail. Nothing.

Of course, they just left and won't return for a couple of hours.

My exhaustion works hand in hand with my overwrought sensibilities.

With that man on the loose, Rand out of town so much, the babies still not sleeping for more than six hours at night, and me in this suspended state of disequilibrium, I can't remember the last time I awoke refreshed.

Fatigue is dragging me down.

Each night, the hours stretch out forever while I hold my breath between the beats of my heart and listen for the crunching sound of footsteps outside our window.

I *know* someone has been creeping around the back of the cabin because the threads have been tangled.

Mother Grace looks like she doesn't believe anything I say, so I hesitate to share new suspicions with her. Did someone look in at us while we were sleeping the other night? Or did Nonni sleepwalk out there, without waking us up, and step on the threads? Or Taffy?

But those aren't paw prints I've found. And the more I think about it, the more unsure I am of my conclusions.

I don't want Rand or Mother Grace or our neighbors or even the sheriff to think I'm an unreliable woman who worries about every single little thing that could possibly go wrong. I'm not that woman. Or at least I didn't used to be.

But a cloud hangs over us, one I've hoped would dissipate or move on.

I yearn for the rainbow at the end of the storm, but the storm isn't over yet. I won't let myself rejoice while the lightning strike of anger and unrest licks at my soul. While that man is free.

I need certainty that he will pay for his crimes, but Rand says that certainty is not always possible.

We argued about this when he was home last week. "Claire, safety is a state of mind." His hazel eyes had bored into me. "We must believe that we are safe."

I feel soul-burning anger at the evil man who took away my belief in the goodness of people and rocked my peace.

We live in a safe place. I repeat this mantra under my breath as I wait for their return.

I need to feel this in my heart if we are to stay out here, away from civilization and without a telephone or other means of communication.

I distract myself by turning on the battery-operated transistor radio that Rand brought home last week. It receives one local station, KQET.

The news is on, and I learn what's going on in our new community.

The library has a summer reading program, which Nonni and Tessa would enjoy. A new drive-in movie theater opened on the other side of town. A peeping Tom is on the loose. There's a swap meet at the drive-in movie on Saturday.

I look forward to my new ritual at the end of the day when the sun sets behind Mount Baldy. I listen to John Charles singing "The Lord's Prayer" right before the stationmaster signs off for the day. That's when I experience a momentary dose of peace in my heart.

But for now, I turn up Frank Sinatra singing his new hit, "Night and Day," and look forward to celebrating the end to our nightmare tonight. When that man's in jail for good, Mother Grace can return home.

Not that it hasn't been helpful to have another set of vigilant eyes and worker-bee hands around. But that woman's worn out her visit with me, and she continually jabs at me with her mental barbs.

I hold my tongue mostly because Rand's still waiting for her to sign over the homestead deed to us, part of his master plan for us.

We finally have a small chicken coop with four chickens and a rooster, and Rand's bringing Nick in as a partner on his up-and-coming chicken business. They've made noticeable progress on the cement foundations for our new home.

Although Rand postponed his contractor's exam because of his work schedule, when he's here for a meal, we ask him a slew of questions from his test prep workbook.

I joke that I'd sign Tessa, whose memory is better than all of ours put together, up for that test in a minute if she could read fluently and if they'd let a six-year-old take it.

Rand's not putting all of his eggs in one basket, so to speak, but is preparing for a dual career in both chickens and construction.

I tell you, that man of mine can dream.

But for now, I put hope on hold and scan the empty road for his return.

Chapter 32
Nonni - The Line Up

Five men stand in a row near the wall in the small, enclosed room.

"Look at each of these men." The sheriff motions me to the window. "You can see them, but they can't see you."

"But it's a window. Right?" What he said can't be right. Is it a magic window?

Daddy winks at me. "It's okay, pumpkin. It's a one-way window. Built that way."

He puts his arm around my shoulder. "Take a deep breath. Ready?"

After I let my breath out, I'm ready. It's all up to me now, and I don't want to see the man. I don't want to *have* to identify him. Or lie.

The sheriff points through the pane in front of me. "Do you see the man who stopped you and your sister?"

I begin with the man on the left side of the line before my eyes drift to the right, and I stare at each man.

"Point him out to me. Take your time, little lady."

None of them is wearing a hat—not a baseball hat or cowboy hat. That's a relief. Maybe the sheriff made them take them off before they entered the room.

As the sheriff gives them orders, they look straight ahead, to the left, and to the right. He asks each of them to say, "Jack's wife." None has that deep raspy sound. The sheriff directs each of them to step out of the line, closer to the window.

Even though they can't see me, they're looking directly into my eyes. I shiver and tap my foot.

The sheriff puts his hand over the microphone. "See anyone you recognize? Just point at him. Or tell me the color of his shirt."

"Relax and take a breath." Daddy puts his hand on my shoulder.

I peer at each of them again, but none of them looks like, or even reminds me of, the bad man.

"Do you see him? Can you identify him?"

I look at the clock on the wall with its secondhand ticking from one small black mark to the next, and I shake my head. "No. I don't see him."

"Try again. Take your time. Once more." The sheriff nods at me.

Again, I search their faces. One by one. Some have dark eyes, others have light ones.

But none of them has *his* eyes. Those icy, pale blue eyes. Or the scar through his eyebrow.

At least I don't have to identify him and bring more trouble on our family. And he knows my name and where we live.

"Can you identify the man? Which one is he?"

"No. He's not there."

"No?" Daddy frowns. "What do you mean? That you can't do this?"

"No. I don't see him. He's not in the line."

"Are you sure?" Daddy wrinkles his brow. "You absolutely sure?"

"I'm sure." I speak with confidence, and I feel

relief. He's not there, and I don't have to think about betraying my family. "No. He's not in the line."

"What does she mean she doesn't see him?" The sheriff looks at Daddy for confirmation.

"She says she doesn't see him. She did her best." He nods his head slowly.

Detective Hunter pulls the sheriff from the room to talk in the hallway. I hear the words "…looking in the window" and "lurking."

The sheriff returns, rubbing his face. "Let's do this once more. Take your time."

I look at the men again, hoping nothing's changed during the last five minutes. I didn't want to have to lie to the police. He's not here. Relief fills me.

"No. He's not there."

The sheriff and Daddy look at each other and move outside. I see them talking in the parking lot. The sheriff points at me through the glass door. His lips murmur something I can't hear. Probably about me.

I close my eyes and wish I could melt through the floor. I so badly want to win their approval, but I feel torn in half. The man wasn't there to identify, but the sheriff acts like the guilty man is standing right in front of me.

But where's the scar? I stare and can't see one. Why don't I recognize his face or his sound? What about those creepy blue eyes?

But even if he had been in that line of men, I wouldn't have pointed to him. I must protect my family. I could point to one of the other men, but it wouldn't be right to get someone else into trouble.

"She couldn't remember the color of the truck, either."

I begin to doubt my memory of the man. My lip trembles. I wish Mama were here.

Daddy puts his hand on my shoulder. "Sheriff. Detective Hunter. She's done her best. If she says he's not in the line, we have to believe her."

The sheriff scratches his head and then shakes my hand. He thanks us for coming.

"Maybe you just forgot." The sheriff looks deep into my eyes.

"Maybe," I said. But I knew I hadn't.

"If you remember something else, little lady, let us know."

I nod and then use my words. "Yes, sir."

Daddy takes my arm and hurries me through the lobby. A woman with silver curls, leaning on a cane, stands at the desk. I hear her speak as we walk by.

"Yes, I'm sure he was the man peeking into our home. I'd bet my life on it."

I stumble on the linoleum floor behind my father. I'm riddled with guilt. Where is that man? He must be out here somewhere, free. He promised he'd hurt me. He'd hurt my family.

I believe him, and I don't know what to do. Tell someone and have him come after us? Not tell? Still have him come after us?

My father strides ahead. "Let's go, Nonni. We're through here."

I follow him through the door to the truck. I step onto the running board and hoist myself onto the seat.

At eight years old, I don't think life can get much worse.

Chapter 33
Randall - The Let Down

I park the truck in front of the cabin and step from the car. My heart is heavy after Nonni's unsuccessful experience with the lineup. I want to be the bearer of good news, but I don't know what to say.

A parent's sacred duty is to protect the children, to make them feel safe. What will I say to Nonni and Tessa to reassure them that the world is safe? That we are safe?

And Claire and Ma? Maybe I should stretch the truth, so they feel it's "being taken care of." They have enough to worry about out here with me gone so much.

And it is true, to an extent. The sheriff is working on the case.

As I step into view, Ma looks up from the garden where she's tending the few surviving plants. She puts down her hoe and takes a step toward me.

Claire cranes her head out of the cabin and hurries to me with questions on her face.

I squeeze Nonni's arm. "Good job, pumpkin. You did your best, and that's all I can ask. Go work on your Zig Zag while we grown-ups talk."

She grabs the rake and scurries out to the front of the cabin.

Tessa reads to the babies in the cabin. She speaks with drama and modulated highs and lows. When did she turn into such a regular little teacher? Or actress?

"Fee fi fo fum!"

Claire and Ma gather around me, questions in their eyes.

"Well?" The worry wrinkles between Claire's eyes are pronounced.

I move my gaze between the two of them before I focus on my wife. "Nonni did her best, and I'm proud of her."

She sighs. "Yes. She's a brave girl. My heart hurts that I couldn't be there with her today."

I smooth her hair, and she leans into me. "Don't feel guilty. I was there. And…"

I lower my hand and look into her trusting eyes. I must deliver the rest of the news. Nothing feels fair today.

I smack my right fist into my open left hand. Hard. "The sheriff asked her to identify the man."

I smack my hand again. "Well, it didn't turn out the way we hoped. Not at all."

I see Nonni with her rake. She drags the tines through the dirt to create a dead-end circle. Her lips move as she talks to herself. I wonder what she's saying. I hope she didn't hear what I just said.

Ma snaps at me. "Cut to the chase, Sonny. What happened?"

"She was definite he was not in the line-up, but the sheriff thought otherwise. One man had already been identified earlier by another woman who saw him peeping in through her bathroom window. The sheriff was sure Nonni would point out the same man. But she didn't. Twice." I amend this. "Three times."

"So, what's going to happen next?" Claire bites her

bottom lip.

"The sheriff says they need an identification from her, or our case remains open."

My jaw clenches so tight I'm worried I'll crack a tooth. "The sheriff wants to interview Tessa."

Ma's eyes widen. "Not Tessa."

Tessa pokes her head out of the cabin. She's been eavesdropping on us. "Yes! Me!"

Claire gasps. "No. Not Tessa."

Tessa trots to the table and does a little twirl, a triumphant smile on her face. "I already told you. I'm not a baby!"

Claire points to the cabin. "Tessa. Please go inside and read *Jack and the Beanstalk* to the twins again. They love it."

Tessa grins and hops back into the cabin.

Claire swivels to me, and her mouth drops open before she speaks. "Tessa? Did you say Tessa? You sure? She's practically a baby!"

I sense Claire's mind race as she pleads with her eyes. "Think about what questioning would do to Tessa. Nonni's still sleepwalking and even made it out the door into the yard at midnight once this week."

"We don't have a choice." I change the subject. "Jack'll be in to look at this line-up, too, once he's back in town. He's bound to add some new information."

Tessa pokes her head out again. She pipes up. "We saw the Jack man that day. Before we ran out to the well to hide. And I fell in."

Claire takes a step toward her. "Back into the cabin. Please." A baby squeals, and Tessa disappears inside.

I pump a small dose of confidence into my

delivery. "That other man who was identified? He's being detained now. At least overnight."

Ma snorts. "I'm confused. A man identified today by someone else? He's in jail now, but he ain't the man she saw? That makes absolutely no sense at all."

"Well, that's all I know. And Nonni didn't change her mind, no matter what."

It dawns on me that my firstborn is more like her mother and grandmother than I thought. As frustrated as I sometimes feel, however, Claire usually has some basis for her stubbornness. I'm not always sure about Ma.

That little girl sure showed her backbone today. She may be wrong, but just on the off chance she's not, we're in bigger trouble than I can imagine.

Ma puts her hands on her hips. "Where's the hamburger?"

"Didn't get it. Looks like we'll be eating crow instead of that celebration dinner tonight."

Tessa comes out of the cabin. She turns toward the mountains and raises her arms in the air. "Lookee! The beautiful sunset!"

We turn toward Mt. Baldy, silhouetted dark against the backdrop of the setting sun. There is a golden squiggle in the corner of the sky as though God Almighty himself has signed this magnificent picture.

I feel my anger drain from my body. In spite of the way the day's turned out, I'm glad to dine with my family. We enjoy the view.

The bass notes bring the song to a close, concluding the broadcast for the day. I feel a brief moment of calm, even if we're not celebrating the way we planned.

This radio was a good idea. My idea.

I look at Claire's and Ma's crestfallen faces. Determination trickles into my soul. We'll get through this. I'll swoop by and pick Nick up in the morning. We'll work non-stop through the next seven days.

By the time I get back home, we'll be halfway through August.

The sheriff said patrols are still in place. The family is safe. One thing I can't afford now is to get fired.

Then, I'll get that man if I have to hunt him down myself.

Chapter 34
Tessa - I Know a Lot

I play with the babies this afternoon. They're even better than Dolly, who sleeps with me every night and waits for me all day when I'm busy.

Tommy and Fiona make motorboat noises, and they smile at me even though Grandma Grace still says it's gas.

The babies like it when I make faces at them, play peek-a-boo, and read them *Jack and the Beanstalk*.

Or at least I tell act out the story with a lot of drama.

After that, I read them a new book, *Good Night, Moon*. I tell them stories about two kittens and the mittens and the moon on the pages.

I know some of the words just by looking at them over and over.

We got these books at the library, and I can read them just like I planned!

This morning I hunted eggs from the hen house. Grandma Grace made us scrambled eggs before Daddy and Nonni left for the sheriff's office.

Mama sent me out to pick a zucchini for dinner. There are only two more left growing.

It's macaroni and cheese night, my favorite. Mama's going to put sliced zucchini in the middle of the Kraft Dinner Ring.

For special occasions like tonight, Mama sets out her special crystal relish tray from when she was a little girl and lived in a mansion that had a fancy bathtub with feet.

She puts carrots, celery, Grandma's bread-and-butter pickles, and black olives on it. Then she lets me arrange them.

Mama says we're no slouches. We're the fancy pants O'Brien Gourmet Restaurant. I'm not sure what that means, but I like how it sounds, especially the fancy pants part.

Mr. Henderson gave Daddy an apple tree in a wooden box for the twins, but Mama acts like it's her tree. I watered that tree today, too, but Daddy says that I'll be in the fifth grade before we can make applesauce from apples that will grow on it.

I can't wait until then for applesauce, so I check it every day to see if it has apples yet. Mama tells me if I talk to it and tell it to hurry up, it will grow faster. But it looks the same to me every day.

The Ritchies visit us with their big black dog this afternoon. Delaware and Taffy chase each other around and sniff each other.

It's too bad that Nonni doesn't like Taffy since my dog took a chomp out of her knee. It was an accident. Taffy's accident. Accidents are okay, aren't they?

That's what they told me about losing my shoe down the well.

Jack stops by to see Mama and Grandma Grace tonight after dinner.

Mama says we are in charge of entertaining the babies for a few minutes. Nonni climbs up on the table next to the window and listens to what they're saying outside.

I shush the babies and try to hear, too, and then I end up singing to them. They really like "Old MacDonald Had a Farm."

After a few minutes, she hops back down. "Mister Jack said he didn't recognize the man either."

I try to figure out what that means. "So what?"

"So what, boo-boo head. I don't know!" The corners of her mouth look like an upside-down smile.

I can't wait to talk to the sheriff. I always remember what people look like even if I see them for just a second.

I can draw them a picture of the man with the red cloud around him.

Nobody ever asks me anything. They treat me like a baby, but I know a lot more than they think I do.

I would know that man if I saw him again.

I would.

Chapter 35
Claire - I'm Ready

It's handy that Nick and Rand work the same schedule most of the time.

When he arrived earlier this morning to pick Rand up for another six-day stint, he hauled a box from the back seat and deposited it onto the picnic table.

"Hey, Claire." He gave me a side hug. "Di sent you these kid clothes. Her two girls outgrew them, and she thought you could use them."

That's putting it delicately. "Thank that sister of yours!"

School starts in two weeks with Tessa in the second grade and Nonni in the fourth, and the girls have grown like wildfire this summer.

They see the box and rush over.

For a few minutes, we forget our troubles. We sing like it's Christmas morning as we divide the contents of the box into two stacks, one for each girl.

Tessa peers into the empty box. "Mama. No shoes here."

It's a school rule that children wear closed-toe shoes to school, and that means no sandals. We already suffered last spring after Rand wasn't able to fish Tessa's shoe out of the well, where it was too deep to reach.

Tessa had bravely nursed her sister's old, too-big,

hand-me-down, holey shoes through to the last day of school.

Nonni peers down at her feet. "Mama. This shoe's broken." She leans over and pushes down on the sole, making it open and close.

Tessa snorts and grabs at Nonni's wriggling toes. She speaks in a falsetto voice. "I want some candy!"

The girls laugh at the talking shoe with its floppy mouth.

Tessa turns her intense gaze to me. "Mama. I have an idea. Nonni's might fit me. I'll wear them if we don't get new ones. Daddy can glue them together."

"They're too big for you, honey, and they're completely worn out. Don't worry. We'll work it out."

I pray there's enough money left in my small stash from the washing machine sale in Santa Monica to buy shoes for the girls.

The truth is that Tessa could wear her sister's in a pinch, if we repaired them. But my oldest girl's feet have grown, and we don't have any shoes waiting in the wings for her.

Over the summer, Nonni's shot up like a bean sprout. All of a sudden, she isn't a little girl but a mini-mom to the younger ones. She reaches my chin, and she's grown up in more than one way since this horrible thing happened.

And it's not over yet. I worry about the girls, but particularly about Nonni, who keeps her feelings bottled up and sometimes goes silent on us.

But I'm also grateful. For the fact that the girls weren't harmed physically. For Rand grabbing Tessa before she slipped all the way into the well. For baby supplies and clothes arriving unexpectedly. Now, for school clothes. For Rand—and his new job that brings in a little more money than we spend so we can save some.

My heart fills with more gratitude than fear. I silently pray for this saga to be over.

After breakfast, I hang diapers on the line, and my gaze drifts up to the puffy clouds, marching across like circus elephants, trunk to tail, against the backdrop of brilliant blue.

I consider cloud formations my personal Rorschach inkblot tests. I smile at my silliness, reminded of how much I love the morning sky.

A breeze whips up, out of nowhere, twisting loose dirt round and round like a mini-tornado rising up from the ground.

I call out, "Dust devil! Dust devil! Close the door and window!"

Tessa pipes up, "Mama, I'll do it!"

She disappears into the cabin to crank the casement window shut so the dirt won't swirl in before she closes the door.

I hurry to join the family inside as the diapers are sprinkled by a fine layer of dirt, which I'll shake out later.

We spend half our time trying to keep the desert from getting into the cabin—and the other sweeping and dusting it away.

We've gotten used to living our lives around the moods of weather, which can be unpredictable. But that means we're constantly on the lookout.

Yes. Vigilance has become a way of life.

No new crimes have been reported since the man was arrested, the man Nonni didn't recognize. Randall is sure, and the sheriff, too, that he *was* the right man even though Jack, who lives a half mile past Annie and Hank, told us he didn't recognize anyone in the line-up, either.

I trust Nonni's judgment, and I believe Jack. I don't have peace about the situation, but I don't want to worry Rand, who's already upset that he's away from home nights at a time.

We neighbors have banded into a little community that watches out for each other. This desert *is* a safe place to raise a family as long as we stick together.

It *has* to be our safe place, our safe zone!

Tomorrow the water truck's coming, and I wish Rand were here. We're always planning everything around deliveries. But I have no doubt that, one day, we'll twist faucets inside our finished home, and water will rush from them into our bathtub and even a water pitcher. We'll flush our indoor toilet, and the girls will water the garden from a hose.

I imagine us doing all of these things. Just like we used to before we moved out here to the land of no services.

As the sun sinks behind the mountains, we gather around the transistor radio on the picnic table for our nightly ritual that concludes our days and begins our nights.

I shiver as I drink in the final bars of the *Lord's Prayer*. The announcer says, "We're signing off for the night, and we'll be back to greet the sunrise."

When the radio falls silent except for the sound of fuzzy static, I flick the knob to turn it off so the batteries will last.

Before the twilight fades, we bow our heads, and I

intone, "Thank you, Jesus for this meal."

I serve everyone except the babies our upside-down dinner of banana pancakes. We hurry to eat before dark descends on us.

At almost three months old, it will be less than a year before the twins can join us in this simple pleasure.

I gather the girls into the cabin after their final trip to the outhouse. We feed the babies one last bottle, chant our little song about "de pot," say prayers, and all lay down to sleep.

Gracie's been quiet tonight, and I'm not sure whether to count that as a blessing or not.

I'm ready now. With the door locked and the thread trap in place.

Chapter 36
Tessa - Sleepless Nights

I slink over to the picnic table where Mama, Grandma Grace, and Detective Hunter are speaking in whispers.

I bounce on one foot and tap my fingers on the table.

Mama looks at me. "Can it wait, sweetie? We're busy here." She sighs. "What is it?"

"Mama. Why's everyone so grouchy? Nonni's inside reading a book to herself and won't talk to me. She won't make a new game. I want to sit here with you. Pleeeeease."

"Everyone's just tired, honey."

"Please, Mama!" I whine, but she still shakes her head.

"Shoo, girl!" Grandma reaches out.

She bangs her hand flat on the table. Mama and the man jump. "The detective's here, and we got grown-up business to talk about."

Mama frowns at Grandma and turns to me. "We're all a little tired, sugar plum. Get your sister and go play Zig Zag with her. And keep quiet. The babies are napping."

I move to the open door. I put a finger across my lips and motion Nonni outside.

She steps out onto the porch, grabs the rake, and

follows me out to the dirt track.

I watch her retrace the outside track where the detective's car ran over it. She works with her head tipped toward the adults, listening in on them.

I'm tired of thinking, hearing, and dreaming about the bad man. Day after day. Night after night. I hum to myself and gather stones, piling them next to the track.

We work for a long time. She still won't talk to me.

The grownups get louder. Mama says, "I'll tell Randy. He'll be there."

The man winks at me as he walks to his car. "It's okay to go back now."

He has a dark turquoise cloud around him. I think that means he's worrying about something. It's the exact color of one of my crayons.

I hurry to the table where Mama sits alone. "He's gone. Are we in trouble, Mama?"

Mama rubs a wrinkle between her eyes. "Everything's okay. Go help Grandma feed the babies. They're just waking up from their nap."

Mama looks up at the clouds. "Do you see that elephant in the sky?"

I look up and nod.

Mama sighs. "Go help with the babies."

I scuttle into the cabin.

Grandma holds a wet diaper out to me. "Take this out to the bucket, child."

I run it out to the bucket by the outhouse. Then, I turn the faucet on to wash my hands before I leap like a silent lizard back to the cabin, ready to help.

Grandma hands my special baby girl to me. "Keep her neck steady. Give her to your mother before you check the hen house for eggs. Here's her bottle."

I feel important as I step outside with my arms full and hand my sister to my mother.

"Here's Fee Fee and a bottle. I have to go to the coop for eggs. Grandma says."

I love gathering eggs. I do it in the morning, and I do it at night.

It's getting dark, so I hurry to the coop with the straw basket.

I take a handful of feed and scatter it on the ground. That way the chickens will peck at it and not at me.

But even the chickens are grumpy today. They cluck and complain loudly, and one chicken chases me around as I check nests.

I lock the gate and take the three brown eggs to the spigot at the water tower. I fill the plastic bowl with water, softly wipe each egg with the wet sponge, and gently place them back in the basket.

I tiptoe slowly to the cabin, so I won't break the eggs. "Here, Grandma."

I hand her the basket and yawn.

I'm ready for bed right now. Mama says I usually sleep like a rock, but last night there was a lot of *yip yip yipping* near the chicken coop. Taffy barked, and the chickens squawked.

I'd gotten up to look out the window but didn't see anything. The wind made a slapping, slapping sound that kept me awake for an hour.

It must have been the outhouse door banging. We're supposed to keep it latched when we're not in it.

Before I'd climbed back into my bottom bunk last night, I heard Nonni cry. I saw a fuzzy dark purple color, not her regular bright yellow one, glowing around her head on the pillow.

I stayed in bed with my eyes open listening to the soft sounds she made until the morning sun came in through the window.

I hope tonight I can sleep without anything waking me up. Tonight, I plan to go to sleep and stay asleep.

Chapter 37
Randall - Torn

"I can't do it. I just can't do it," I explain to my boss for the third time. "We have another appointment with the sheriff. I *have* to be there."

Mr. Henderson shakes his finger in my face like he's brandishing a knife. His face darkens to a deep purple.

"This whole project will go under if we don't meet our deadline. Everyone's putting in the extra hours. You know that!"

I rub the twinge in my left shoulder with my hand, torn between two obligations with similar urgency. Leave work to join my family at the sheriff's office.

Or stay here and, metaphorically speaking, throw my family under the bus.

I better choose my family. I choose my family.

"How about I come back later this afternoon? I'll work double shifts through this weekend.

He considers my proposal, and the color in his face fades.

I don't blame him for being upset at me. I visualize the gears in his brain turning. I am an efficient worker. I need this job almost as much as I need oxygen. I have babies and a family.

I haven't ever complained about working sixty- to seventy-hour weeks, away from home, while going through this necessary, legal family stuff.

I know this job is the master of all of us. He needs me, too. With this looming deadline, he'll suffer financial penalties if we don't meet our deadlines.

But what if he fires me anyway?

"Okay. And through the next week?" That means I'll be away through the weekend and maybe on Labor Day.

He sucks on a wooden match and nods. "Okay. Come back after. Double shifts."

I stick out my hand, and he shakes it.

As he pushes the door of the construction trailer open, he looks back at me. "Good luck, man."

I dip my head in thanks, and he leaves. I wait about fifteen seconds before following him out.

Grabbing my lunchbox out of my truck, I head to the thin strip of shade by the trailer.

I join the guys, who're already eating on a thirty-minute timetable. If we had a union out here, things'd be different. But jobs are scarce.

I'm grateful for this temporary employment, which is nearing an end in about six weeks.

Nick's voice is low. "You okay, man?"

He's the only one who knows what's really going on with the family and me. That's because we're more than carpool buddies. We worked together at the corporation. He got me that writing gig at the Rock.

And then he got fired from the company because of me and that writing gig. We've exchanged labor on our home building projects. He helped me pour a cement foundation. I helped him build a porch.

He's my new partner in the chicken business. We already have a small coop at the cabin so I can try out my new design. Useful by-products include a few eggs and an occasional chicken for eating.

Generally speaking, I don't like people knowing my personal stuff, but he's the exception. Because he's been here as it's unfolded.

"Yeah." I bite into the bologna sandwich.

One guy mentions it might rain this weekend, but I tune him out. I don't want to come across antisocial, but I don't feel like talking.

Nick eats his own lunch without a word.

I consider the interview with the sheriff and the new lineup tomorrow. I hope it goes well, so we can meet with the district attorney.

Last time we were there, a man was identified as doing some weird peeping Tom stuff. The sheriff temporarily locked him up even though my frightened little girl didn't point him out. She couldn't, or wouldn't, point to anyone. But someone else did.

I'm all about targeting the problem, solving it, and moving on. Especially when it's that ugly-hearted creep who bothered my little girls. Kidnapped other women. Left them tied up in bags.

This has to stop.

I haven't been home with the family much lately because of the final deadlines for the resort. I'm here at the site days and nights at a time.

That means I'm not at home where I could be running patrols on our cabins and those of our neighbors.

Claire told me Tessa's wetting the bed again. Nonni's sleepwalking. Ma's staying with the babies tomorrow, so Claire and the girls can meet me at the sheriff's office for this new line-up.

Since Nick drove us in this week, he says I can borrow his truck to get to town.

I'm sure Nonni'll identify the perpetrator this time. Maybe even Tessa. Although I don't want her there at all. She's just a baby herself. My fiercest hope is that we'll be moving out of this nightmare.

Nonni'll probably have to testify even though I know she's scared to speak up in front of strangers. Or, sometimes, even in front of us.

This time, she'll point him out in the lineup. We'll kick this ordeal out of its holding pattern. The beast will be locked up, and I'll throw the key away myself.

Just the thought of seeing that bastard who threatened my kids makes me angry. Adrenaline surges through me.

My sweet girls.

I smash my hand against the hard ground and wince. That shock's nothing compared to the pain and rage I'm stuffing down about what happened to the girls. He's one sicko who needs serious punishment.

Not smart. Keep my cool.

A line of blood drips from my knuckles. I raise my hand to my mouth and suck the blood.

I envision Claire's face and wish we had a phone, like we used to in the city, so I could call her.

Last thing I'd said to her was that I'd try to be there, but not to count on me.

She'd snapped back, "Well, trying's not enough!"

We'd left it at that, and I haven't had time to feel remorse about it until right now. I imagine. No. I know she feels abandoned to my mother, her toughest critic.

That's another thing. I don't understand why the two women I love most don't get along.

Damn! The bread I'm chewing tastes like cardboard. My mouth waters, and I gag a little.

Repress, repress, my mind screams.

I take a few deep breaths. I force myself to swallow another swig of stale, sun-heated water. I clear my throat with a cough.

"You okay, man?" Nick turns to me.

I nod. Take another nasty swig. Close my eyes. Force my shoulders to relax. I picture my "go to" place: Orion against the dark sky in the still, desert night.

I look for that constellation of the hunter every night, whether I'm here or at the cabin, and it always calms me. To feel like he's looking down on us with his sword ready for action.

I didn't used to feel we needed protection from anything menacing. But my thoughts have changed, and this star visualization strategy isn't working for me today.

Deep breath.

I rub a knot in my shoulder. This stress is eating me up. Not a good thing. Not a good thing at all.

Calm down.

I unroll my T-shirt sleeve. I pull out one of my rationed cigarettes and the book of matches. Cupping my hand over the tip of the cigarette, I puff to ignite it and draw in a lung full of smoke.

My shoulders loosen. For one ridiculous moment, I have a mental flash of myself smoking with Lucille Ball in her television sitcom.

I thank my luck stars, or should I say, Lucky Strikes, that America has advocated this healthy method of relaxing. Even if it's a little pricey.

Hence, the rationing.

And my life *isn't* a sitcom, sorting candy on a conveyor belt.

It's an impending trial, never-ending work, a partially finished home of cement slabs and exposed pipes, chickens and coyotes, and a family of seven, if I count Ma.

Everyone depends on me for so many things.

How in the world is one man supposed to do all of this on only four hours of sleep a night? Without cracking into tiny pieces that can't be glued back together again?

How?

Chapter 38
Claire - Traps and Clues

I do everything possible *not* to fidget or pace. I must exude confidence and a peaceful spirit for Nonni. And for Tessa, too, who's going with us in case they follow through with their request to question her.

This time I'll be there with them. I pray to God that Randall's boss lets him off to be with us.

"I need you here!" I told him last time I saw him. "I can't do this alone!"

Our parting was contentious. I hate it when we part on disgruntled terms, but I'm tired of fighting everything alone.

I'm so exhausted I could crumple and fall dead unconscious before hitting the newly poured concrete.

For one thing, Nonni didn't sleep much last night—or any other night this week. Her bed creaked, and then I caught her trying to sleepwalk out of the cabin.

The chair I'd placed in front of the closed door to keep my nightmares out kept her in and gave me time to get her into bed before she woke anyone up.

That was followed by Tessa's nightmare and her mumbling, "Red! Red!"

Thank God, the babies and Mother Grace slept through it. Or at least I think they did. Mother Grace is pretty quiet this morning with dark circles under her eyes, so it's hard to tell. That woman may criticize me, but she doesn't complain. And that's an unexpected blessing, for sure.

Through the soughing and whooping of the wind, I heard sagebrush crashing against our cabin, coyotes howling, and Taffy barking. The door to the outhouse banged open and shut all night.

"Girls." I shake them awake.

It's unusual for them to sleep once the twins are up, but they must be as tired as the rest of us.

"Rise and shine! Grab a granola bar that your grandmother made yesterday and come on out."

Tessa opens an eye, bats her eyelashes at me, closes her eye, reopens it, and flings herself off of her mattress. It's like watching a butterfly come to life.

On the bunk above, Nonni rolls over to face the wall and covers her head with her pillow.

I pull her sheet back and touch her shoulder. "We leave in an hour, honey."

The girls stumble around inside the cabin, getting ready for the day. I stroll outside to check on the wind damage, and everything appears calm.

I see the cloudless, blue sky and smell a slight eucalyptus scent.

The early morning temperature is mild. Chickens cackle in the distance, and Taffy snoozes on the porch.

I continue around the perimeter of the cabin until I'm near the outhouse. The latch is broken, maybe from the wind. I thought I'd secured it before cozying us up in the cabin for the night, but that's the cause of the repetitive banging sounds.

Rand'll fix it. Or, better yet, I'll ask Mother Grace. She's handy with tools.

After I check our last withered squash plant, I gaze in at the hens and rooster pecking corn from the dirt in their coop. I walk around the house and check my sneaky trap. The threads are wadded up. Could the wind have scuffed it up into a pile like that?

That's when I observe a clear print of a man-size footprint next to it. The funny—no not funny, but dangerous—thing is that I *know* I brushed that sandy area clear and flat before laying the trap last night. I know I did.

I am not making this up or dreaming up hysterics about it.

Wind or not, this is new. And it doesn't belong to any of us. It's way too big, and Rand's been gone all week. A chill shivers down my spine.

Someone's walking on my grave, I think, with Mother Grace's voice in my head saying the words.

Someone's walking in my yard, I reply.

I circle the cabin, examining every inch but don't see anything else unusual. I take stock of the empty land surrounding us.

Is someone hiding behind one of those Joshua trees or creosote bushes? I scan the land for clues and question myself.

When did I turn back into the type of person who waited for the serpent to strike? I inch around to the dirt drive and down to the corner where the road begins.

No fresh tire tracks. Nothing. Maybe the powerful winds last night whisked them up into the air.

Returning to the cabin, I take a piece of newsprint from a shelf in the cabin and return to trace it close to the outside wall. I scooch down and notice a notch across one of the heels.

Is this a shoe or boot? That foot's a lot bigger than mine. How'd it get here?

I'll take my tracing with me today, but I wonder what they'll say. Will they think I'm a clever detective protecting my family?

Or that I've turned into an obsessive mother who is losing her mind a little bit at a time?

I don't want to admit it, but the stress is getting to me.

Randall's away more than he's here, and I can't rest while he's gone at night. I sleep with one ear listening to sounds in the night.

And while I do that, I worry about the babies. Food. Clothes. Our home. Footprints. Coyotes. Nighttime noises. Mother Grace watching everything I say and do—and probably reporting it to Rand. Nonni's stubborn behavior. Even Tessa was restless last night.

I decide to talk to Mother Grace, away from the kids. We must put our differences aside to figure this out. Together.

And I don't want to worry the girls. They're already experts at picking up clues from us and then acting out these emotions. If we're worried, they're worried. If we're snappy, they are, too.

Rand better be there today at the sheriff's office. He has a calming influence on the girls, too.

He isn't intimidated by the legality of it all, which gets my back up and makes my skin crawl.

"She'll identify him this time," he'd said with confidence. "Nonni was distracted by the line-up process last time, and I think the one-way window made her nervous."

"How's it that the sheriff arrested a man that

Nancy Brashear

someone else identified, and somehow he's not our guy?" I'd said this to Rand when we were alone because I didn't want Nonni to hear my doubts.

All we could agree on was that we had no answers and that soon everything would be sorted out and make sense.

I pray that she recognizes someone, anyone, in the lineup today, so we can reclaim our lives. The detective asked for Tessa to be there, too, but I can't figure out what good she'll do.

My mind circles back to that question, worrying around it like a tongue exploring a sore tooth. There can't be more than one crazy man out here, can there? And who belongs to that print by our cabin? It couldn't be him because he couldn't be in two places at the same time. He's already in jail!

My jumbled thoughts exhaust me, and I try to banish them.

I finish tracing the footprint and tell the girls we'll be leaving soon. Tessa's dressed and eating a square of Mother Grace's no-bake breakfast bars.

Nonni pokes her head out of the door, still in her nightie, and looks at me with a puzzled expression.

Tessa darts back, tags her, and calls out, "You're it!"

Nonni reaches out automatically and smacks her on her wrist. "No, *you!*"

They take off with Tessa chasing her around the cabin, screaming and laughing. Taffy gallops after them. I think back to Taffy nipping Nonni in the knee last month.

"Don't rile the dog!" I call after them. "Don't scream! Remember last time."

194

They make a complete pass around the house, and Nonni passes by so closely she brushes my elbow. I feel like I'm living in a three-ring circus.

"Stop running! Nonni, get dressed," I call out. They're already around the corner.

I follow their path. Nonni is nowhere in sight, and Tessa's huddled over the print, her face pale and her large freckles pronounced.

She whispers, "Red, red, red."

"Honey." I speak in a soothing tone, taking her hand in mine and pulling her up onto her feet. "It's okay. Really. It is."

She lifts her head and looks up into my eyes, sadness flooding her face. It's like she's in some kind of trance or something.

"No. It is not, Mama. It is *not* okay."

A squeal from one of the twins breaks the spell, and quick as lightning, Tessa's face changes, her eyes brighten, and she shakes her head.

One minute, she's like a wise but spooky old soul, and the next she's a little girl running to help her brother.

What's that all about? I try to shake off the feeling of foreboding that sticks like a cobweb. I follow her around the corner.

"I'm coming, Tommy!" She scoops his toy from the ground and hands it to him in his makeshift highchair outside.

Fiona is snugged with blankets into the seat next to him.

Tessa nestles the rattle into his fingers, and he clutches it. She kisses Tommy, and then Fiona, on their chubby, red cheeks.

I take a breath. "Peace," I whisper and turn my face toward the morning sunshine.

Nonni lounges on the bench chewing on a breakfast bar, her eyebrows lowered and expression somber.

I move over by her. "Honey," I tell her, "just tell the truth. Tell the truth, and the truth *will* set you free. You don't have anything to worry about. I'll be there, and so will Daddy."

Tessa's head is tipped toward us, listening. Her eyes shine. "Me, too. I'll be there, too!"

I wondered how my two big girls are so different, Nonni who hides her feelings, and Tessa who wears them for all to see.

Nonni hops from the bench and gives me an unexpected hug, really clinging to me, and I hug her back.

"Honey, get dressed. Pick something from the new clothes Uncle Nick brought the other day."

She skips to the cabin. I look over at Tessa who's playing peek-a-boo with Fiona.

"Tessie, bring me a brush and a ribbon, and I'll braid your hair."

"Mama." She calls to me from doorway. "Can I wear this today?"

She holds up blue pants and a checkered shirt in one hand and a pink plastic headband in the other from the box of clothes Nick had brought from Di to us.

"Yes, sweetie. I bet they fit you perfectly."

She smiles from the doorway, the clothes clutched in her arms, ready to change into them.

I glance over at Mother Grace who's hanging up wet laundry, clothespins lined up between her lips. A small breeze whips up a miniature dust devil.

To any passing neighbors, of which we have none, we'd look like any regular old family, enjoying the early morning.

Little would they suspect that we are not as we seem. Instead, we're disoriented. Falling apart at the seams. And yearning to end our reign of terror.

I call to Mother Grace. "The babies should be ready for a nap in a few minutes. Can I talk to you for a minute before I leave?"

She squints at me as she hangs the last diaper. "I'll be finished up in a minute."

I sigh, finally ready to tell her about the shoe print. I can almost hear her sharp judgment declaring, "Claire, you're crazy."

I've only taken a few steps toward her when I heard Nonni sobbing, "No, no, no!"

I bolt back toward the door as Mother Grace pivots, clothespins scattering.

Chapter 39
Gracie - The Bunker

Here I am, doing what I do best. Hanging out those never-ending diapers. I may only have graduated high school, but I do know how to multiply.

Those twins are everything times two and more.

Then there's the rest of us. I'm barely halfway through hanging up the wet clothes in the big wicker basket at my feet.

The air is warm enough they should dry, full of Vitamin D, before nightfall if the wind doesn't dust them up. Nothing I can do about that.

Out of the corner of my eye, I spy Claire sneaking out back of the cabin. I'm sure she's checking her thread traps, which she doesn't think I know about.

She reappears and then disappears, very mysterious like. I turn my back and pretend to ignore her.

She rounds the corner, calling out to me. I turn and notice the grooved lines between her brows, sunken in like tire tracks.

"I need to tell you something. Away from the girls." Her face is more pinkish than usual, and she's panting like a puppy.

My hand is paused mid-air as I wait for her to get to the line when I hear Nonni's wail from the cabin. I drop the diaper back into the basket, hightail it to the cabin, lickety-split, my heart pounding as hard as my feet, but Claire beats me there by a hair.

She's hunched over, howling, and rubbing her eyes.

I push my way past Claire and pull the child to her feet.

"Child! What'sa matter with you?"

"Spider."

"Where?"

"Musta crawled away."

I drop her arm and hustle around looking for that spider.

Claire wraps her arms around her. "Spider? Honey, you okay? You get bit?"

We're always on the lookout for spiders. Inside shoes. Under blankets. In corners. Black widers and scorpions are the worst. None of us aim to get bit by them.

I peer in beside the icebox.

For certain, there is a big, fat, blonde tarantula there. I stab at it with a broom handle, and it hustles to the wall. I hover over it, swooping a canning jar down on it, trapping it.

Claire is a total coward of spiders and snakes, and just plumb useless around creatures such as these.

I'm puzzled about Nonni, though, who ain't usually afraid of spiders. She captures them, letting them loose out in the brush.

Mebbe her nerves have gotten to her, too, and weakened her courage. And she needs as much of that as she can scrape up today, so's I hope she hasn't used it up ahead of time.

She's surely a child of many moods nowadays.

"Honey, it's okay." Claire cups her hand under her

chin and tips her head up so she has to look at her.

"Don't want to go today." She squirms out of her mother's grasp.

Claire touches her shoulder, turning her around. "What's going on, honey?"

"Don't want to go."

"What brought this on, honey? You were fine a few minutes ago. You'll identify the man this time."

Nonni glances up at her mother from under her damp blonde eyelashes. "It was the...spider."

Claire's eyes focus on her pale face. They're a fine kettle of fish, those two.

If I was the one taking the girls off to the sheriff today, I wouldn't put up with such shenanigans. I don't have time for that kind of nonsense.

"Hmmmph! Don't throw a fit. I captured it." I point down. "I saved you. All of you!"

I pick up the jar, flipping it over and praying that nasty critter won't be jumping up onto my face before I get the lid screwed back on. Because that's what they do, leap straight up.

I straighten my back and march, quicklike, out through the creosote bushes as far away as I can get from the cabin in about two minutes.

I open the lid and fling the tarantula out into the brush with all my might.

"Don't you never come back here, you no-good, rotten spider!"

I wish I could take banish all our problems that way. It feels good to throw something and yell a little.

To tell the truth, we're all as nervous as stray cats today. Mebbe Nonni's nerves are fried, too, like her mama's, and even mine.

I do feel kinda bad for that little girl because she'd got a lot sitting on her small shoulders today. Maybe Tessa, too.

Claire hustles them into Sally, and they set off for their meeting with the sheriff with a list of things to pick up on their way back. Potatoes, goat's milk, block of ice, Gerber's rice cereal so the twins can sleep longer during the night.

Claire's gotten absent minded, and I hope she remembers.

And I surely pray that Randall will be waiting there for them for moral support. Best of all will be when Nonni, or even Tessa, identifies the man.

Claire's bringing back Sonny's pay for the week, just in time for the tank to be half-filled this afternoon.

I'm still working on hanging the laundry when I hear truck tires crunching across our gravelly yard. He's earlier than expected.

I poke my head into the cabin where the babies are slumbering. There's no way around it. The noise is gonna wake them up.

I tug off my apron, hang it on the hook by the door, and hurry to the truck where the man is already half-way out.

Lordy, Lordy! It isn't even same man as last time. This one here has shiny white hair to his shoulders, like Santa Claus.

"I'm Ted, owner of Water Works. Here with your delivery." He steps toward me with his hand out.

"Where's the other feller?"

"He doesn't work for me anymore." He opens his mouth and then closes it without saying anything else. He dips his head toward me and then hurries to the

201

truck where he hooks up his filler hose to our tank.

He gets things going and returns to stand by me. After a few silent moments, he turns to me. "Did you notice anything odd about the other man?"

"Well, he was a mite nosy. Caught him trying to talk to one of the granddaughters. Don't want no strangers talking to my girls."

"Yeah. Everyone's jumpy now."

"Why you asking?"

"Two customers told me they got bills for water he never delivered. You get yours?"

"He came here. Twice. Yep. Pumped water each time."

"Well, you're not going to see him again. He quit and took my tools with him." Ted pulls a slip of paper from his shirt pocket and points to the amount due. "You have the money today?"

I shake my head. "Nope. Thought you were coming this afternoon. Claire's bringing it back."

Ted hands me the invoice. "That's okay. Send your check to the post office box. Or drop cash by my office."

He points to the address along the bottom of the paper.

I nod. "Okay."

Ted points at the paper again. "My name and phone number. Call if you see him again."

He gives me a long look before he winds up the hose, which he snaps into place on the side rail.

I hold the bill in my hand and watch the dusty tail follow the truck to the highway. Somehow, I cain't help thinking there was still something else he wanted to say and maybe something else I needed to hear.

But I ain't much of a talker and, evidently, neither is he.

His visit leaves me with a sense of unease. My thoughts drift to what he said about the other fella.

A thief and cheat? Good riddance! He's probably already to Nevada with the stolen tools.

I take a clothespin from between my lips, pinch it open, and stab it onto the remaining sheet.

Unexpected remembrance rolls through my body, and I consider the strangeness of this summer.

Before Pops took sick, we always had something interesting going on. Weekend trips out here to the homestead with a rush back so he could get back to work.

Lotsa projects to work on like the cabin and shelter. I'm handy with my hands that way.

Those were different times with splashes of excitement, and now I feel like I'm stuck. I push those feeling away. No time to be a sentimental old fool.

Out here, one day melts into another with the temperamental weather dividing up the week.

And that darn thing still hangs over our heads with that blasted man. I pray Nonni or Tessa identifies him today so's we can get back to a regular old life.

Claire's been as high strung as one of those electric lines we want to bring in, stretched to a breaking point. She wanted to talk to me this morning when Nonni began howling, and I cain't imagine on what.

Mebbe one of her hair-brained schemes, but I'm not encouraging any more chitchat.

I hang a damp diaper on the line. As I'm about to stab the clothespin onto it, a gust of wind snatches it plum out of my hand. I chase after it, hoping that I can catch it before it is completely covered in dirt.

It tumbles farther away, like it has feet of its own, right out to the edge of the bomb shelter, located away from the cabin and hidden by the brush.

Sonny padlocked it to keep the kids out and made them promise to stay away from it. Nothing's down there now except for a few building materials and some of my canned preserves and some construction supplies.

I stare at the broken lock and shake my sorry head. I see footprints around the door in the dirt, and they look bigger than Sonny's feet.

But mebbe I'm wrong. They must be his. I swing the door open and peer down into the dark interior but cain't see nothing.

I head back to the cabin and take me a peek in at the sleeping babies before I grab the flashlight on top of the ice box and hurry back to the shelter.

I pull the metal door open wide and lay it flat against the ground. The bunker itself is underground. I scooch close to the opening and aim the light beam down into the dark.

Hanging onto the wall rail, I use the tip of my shoes to feel my way down the metal ladder until they finally touch the cement floor.

I scan the small room with the dim beam and see a battery, boxes of nails, a few bags of cement, and an old kerosene lantern Pops had after we had installed the shelter.

Shelves rest against the wall with jars of canned goods from home: tomatoes, apricots, strawberry preserves the kids like best, and fig jam from that giant tree in my backyard. My favorite.

I grab two jars of stewed tomatoes and place them

in a flour sack, leaving them on the shelf next to the jars of water.

We was so worried the communists and Castro shooting missiles or dropping bombs on us that I'd boiled up a big batch of water, bottled it up, and dragged it out here last year. Just in case.

I don't know what to look for. There's jumbled stuff from Pops and newer stuff from me mixed with some of Sonny's construction fixins.

I step closer to the wooden crates with bags of cement balanced on them and spy something dark shoved tight between them and the wall.

I tug out a knapsack of some sort, sure I've never seen it before. Not that I know everything Randall and Claire have, but I know for a fact neither Pops nor I put it there.

I stick my hand in and pull out a red-and-black checked blanket. At this time of the year, some of the nights are warm and others drop to freezing.

I sniff it and smell dog and something else I cain't identify. With a little boiling, it'll be good as new.

I shake it, and a picture drops to the ground. I pick it up, my mouth wide with shock. In the light of the flickering torch, I make out a picture of a nekked woman. I'd never seen such a picture before.

What in the Sam Hill is it doing down here? If it is Sonny's, I don't care if he is a grown man, so help me God—I'll throw him over my knee and give him a strapping.

I dig deeper in the bag and discover ropes, a necklace, a woman's watch. There's also a baby bottle filled with rocks like the one that Sonny brought back that day.

I retrieve a stuffed gray sock. Nothing makes sense to me. Not at all.

Underneath it all is a tightly-rolled bundle. I grab it by a corner and shake it out. It's about three feet long, two feet wide. Its texture is rough under my hand. I look at it in the flickering light, and horror creeps into my bones.

Could this be a gunnysack?

I shove the whole kit and caboodle into the backpack and begin my slow climb up the ladder. I swing the flat metal door closed and adjust the broken lock to the closed position before marching back toward the cabin.

I am plumb out of patience. And I am in a hellacious, and I mean a hellacious, mood.

Claire wants to say something to me?

Just wait 'til she hears what I aim to tell her when she gets back.

Chapter 40
Nonni - Another Try

Daddy arrives at the sheriff's office alongside us. The sheriff and Detective Hunter herd us back toward that room, just like last time when I looked through the special window at five men standing in a line.

And they looked straight back at me, and I'd wanted to run right out of the room. But I didn't. And that hadn't turn out so well anyway.

Be strong.

The sheriff wants to begin with Tessa, and Mama protests. "Let Nonni go first."

He shakes his head. "Nah. I want to get the little one's response before Nonni tries it again."

He tells me to sit down on the bench outside the little room, but he doesn't close the door.

He gives directions to Tessa, who has never gone through this before. "Look closely at each man. You can see them, but they can't see you."

That's exactly what he told me last time.

Although I can't see through the window from where I'm sitting, I have a good view of Tessa. She wrinkles her forehead, and I imagine the gears in her head spinning.

Her voice squeaks out small. "Why can't they see me through this window if I can see them?"

I'd heard the explanation last time. I think this is a

good question on her part. Even though she's still small, she's nobody's fool, as Grandma Grace says.

The sheriff sighs. "It's a magic window. Believe me when I tell you that they can't see you."

Tessa looks up at him, her expression serious but believing. After a few quiet seconds, she nods and presses her nose against the window. "Okay."

"Do you see the man who stopped you and your sister?"

I study my sister, who is eager to do her part.

My heart feels like it's being torn in half. Should I tell the grownups what I know? Especially if that man is on the other side of the window?

If Tessie can be brave, I can be braver. Being silent hasn't helped me or my family.

Maybe I should step forward and be the hero of the day. I can't maintain my silence much longer, or I'll explode.

If I see the man and save my family, the police will protect us from him. Won't they?

Tessa's jaw juts out as she concentrates, her chin barely clearing the windowsill. She stands with her feet firmly planted on the ground and arms crossed against her chest as she swivels her head from left to right and back again.

"Nope. I don't see that bad man. But I do see *other* bad men. They are red, too."

She lets out a long, grown-up sounding sigh that sometimes bugs me but not today. I know what she means, and I'm proud of her.

The sheriff turns to Mama and Daddy. "Red? She isn't making any sense. Sounds like she can't identify him either."

Mama's face fades from pink to white.

"Where is he?" Tessa raises one eyebrow at the sheriff. "You're the sheriff."

She turns to the detective. "You're supposed to catch the bad guy, right?"

He looks at her, a kindly expression on his face, and shakes his head. "Well, do you see the man from *that* day?"

Tessa drops her head and closes her eyes. She keeps her hands on her hips and appears to be in deep thought. "No."

"Are you sure? Absolutely sure?" The detective is on one knee looking directly into my sister's eyes when she opens them.

Daddy faces the sheriff with exasperation on his face. "C'mon! She's just a young child. I told you she couldn't help. It's bad enough that we have to bring Nonni into it, again."

The sheriff turns to me. "Your turn, little missy. You know the drill. Come on in."

I enter the room and step up to the window as Tessa moves back. I can do this.

"Look at the men. Point to the man who stopped you and your sister. Take your time."

All but one of the men are different than last time. The man they had me look at twice last time is there, a kinda short, round guy compared to the others. But just because I saw him in a lineup twice doesn't mean that he's the guy who stopped us.

I stare at each person standing in front of me. I can't point him out even if I want to.

"Do you recognize any of these as the person who stopped you on the way home in May?"

I shake my head no.

"You need to say it aloud. Yes. Or no."

"No." My face flushes with embarrassment.

"Are you *absolutely* sure that you don't see that man standing in the line?"

No matter how many times he might ask me, it won't change what I see. Or don't see.

The man in the truck who stopped Tessa and me is not in the line-up.

The same man I saw later with the water truck is not here in front of me.

The same man who knows my name and says he'll hurt my family if I talk is not here.

That same man with the scar on his eyebrow and blue eyes that look like they might slice through me like a knife is not in the lineup.

To try to please the sheriff, even though I know it won't make a lick of a difference, I study each face, again, and will myself to recognize the man.

It doesn't happen. It can't happen. He's not there.

"No. I don't think so." My voice shakes. I so badly want to say, "Yes! That's him!" and for the sheriff, the detective, Daddy, Mommy and Tessa to beam at me with pride. For someone to shout, "Good girl!"

But I can't lie to them, so I stand there feeling stupid and wishing that I could melt onto the floor, just like the Wicked Witch of the West in the *Wizard of Oz.*

The grownups look at me, disbelief on their faces. I can hardly force the air in and out of my lungs. I begin to doubt my memory, just like I did last time. After all, I'd had trouble with the color of that truck when we described it to the sheriff that day. My mind had tried all kinds of colors and combinations, and, in the end, I ended up confused.

It was Tessa who was positive about the color, not me with my incorrect recollection. She always had that color thing going.

But now, her mumbling about "red," that same word she mumbled in her sleep and also outside our cabin this morning, makes no sense to me or the police here, either.

"Are you sure? Absolutely sure?"

"Yes." My certainty slips away. "Maybe. No. I mean, yes. I'm sure. I don't see him."

"Wait here." He points to a bench outside the room.

Tessa and I boost our bottoms onto it, and our feet swing, not touching the linoleum floor. We huddle close to each other.

He motions my parents to the far side of the room where he speaks in a low tone.

One of my gifts is my keen sense of hearing. And sometimes I hear things I'm not supposed to and that I wish I hadn't.

"Without a positive ID, we can't use either of your girls as witnesses in your case." He sighs and scratches his ear.

"However, two other witnesses earlier today definitely confirmed a suspect as the man they saw peeping into their windows. And we had that earlier confirmation on him by another witness from the first line-up. We've had enough evidence to hold that man in jail based on these identifications. But it's a shame we don't have confirmation from either of your daughters. For your case."

They're mad at me now. I can tell. Or maybe it's

just supreme disappointment. Again. I don't blame them.

It's my fault. I feel my bottom lip tugging itself down with a resigned quiver.

Mama motions the sheriff and detective to follow her to the other side of the room. She reaches into the bag she lugged in with her and pulls out a piece of newspaper. She unfolds it, handing it to the sheriff. He and Detective Hunter look at Mama's paper.

"I traced this from an indentation in the ground outside our window last night and then drew in the scrape across one of the soles." I can barely hear Mama's low murmur.

Detective Hunter takes the newsprint into the room with the men from the lineup, who are still waiting in there. He says something to them, and they slip their shoes off and turn them over. He holds the paper up to each and checks for a match. He shakes his head. There isn't one.

He leaves the room to return to our mother. "May I keep this, ma'am?"

Mama nods, and he refolds the paper before placing it on the table. "Thank you. It's not much, but it might be helpful. You never know."

The detective asks me to look at the men one last time.

"She did the best she could. Don't pester her any more. And Tessa didn't recognize him, either. Please. This is just too hard for all of us. We have to get on with our lives." Daddy raises his shoulders and clenches his fists in frustration.

"It's okay, Daddy. I'll try one last time." I hope in my heart of hearts that something has changed in the lineup in the last few minutes.

I position myself in front of the window and stare again at each man. No. If he's there, I can't identify him as much as I want to.

There's nothing left in me to give after finally deciding to identify the perpetrator, in spite of his threats. The letdown is heavy on my soul, like a big, wet, hairy blanket being draped over me. I can hardly stand up, my knees knock together so hard.

I shake my head. "No. No. He's not there."

Mama sighs and lowers her eyebrows, her worry wrinkle forming between her eyes. The detective and sheriff confer, mumbling and shaking their heads. I can't hear them this time even though I strain, but their body language tells me enough.

This much I know. I'm a failure as a witness. The weight I bear as an almost-snitch is almost too heavy for me.

The sheriff marches over to me, takes my hand in his, and shakes it. "Thank you, Nonni." He does the same with Tessa.

Detective Hunter stands behind him and makes eye contact with my parents. "I'll let you know if anything new comes up."

He shakes our hands before leaving the building. Through the window, I watch him climb into his car.

"If you remember anything else, tell your parents, you hear me?" The sheriff holds his gaze, now kind, on me, and a blush rises up from my neck to burn my face.

My bottom lip trembles, and my vision blurs with tears. I nod and focus on my feet. No one speaks for a few seconds.

Mama reaches over and gently rubs my shoulder. I

jump. "Nonni, baby. You did good. You, too, Tessie." She stretches out her other hand to smooth my sister's hair.

Then she looks down at our feet, which are clad in our old flip flops. "Let's go get your school shoes now. Okay, girls?"

Daddy picks me up by my armpits and blows a raspberry on my neck. "Gotta go back to work, pumpkin."

I feel my face flush. I'd disappointed him before, and now I am a fraud. And he doesn't know. What will he do when he finds out?

He sets me down and does the same with Tessa. "Love you, sweet cheeks." He swivels and walks toward the door.

"Hey! Aren't you going to say goodbye to me, too?" Mama's eyes spark.

He returns and gives her a quick hug.

"And the check?"

"Sorry. I forgot." Daddy reaches into his pocket and draws out an envelope. "I've already signed it," he says. "Go ahead and cash it at the bank."

"Mother Grace is planning to pay the water man with part of it. He's coming sometime today with the new delivery."

When I hear her say that, I can't help it. A squeak escapes, followed by another. As much as I hate to cry, I've done it twice today. What's the matter with me? Where's my stoic O'Brien self-control?

Tessa sniffles, grabs my arm, and squeezes it hard. "Nonni!" She cries a little, too.

Mama puts her arms around both of us, drawing us close to her. "They've had a hard day. This has been too much for them."

She gives Daddy the "look" that says there's more to be said on the subject later.

If only she knew what I know, that conversation would have begun on the spot.

Chapter 41
Claire - Secret Stash

Nonni, and now Tessa, are crying, so Rand and I hustle them by the bench and into the observation room. The men in the lineup are gone, and the room feels safe. I'd been afraid that something like this might happen.

"What's wrong, Nonni?" Rand stoops down to her level and looks into her green eyes.

"Nothing, Daddy," she whimpers. "I'm sorry!" He rubs her back in a couple of slow circles.

I put my arm around Tessa, and she sniffs into my side. The girls' outbursts are evidence of the stress we've been through. My nerves are certainly shot, but I do my best to tamp them down, so they won't get the best of me.

With both girls upset and Rand heading back to the job site, I'll talk to him later about the footprint. He was standing with the girls when I turned it over to the sheriff and detective, and he gave me an odd look. I don't think he overheard my conversation, but he has to be wondering what I was doing.

Rand's voice is strained. "Gotta go. I already begged my way out of time to do this. Don't wanna get fired today."

I wheedle the check from him, and he gives me a worried look before he hurries out to the truck to return to work.

"Girls." They turn their sad eyes to me. "Let's go get lunch here in town, down the sidewalk to the diner."

Their faces register surprise, and then small smiles tug at the corners of their mouths.

The girls and I sit at the counter. We split two hamburgers between the three of us. They are served with mayonnaise, catsup, fresh lettuce, and tomatoes. There are a couple of dill pickles and a mound of French fries on the side to share. I can't remember the last time we ate an honest-to-goodness grilled burger.

We each are served a delicious ice-cold glass of water with ice cubes. What a divine luxury. Ice cubes! And water without a metallic aftertaste.

In spite of the disturbing experience with the line-up, I want to turn our day into an adventure.

That's the way to move through life, and I want to model that spirit to the girls. And to erase the negative feelings from the lineup. Here we are, away from the cabin and eating out, just like the city folks we used to be.

After we finish, the girls lick their fingers, and we walk down the sidewalk to the thrift store. I'm on a hunt for school shoes. That's something I miss from Rand's Chrysler days. Having time and a little money to meander through a store looking for something I need, or simply want, to buy. Or even just to window shop.

Our days living in the city seem like downright luxury compared to the life I'm living now. This afternoon, with money in my purse from my secret stash, we search for school shoes.

A new year with new grade levels and new teachers begins right around bend for us, and I want to be ready.

Nonni discovers a pair of barely scuffed red tennis shoes and two pairs of slightly used white socks with ruffles for herself. Tessie immediately gravitates to pink tennies, practically new, and Nonni locates a package of matching socks for her.

"Thank you, Jesus," I whisper. Excited, they skip down the sidewalk in their "new" shoes. The "me" of a year ago wouldn't have recognized the "me" of today.

Living as we do, mostly off the grid, puts material goods in perspective. When we moved out here, we were relieved from the never-ending feeling of having to keep up with our neighbors even though I did love my modern appliances!

Now with the delivery bill and hospital paid off, clothes from Nick's sister, and practically new shoes for the girls, things are looking up.

"We can be twinsies, too!" Tessa points down at their shoes. "Tennies and tennies! Twinsies!"

They both giggle, and it warms my heart to hear this musical sound that's been missing for far too long.

When we get back into the car, I smile back at Nonni from the rear-view mirror.

Good. With school beginning in less than a week, maybe we can settle into a normal routine.

Tessa chatters all the way down the bumpy, dusty road about how she plans on being the tetherball queen of the school during lunch recess now that she'll be in the second grade.

"I'll beat Bobby again this year! Every day!" Her enthusiasm is contagious. "When's Daddy putting up our tether ball? He promised!"

"I'll remind him when he's home again. He's been

pretty busy, you know." His hours away at the job have increased over the last couple of weeks, and he's promised Mr. Henderson to work overtime in exchange for being with us at the sheriff's office today.

It's a sacrifice, but Gracie's still here. We need every penny he earns.

"Nonni! Play tetherball with me!" Tessa challenges her sister. "I bet I can beat you, and I'll be the tetherball champion of the world! That's what I want to be when I grow up!"

"You can't be tetherball champion when you grow up! That's not a job, is it, Mama?" I see the reflection of Nonni's earnest expression through the rear-view mirror.

Before I can answer, Tessa demonstrates. "You make a fist like this." She clenches her hand into the shape of a boxing glove. "Then, when the ball swings around, you hit it down, I said *down,* as hard as you can."

"But you must never touch the rope, or you're out." Nonni side-eyes Tessa who nods at her and leans back in her seat with a sigh.

The silence doesn't last more than a minute before Nonni says, "Let's sing!"

She begins, off key, and we empty our lungs with "Cry me a river. Cry me a river."

She croons, "You cried a river over me," and Tessa fake cries. We all laugh until real tears roll down our cheeks.

"One more time!" Tessa begs as we near the cabin. She holds onto the note as long as she can, her voice wavering toward the end with her effort. "You cried a river over me!"

We had learned the words from listening to our new transistor radio that Rand had brought home. For a few moments, normalcy has returned to our family. I feel the corner of my mouth dance with a small smile.

As Nonni opens door to leap out, I look down and see the grocery list flutter on the seat. A frown bunches up on my forehead. With everything that's happened today, I forgot to stop at the market and drove past Jolly's without a blink.

I know Mother Grace is going to give me fits for this. And after the lineup today, I'm not in the mood to fight with her.

I make a decision. "Out! Quick!"

Nonni jumps out, followed by Tessa.

"Tell your grandmother I'll be back in a few minutes. Going back to the market."

Tessa slams the door, and I back up in a hurry. I'm going to get what we need at the store and deposit the check. I also need a few quiet minutes alone to think about what happened today.

As I crank the steering wheel, I take one last look in the rearview mirror. There's Mother Grace waving her arms at me.

I stick my arm out of the window and wave back as I gun the engine and bounce across the ruts onto the road. I pray she has enough sensitivity to leave the girls alone until I get home.

My brief interlude of happiness evaporates. How will we proceed with what happened today at the station? With what I discovered this morning outside of the cabin?

There's a good chance that Mother Grace will call me crazy after I tell her what I know. But for now, I need time to think. Alone.

Coward that I am, I cling to the wheel and spin off in a cloud of dust.

Chapter 42
Gracie - We Hafta Talk

I'm anxious to get Claire alone to show her that backpack. There's a lot of things plum wrong with it. I worry about it all day long. It's not Rand's. I know it in my soul.

My son may be hard-headed like his dad, but he is not into that kind of secret nasty stuff. And what about that money in the sock? And those other things? I've stuffed the backpack under my bed where the kids won't find it.

The car pulls up in front of the cabin right while I am changing Fiona's stinky diaper, but by the time I get outside, Claire's pulling away with dirt and rocks spinning under her tires. She's in some kind of a flat-out hurry.

The girls run toward me, chattering and pointing down at their new shoes.

Then, while I attempt to flag her down, Claire takes off down the road. Just keeps going!

After months of me not having much to say to her, 'cept in my head, now I am ready to talk, and she takes off! Driving like a crazy person.

"Where's your ma going?"

Tessa jumps in the air and clicks her heels together like a leprechaun. "Mama's going to the market. She'll be right back, and then she can cry me a river, again."

Sometimes that child plum doesn't make sense, but I could almost predict the foolish actions of her mother. Does this mean Claire is upset?

I'll talk to her about the lineup when she returns with the stuff she forgot to get at the store. And I could have bet a bushel of our fresh-laid eggs she'd forget. We're almost out of that goat's milk, and she was supposed to pick it up at the dairy.

My mouth is parched, and I could kill for a frosty Coca Cola. That'll never happen. I'm staying away from the sugar water whether I want to or not.

But, dabnabbit, I need to talk to her. And I need a big, tall glass of water right now.

I shoo the girls to the picnic table, setting them up with one of my world-famous-no-bake oatmeal cookies and sun tea.

The babies, propped up by pillows, gnaw on hard crusts of bread because they have sharp little biters brewing in their swollen gums. Even if they haven't broken the skin yet.

If we had ice, I would chop some up, wrap it in a tea towel, and let 'em chew on it. And if we had some brandy, I would dip the chewing cloth into it, too. We don't have none of those items, so my homemade teething biscuits will have to do.

I'm guessing Thomas Patrick will be the first to burst one through, but time will tell.

Tessa hovers over the babies. Nonni's lost in a daydream and drawing a figure eight with her finger on the picnic table.

"You sure you couldn't point at that man?"

They shake their heads. I'll wait to talk to Claire about that, too.

223

My mind churns. If Sonny did not put that stuff there, then who did? Mebbe Claire's sneaky, secret traps are not so crazy after all. Mebbe that earlier footprint's connected to the broken lock and backpack?

But if they are connected, whose'n are they? And why couldn't they identify him today? I have a very bad gut-level feeling about all of this.

We need a new lock on the shelter. In the meantime, mebbe I should get me some twine and tie the latch so that the kids cannot get in there.

That's all we need, them falling in and breaking their necks like Tessa almost did with that well.

Do we even have any twine? I s'pose I could use some of that rope I found in the backpack.

I look up at the sky with high clouds skittering across and wonder if that rope is too thick to thread through latch.

"I'm going to make us a new big old Zig Zag. Where's the rake?" Nonni turns away from the table.

"Zig Zag!" Tessa's eyes shimmer with excitement.

"I'm gonna start it now." Nonni grabs the rake from its resting spot along the cabin wall.

"Go, Nonni. Tessie, keep an eye on the babies." Zig Zag is a surefire way to keep Nonni busy while Tessa watches from the table.

What I do need is another look at that backpack before all Hades breaks out.

Chapter 43
Claire - Honesty

I crank down the window and wave to Nonni as I near the cabin.

I made it to the dairy before they closed and bought a bottle of goat's milk. The groceries from Jolly's are the front seat next to me, and the ice is wrapped in paper on the floor in front of the passenger seat.

I also picked up the last Sunday Times, which was still on the shelf. The kids love the funnies, and it's the main way we keep up on what's happening out there in the world other than that little transistor radio.

I've had some time to think about the lineup and what I've discovered. I'm still not sure how much I want to tell Gracie about my thread traps and the new footprint this morning. She's likely to tip her head back and stare at me like I'm crazy.

I pass by Nonni and croon. "Sweetie! You're working on a new game!"

She flags me away from her design, and I park on the west side of the cabin. She's already sketched the outer perimeter, exactly two rake widths wide. Her safe zone's plotted out in the middle.

She'll be working on it for another couple of days before she finishes it to her satisfaction.

I smile and wonder how this child of mine was born with such a streak of creativity, and I suspect it's what she needs to calm her spirit. That and the stories she writes for Tessa and the babies.

It suddenly strikes me that she's a lot like her father with his construction projects. They're both always creating something new.

As I step out of the car, Gracie rushes up to me and grabs the wrapped block of ice right out of my arms. "Got to talk to you." Speckles of spit shoot off her lips.

I pull the other two bags of groceries from the front seat and head for the cabin, my curiosity fired up. I don't want to show it to that woman, so I follow her into the cabin at a leisurely pace.

Tessa's practicing her school skills at the picnic table, tracing words, and drawing a picture with her crayons.

I call out, "Stay there, honey! Keep working!"

She looks up and smiles before looking back down at the paper in front of her.

"I want to be the smartest person in class this year! I'm practicing 'cuz the teacher might make me take a test on the first day of school. I'm gonna be ready." She hums as she concentrates on her work.

I tiptoe into the cabin where Gracie is sliding the ice into the icebox. The babies sleep as I add the goat milk, cheese, and bologna to the icebox.

I don't want the crinkle of the paper bag waking them up, so I lean over and place it on the floor to finish unpacking later.

Outside, she motions me to walk with her to the clothesline where today's clean sheets and diapers flap next to a blanket I don't recognize.

I follow her to the end of the line, and she places her hands on her skinny hips, squinting at me with a wrinkled brow.

A cloud shadow skitters across the desert floor around us. "We need to get these down. I feel a storm a coming."

I feel a shiver as I pull a wooden pin from one end of the sheet.

She touches my elbow. "Well." She pauses.

I wait. She usually isn't at a loss for words, at least with me. This isn't a game we play.

"Well. Whiles you was gone, I walked on out to the shelter. Thought I'd get us out a pot of preserves for tomorrow's breakfast."

I stand, puzzled, not knowing where she's heading with this conversation.

"The lock was broken." She nods for emphasis.

"What?"

"Yep. The lock was broken."

"The lock to the outhouse?" I pause. "I know. I was going to ask Rand to get us a new one so that darn door doesn't keep banging all night in the wind."

"No. Not *that* lock. The lock to the shelter. Mebbe Sonny broke it and forgot to tell us." She blinks rapidly several times. "I didn't know about the other lock."

I'm confused. What in the world is she talking about?

"I climbed down the ladder into that dark box and found this." She points to a red and black blanket pinned next to the sheet. "Stuffed in a backpack. You seen it before?"

"No. Never. Or any backpack down there."

"Well, I washed the blanket good so's we could use it." Her pronunciation of "warsh" accentuates her intensity.

227

"Maybe Randall got it at the job and left it there." He sometimes brought home items he collected when he was out and about.

Gracie's eyes flit to me uncomfortably. "That's not all."

She reaches into one of the deep pockets of her apron and pulls out a big roll of hundred-dollar bills banded together.

My eyes almost bug out of my face.

"That's still not all." She shakes it in my face. "There was another roll of them, just like this one."

My heart beats erratically, and I place the palm of my hand on my chest before I reply. "I know for a fact we don't have any extra cash laying around except for that bit in the bank for the chickens and for building the next piece of this home."

It doesn't make sense to me. It's like she's talking a foreign language. "You know. Randall's been breaking his back working double-time to provide for us."

Gracie's eyes dart back to me. "There's more."

I hold my breath.

"Jewelry. A footprint. A dirty picture. Didn't think Randall would dare look at that kind of thing."

I can't help it. I gasp. "Oh, dear God. No! No, he wouldn't."

"Men sometimes change over time, though. You sure?"

"Sure. He wouldn't." I fight for words, but they stick in my throat.

Despite the fading warmth of this late afternoon, a chill trickles along my arms. I would almost swear that it's spelling out "danger" in goosebumps.

It's time to tell her about my last trap and what I'd found this morning, the new footprint, the one I'd turned over to the sheriff.

Gracie struggles to fold the last sheet without letting it drag on the dirt. At four feet ten inches, that's quite a task for her since the breeze keeps ripping it from her grasp.

I grab one end and, together, we fold crease over crease, corner to corner, ending up with a folded flat bundle. That's the way I like my sheets—and my life. Clean, folded, safe, and under control with loose ends tucked in.

Gracie plunks it down in the laundry basket.

"Follow me, child." She marches to the bunker, stopping by the metal door and points her toe at an impression of a shoe in the sand. "That's not Randall's. Too big."

I squat down and examine it closely.

Gracie follows suit.

"See this?" I point to the ridge across the heel of one of the prints. "It's just like the one I traced from a print by the house this morning that I gave to the sheriff today."

I see shock register in Gracie's eyes as we come to the same conclusion.

"Someone's been out here. At night. By our home. By the shelter. By our window! The same person with the same shoe!" I shiver. "Who is he? What does he want?"

I shiver again as I picture someone slinking around in the dark, spying on us. And we don't even have a phone to call for help.

"Well. For starters, a place to stash a backpack

with this here money and other stuff." Gracie shakes her head.

"I wonder when he's coming back for it." My eye twitches, and I rub it.

"Well. I hid it in the cabin where no one can find it."

"We should tell the sheriff. I'll drive there right now." I'm ready to take action with adrenaline coursing through my veins. I'm sick and tired of feeling like a jackrabbit paralyzed in the glare of headlights.

"You told them about footprint today? Right?"

"Yes. Showed them the tracing I made on newspaper. The sheriff compared it against the men's shoes in the lineup. No matches."

Gracie chews her bottom lip. "Mebbe it *is* Randall's. Mebbe we should wait to ask him before we go running off to the sheriff. They think we're mighty flighty anyway. He'll be home in a couple of days, and then you can go down there with him to the sheriff. Or I can go. Unless you think we should go today."

"No, he's not back until the end of next week. I don't know if we should wait or not. No. We should talk to him first unless something else changes, and we need to go early. The patrols are in place, and the sheriff said he'd tell us if something happens."

"Yes'n. Let's play it by ear. If'n something feels extra fishy, one of us can go. Okey doke?"

"And if those things you found are his, I'm going to kill him!"

How could I doubt him?

There had been that one time in Santa Monica that I'd found a picture in his pocket when I was doing the laundry, but he'd promised me it was a joke someone played on him in the office.

I bring myself back to the present. Is this an emergency or something we should talk about before going to the sheriff? Once these things are in the hands of the sheriff, they'll be out of our control.

They *might* set things in motion that we can't stop. There *might* be explanations for what we've uncovered.

Might is the operative word.

"And that's not all." Large, soft drops begin to plop down from the sky before she can say more.

Nonni shouts, "No-o-o-o! Do not rain on my game!"

Gracie and I turn in unison to grab the blanket from the line.

"Let's get it out of sight."

Chapter 44
Nonni - A New Beginning

Yesterday was Monday. Labor Day. The first day of school is today, and I won't be the new kid in class this year.

I skip out to breakfast in my almost new flat-soled Keds and white socks with fancy ankle ruffles. From the bag of clothes Uncle Nick brought us, I had chosen a green corduroy dress with yellow shorts so I could hang upside down from the monkey bars after lunch.

Mama has already threaded yellow ribbons through my two braids, Annie Oakley style. Everything I'm wearing is new, or at least new to me. If Annie can ride a rodeo horse, I can reinvent myself in the fourth grade.

It's a spanking new year. Anything can happen, and I'm ready.

Mama sets the platter of scrambled eggs on the picnic table. Our hens are laying big, beautiful, brown eggs.

Tessa and I take turns going into the coop to retrieve them while they're still warm, and our breakfast menu alternates eggs with our standard oatmeal breakfasts. I bet we get hard-boiled eggs in our lunches today, too.

For this first-day-of-school breakfast, Grandma Grace plunks a plate of pan-fried toast in front of us, spread with her sweet homemade strawberry preserves.

My mouth waters.

Tessa's wearing my favorite blue-checked dress from last year.

I point out, "That dress is too long for you to wear. Maybe you should switch into something smaller."

"No. I don't think so, and I don't care." She twirls around, laughing. "I look like Dorothy from *The Wizard of Oz*. I love her!"

Mama and I read that book aloud at bedtime by the light of the kerosene lantern, and Tessa's always keen for the next chapter.

Mama's pulled Tessa's brown hair, with its glints of red, up into a tight ponytail, and she's wearing her favorite silver plastic headband.

Excited, she kicks one of her new pink tennies toward my face and almost hits my nose.

"Stop that!" I back up and wave a hand in front of myself.

"I'm the Dorothy in the second grade!" With her foot back on the ground, she uses the tip of her shoe to trace a number two in the dirt. Those feet are everywhere.

"Watch out! Or you'll have to wash those new shoes every night to keep them clean." I twist my feet around to admire different views of my fancy tennis shoes.

They are much lighter on our feet than our old saddle shoes we've grown out of (or in Tessa's case, dropped down a well), so it'll be an easier walk home.

Then I remember. After the encounter, which is what Mama calls it, last spring with that man and the abandoned well, I'm not sure we'll ever be allowed out on our own again on that road.

I'll miss running part of the way, which is what I like to do when I'm not kicking a rock. Either Mama or Grandma Grace will be picking us up in Sally while the babies take their naps.

No more "Sammy Snake" games for us on the way home.

No wells.

No strangers.

Or anything else.

"Hurry up!" Grandma hovers nearby.

I use my fingers to push the last bit of scrambled eggs onto my last bite of toast and shove it into my mouth. Licking my fingers, I hand Grandma my plate.

"I see him and his kite-tail coming!" Daddy points at the truck bouncing toward us, dust in its wake.

"Hey, bud!" Our father waves at him and heads to the table to pick up his things for work.

Uncle Nick greets us with his slow drawl. "Hey, kiddos. Your daddy said we should take you straight to school since it's the beginning of school and all. Hop on in!"

Daddy puts his sleeping bag and supply bag into the back where we're riding and climbs up into the cab with his steel lunch box and a big jug of water.

Before we know it, we've arrived in style, just like the rich kids in class, but our ride was probably a lot more fun out in the truck bed, bouncing around.

We climb out, and Daddy hangs his head out of the passenger window and motions us to him.

"Either Mama or Grandma'll pick you up after you get off the bus. Tomorrow morning, one of them'll take you to the bus stop since I'm out here at the job all week. Don't talk to anyone while you wait. You hear?"

"Yes, Daddy. Bye, Daddy." We chime together and laugh.

A shadow, a reminder of last year, flits across my heart, and my smile fades as quickly as it appeared.

There's no time to dawdle. We dust off our dresses, pat our hair into place, blow kisses at Daddy, and scamper to the blacktop where our teachers wait for us.

I line up next to Room 4, and Tessa is a couple of rows away by Room 2.

My fourth-grade teacher greets us while we wait, smiling and shielding his eyes from the sun with his hand.

When the bell rings, we follow him to what will be our new home-away-from-home.

"Take any seat for now." He points to an unusual formation of desks, a big, roundish pattern that is open in the middle.

It reminds me a little of my Zig Zag games. This is a good sign. I hurry to the desk closest to the door.

"My name is Mr. Parra." He picks up a piece of yellow chalk and writes it on the blackboard. "It means vine. Like a grapevine."

I wonder what O'Brien means? I've never thought about that before. And I've never seen a man teacher in school before. My chest puffs out with pride that I've been assigned to him.

"This is my first year of teaching. Follow my lead, and we'll get along great."

I guess it's a first-kind-of day for him, too. He's full of energy and has lots of ideas like organizing our classroom after King Arthur's Court and his round table.

"That way the knights could all see each other and

settle their problems in a civil way." He takes a minute to look directly in our eyes.

"Civil means without yelling or bullying. This year, you'll learn how to use problem solving techniques to solve your issues by talking about them." He glances at us again. "Any questions?" No one raises a hand.

"That's okay. You can ask questions later. And that's not all that we'll be doing." He points to a chart on the wall that lists activities like running, jumping, pull-ups, and rope climbs.

"You're going to have Physical Education every day and Square Dancing on Fridays."

I hear Barry groan.

"I know you all learned how last year." He smiles. "It will be fun. I guarantee it!"

I'm a pretty good square dancer, but I'm an even better runner. When I grow up, I want to be a track star, like Wilma Rudolph, in the Olympics.

"And at the end of the year, we'll have a contest with the rockets you're going to carve out of balsa wood! More about that later!"

A buzz of excitement erupts. We're a combination classroom, and there're only ten of us fourth graders. The other fifteen are fifth graders.

I look around for Trina who's sitting next to a girl I don't recognize.

The day passes quickly. Sherri's the girl in the desk next to Trina in class, but we all sit together at lunch outside under the shaded patio.

"The teacher assigned me to help Sherri because she's new," Trina whispers.

I don't think the new girl needs much help because

she's already acting like she's been at our school longer than I have. She tells us that everything she's wearing is brand new and that she loves store-bought clothes.

I wonder what she'd think about my hand-me-down clothes, if she knew. I sit there and eat my peanut and grape jelly sandwich while she and Trina chat away.

After lunch, Mr. Parra calls on each of us to read aloud. I'm a fast reader and can read almost anything silently, but I don't like how I sound.

Sometimes, I feel like I'm literally swallowing my words as the ends of my sentences vanish down my throat.

I hope he won't tell me to speak louder or read my passage again. Instead, he smiles at me when I finish. The little knot in the middle of my tummy relaxes.

Back on the bus with Tessa sitting next to me, I realize I missed seeing her on the playground today even though she's sometimes a pest.

And I didn't think about the bad man at all today.

The summer had dragged on with too much thinking time, and I like having a brand new year and class and teacher and being busy.

I have a good feeling about this year and my new teacher. He told us that things we could never imagine would happen, and we would be brave and wise in ways we couldn't anticipate. That he is here to help us.

Even he would never have anticipated what happened next. When it did, I was glad that he was the one I told.

Chapter 45
Claire - The Unveiling

How did October slide into our lives without notice? Well, in a couple of days, we'll be halfway through it.

We've been in a constant state of motion with the girls in school, Rand away more than usual, and all the tasks that have to be completed daily without electricity or running water.

When I snug the babies down for the evening, they now sleep for at least a six-hour stretch before they wake up hungry.

Gracie and I've put off any decision-making until Rand is back in a couple of days. Then we'll go to the sheriff with the new evidence we've gathered.

In the meantime, neighbors and law enforcement are patrolling, and there haven't been any new crimes.

I prefer to think that we're back to normal, and that crazy guy is out of commission or in another state.

Tomorrow is Columbus Day, the last day of the school week. The kids don't have school. Rand's job is almost finished, and we're excited for the grand opening, which we're all invited to.

It's still warm enough in the daytime that Nonni and Tessa will be able to swim in that lake during the festivities. Or at least paddle around the edge of what Rand calls "Baby Beach." There will be lots of glorious food. A big barbeque with all the fixings.

My thoughts are interrupted as the car arrives, and the girls jump out. I rub the feathers from my hands.

Gracie pulls a large paper bag from the front seat and heads toward the cabin.

She glances over at me. "Got the goat milk. And some cans of cream of mushroom soup and a bag of rice to make a couple of meals from that hen I kilt this morning. It'll save in the icebox until he gets home this weekend if'n we keep that door shut and if'n I get some more ice tomorrow afternoon to keep it cold. You finished plucking it?"

I swear, that woman can speak a nonstop paragraph and not even end up winded.

"Almost." I had scalded the chicken for a couple of minutes before gingerly extracting most of the recalcitrant feathers while trying to not tear the skin.

The thought of it makes me shiver, even here in the heat. I don't think I'll ever get used to the whole prep process, from living creature to main course. It's enough to turn me into a vegetarian.

I'm a city girl at heart. "Here, you take over the rest of it."

Gracie nods, a gleam in her eye proclaiming me to be a less competent woman than she'll ever be.

Mentally, I concede she's got me beat in this category since she grew up picking cotton for her father, a sharecropper who kept chickens, too.

And she had no trouble wringing that hen's neck earlier.

Tessa brims with news about her tetherball victory. She demonstrates with her fist in the air making a downward arc.

"I'm going to be the tetherball champion of the world. No one can beat me this year. I already beat Bobby at lunch today!" She springs high in the air.

Nonni hugs me before she grabs the rake. "Mama, I just have a little more to do on my Zig Zag, and it will be finished. No homework!"

"I'll call you in when it's time to set the picnic table for dinner."

I hum a refrain from my new favorite Andy Williams song, *Moon River*, and follow her out front. I love that transistor radio bringing culture back into my life.

"Look, Mama!" She points to the outer circle in place and the safe zone in the middle.

She's already laid one of the smaller tracks leading from the outside to the safe zone and created several dead ends with their rounded circles.

Rand isn't expected tonight, so Nonni isn't worried about him running over her elaborate work with his truck in the dark.

I can tell by the determined look on her face that if I let her, she'd work on it until the tracks faded into darkness. A little distraction goes a long way.

I look beyond her toward the Colony and the bus stop. A small red car picks its way down the long, windy road to our cabin.

By the time it arrives, Nonni, Mother Grace, and I are standing against the cabin out front. The driver's door swings open, and out steps Nonni's teacher.

I walk toward him. "What a surprise! Mr. Parra! A home visit, just like you promised at Back-to-School Night.

"Yes. I'm calling on each student." He moves

forward and shakes my hand. "It's good to see you again."

He smiles at me before turning to Gracie and taking her hand.

I'm surprised she doesn't flinch since she generally doesn't like to be touched by strangers.

"Ma'am. Glad to make your acquaintance."

She flashes him a rare smile and flutters her eyelashes. I can't believe it.

I lead him around the cabin to the picnic table. "Welcome to our...home."

Gracie hurries inside to check on the babies and returns with a pitcher of sun tea, which she also calls Mormon tea, no ice, and some of her no-bake cookies.

"Thank you. This looks delicious." He picks up one of the cookies and takes a big bite of it. "Mmmmm."

I swear I see Gracie blush.

He turns to Nonni, who has followed us to the table.

"But I have a special reason for coming today. Do you feel up to talking to your mother and grandmother about your writing project?"

Nonni hesitates. "Yes. I think so."

I crook an eyebrow at her. "Honey, what's up? What does your teacher want you to tell us?"

My alarm system is revving up. Out of the corner of my eye, I see Tessa through the open cabin door holding up a picture book and telling a sing-song story to the twins.

He takes a folder from his briefcase and lays it on the picnic table. He pulls two papers out of the file, one with writing and one with drawing on it, and then he turns to Nonni, whose face has paled.

"Please read it aloud to us, Nonni."

He looks at Gracie and me. "We've been working on ways to solve problems in class, and this was a writing exercise about fear. Each student identified something that bothered them and then proposed a solution. Please listen to what Nonni wrote. She needs to share it with you."

Nonni's hand shakes as she picks up the paper with her tidy printing on it and silently places it next to the picture she's drawn.

From where I sit, I see a primitive line drawing of a pickup truck. Although it contains a stick-figure man, I recognize that he's holding a bag in his hand.

Chills creep down my spine.

After only a few seconds, she reaches for the picture and turns it upside down so none of us can see it.

Gracie looks over at Nonni with an incredulous look on her face and then addresses the teacher.

"What's going on here? I cain't believe Nonni did something wrong. She's a might quiet, but, generally speaking, she's a hard-working child."

"Oh no. She's incredibly brave." He locks his gaze on Nonni. "You, you can do it. Take a deep breath and then read it to us."

She slowly flattens the top page, holds it in front of her, and gulps air. Without giving us eye contact, she reads in a soft voice that sounds like she's swallowing her words before they can reach our ears.

"Speak up, girl." Mother Grace sits upright with her arms folded across her chest.

"You can do it, Nonni." Mr. Parra nods at her.

Nonni begins anew, stumbling over her words before lapsing into a robotic tone.

I hold myself rigidly upright, and before she's finished, a tear rolls down my cheek. I bite my bottom lip to keep myself from distracting her.

"The bad man told me he would hurt me and my family if I told anyone. Two different times."

She pauses and wipes her nose on her arm. "On the way home that day and at our water tank. I couldn't tell because I didn't want anyone to get hurt. He knows I live here, and he heard Grandma Grace say my name that day he delivered water to us. He said my name, too."

Nonni rests her head on the table, exhausted. After a minute, she sits up and shakes her foot hard. "He said I would be responsible for him hurting you. It would be my fault."

I want to leap over to her, but she turns the paper over to read more. I sense that if I interrupt her, she might stop reading, so I stay where I am.

I look over at my mother-in-law, who is speechless, her face drained of color, and then back at my girl.

My mind races.

The teacher has his eyes trained on Nonni.

She chews on her bottom lip. "The last time we went to the sheriff's office, I'd decided I wasn't going to be afraid anymore. I was going to pick him from the lineup so he could go to jail. But he wasn't there." Nonni hangs her head and scratches at the table with a broken fingernail. "He wasn't."

This is the most she's said in any one burst for at least three months. If I can hardly believe what I've just heard her say, then Gracie probably can't either.

Her teacher says, "I'm proud of you for facing your fears and sharing them with your family."

Finished with reading the paper, she bows her head and stares at a spot on the picnic tabletop near her. She speaks in a whisper. "I was afraid to tell anyone. Will the bad man hurt my family?"

"Over my dead body." Gracie slams her fist on the table.

I clench my hands so hard I feel my nails digging into my palms on both hands. I begin to stand.

He holds a hand up. "There's just a little more. After Nonni wrote this in class, I read it at lunch, and I brought her back to the room to talk about it."

Mr. Parra describes how reluctant she'd been to talk about what she'd written until he'd described how keeping secrets makes us our own prisoners.

He'd asked her if this was true story? "A real problem?"

He pointed to the words she'd written and the primitive picture, drawn with colored pencils, of the stick man with the bright blue eyes, the scar through his eyebrow, and a cowboy hat.

Finally, she'd looked at him with a furrowed brow. "I don't know how to fix this problem."

"This will be the ultimate problem resolution, and one with a punishment," he told her. "Not a punishment for you. You're the courageous one, and you do have a seat at…"

He'd paused to hold his fingers up to represent air quotes, "'King Arthur's Round Table, figuratively speaking."

After Nonni had told him she could identify the

man, he had given her courage advice. "Stand tall and be brave. This is one problem that's going to be solved, and I'm going to get you some help."

Gracie and I look at each other. We've added a few more pieces to this jigsaw puzzle, and I'm glad that Nonni's teacher made her share this information with us.

She shouldn't have had to shoulder this burden by herself, and I wasn't sure she would have told us this on her own yet. Not if she thought she was protecting us from harm.

All the while we thought we were protecting her, she was doing the same for us.

Mr. Parra's gaze lingers on me and then on Gracie. "You know, don't you, that I have to bring this information to the attention of the school?"

"I'll make a visit to the sheriff as soon as Rand gets back into town, okay?" My face burns with embarrassment.

"I'll bring him up to date, and then we'll make a visit to the sheriff. This weekend. I promise."

He taps his fingers on the folder. "I'd rather it was tomorrow, but I understand. Just take care of it before school resumes on Monday, okay?"

I nod at him and feel my eyes dampen. I move over next to Nonni and wrap my arms tightly around her.

I know in my heart Rand isn't going to be happy about what Nonni's disclosed. Or what Gracie and I haven't told him.

More than anything, he wants to protect us. It's not his fault this happened, but he'll be angry at himself that he wasn't here with us when he finds out.

"Okay, then." The teacher gathers Nonni's papers,

slides them into his briefcase, and stands up. He leans over to look into her eyes.

"You did the right thing, young lady. You've released your secret, and we can help you now. Sometimes you have to let your words speak for themselves. Your words, written and spoken, matter."

He turns to Gracie and me. "I'll talk to the principal early Monday. Send a note with Nonni to let me know the actions you took."

My face still feels flushed as he gently puts his hand on her shoulder. "See you in class on Monday, Nonni."

He gives us a compassionate smile, pivots, and heads to his car.

I scoot over to her and hold her in my arms. Her body is limp as though she's used up the last of her energy sharing this information with us.

"It will be fine, sweetie. I promise." I murmur into her ear.

Suddenly, this weekend doesn't seem soon enough.

Chapter 46
Randall - The Surprise

We've worked for seven days straight, and we're about finished. Mr. Henderson announced we can go home today after our work is completed. Today, Thursday. Claire isn't expecting me until possibly tomorrow or later.

I'm hoping this will be a good surprise for her. I'll be home a day earlier than we planned, Friday night and all day Saturday. Then, we'll all go back together, as a family, on Sunday afternoon for the grand opening to the lake.

But before that, my two most important priorities are to be with my family and catch up on my sleep.

"Hey, man. It'll be a relief to get out of here and take a real shower! Can you hold out for one more stinkin' day?" Nick grins at me.

"A real shower? You mean a hot shower?" I raise my arm to sniff my armpit. "I only stink when I'm broiling. Those cold showers aren't cutting through the sweat the way they should. How about I take one at your home before heading to mine?"

"Depends on how fast you want to get home to your sweetheart. Well, when you join the human race with inside plumbing and a water heater, you, too, can have your own hot shower at your own home any time you want!"

I think about the effort it takes to heat the water on the wood-burning stove for a tub bath and sigh.

"With this project finished, we'll get the new house built more quickly, but we'll still have to wait for new neighbors to move out so we can bring in water and electricity lines."

"What we?" Nick smirks. "You want help?"

He pulls out a cigarette. "But only if you come back to help me finish my patio."

"Bud, it's a deal." I unroll the cuff of my T-shirt and extract the package of cigarettes. I shake one out with a single flick of my wrist. "After this short break, we work prison work-gang style until we finish up. I'd like to get home sometime before midnight tomorrow night."

"Hah! Good thing you drove this week. Drop me off on the way, and scoot on home. I bet the little missus, well, all your folks, will be glad to see you."

"They'll probably be asleep before I get there. I'm sure I'll have to do some groveling before Claire'll be glad to see me. That last visit didn't end so well." I admit this to Nick sheepishly.

I grimace as I think of our last encounter at the sheriff's office when Nonni still couldn't identify anyone in the line. Even though someone from town had pointed a man out of that same lineup.

"I hate to admit it, but I haven't been the most attentive husband to her—what with working these extreme hours here and all of the chaos over legal things. Plus, Ma being there."

I take a drag and blow out a smoke ring that floats above my head.

"That's why I live alone. Too much drama." Nick

takes a final drag, throws the butt on the dirt, and grinds it out beneath the heel of his work boot.

"Besides, women are a lot of work. And you have four of them living with you. Plus, those two babies, and one of them's a girl. Don't know how you do it!"

"Well, bud. You're still somewhat of a youngster. In time, you'll get it all, too."

I blow another smoke ring before dropping the butt and stepping on it. Bending over, I retrieve the butts for the trash bucket.

"Remember, knucklehead. We're supposed to be cleaning up. Not messing up. Old man Henderson'll be through here with a magnifying glass looking for reasons to keep us through the weekend."

"Yeah." Nick knocks himself in the head with the palm of his hand. "But you're going home to outstretched arms, and I'm going home to a backyard full of rattlesnakes."

He chuckles. "Maybe I can go to your place soon for a barbecue with one of *our* chickens. I'll bring the beer!"

Nick's my silent partner, meaning he's provided the financing for the materials like the construction and chickens.

I've chipped in the brainpower, muscles, and location, trying out the new coop design with its inmates at home.

With my junior college classes in engineering, my stint in the Army, and my job at Chrysler, I have definite ideas about how to create efficiency in my environment.

Ma's reported that the beginner coop, as we call it, is working pretty well but that there are still some issues to do with the basic mentality of a herd of chickens.

I'll be able to judge it myself when I can keep my eyes on it for a week or so. Once the bugs are out of the system, we'll set up our venture on the back of our acreage with the new, fully-functional coop. Soon, 13,000 chickens will bring us a living as we raise them from "coop to kitchen."

"It's a deal." I give Nick a mock salute. "But we gotta finish up the doors and locks on the filter system."

"Yep. Home for one day and night. Fancy picnic this weekend. Then back again on Thursday to finish up anything the boss found lacking. My sis and kids are coming down from Big Bear for the celebration."

He smirks. "Won't they all be surprised at this Disneyland-type-of-resort for the rich and famous water-skiers and campers, right out here in the middle of the desert?"

"Yeah. And we'll never be able to afford to step a foot into it again once it opens."

For all intents and purposes, we've met the deadline. Even with unexpected delays caused by the unreliable weather, breakdowns of equipment, the flu, and unplanned emergencies including Joe who'd had an emergency appendectomy and hadn't returned to our crew, we're close to finishing.

One crew is hauling the trash to the dump. We've almost completed our part. If everything's finished on time, there'll be no penalties for Mr. Henderson to pay.

Claire and I are almost in the clear with that last paycheck, and with the bonus for finishing on schedule, we might have enough to raise the walls and move ahead.

Maybe I'll even send Ma back home soon. She's welcome to visit any time she wants, but I'm anxious to begin living my life in our new home with my own family.

I envision our home finished with a real refrigerator and indoor plumbing. Claire and I'll nestle into a more comfortable relationship without all of the crises we've been facing.

Maybe our dreams are closer to coming true sooner than I imagine.

Which reminds me I still need to get that deed from Ma.

Focus.

I struggle to banish these thoughts and pay attention to what we need to do today. First things first. Mr. Henderson exits the construction trailer as I pull on my work gloves and bend down to grab the handle of my toolbox.

Maybe he'll hire a few of us, me and Nick in particular, to work on new projects in the future, which would bring in extra income while we get the chickens up and going.

We've worked through the hottest months of summer to meet this tight schedule even though we came on crew toward the end of the project.

Although the completion of the resort doesn't coincide with the summer season, Mr. Henderson and his investors plan to make it a year-round resort.

It stays warm out here until Thanksgiving, so it makes sense that people might want to camp and ski well into the fall.

The idea of a year-round resort experience is a new one. Wet suits, though pricey, are becoming more popular for keeping swimmers, water skiers, and surfers warm in cold water. Mr. Henderson said he thinks we'll see them on the folks using the lake in the winter.

All this is to put salve on my conscience. Being away couldn't be helped. I've sacrificed the peace of mind of my family by having to stay away for days and nights at a time in order to bring in a steady paycheck.

I've hoped we could put this crazy, evil man stuff behind us by now. That patrols are only a formality. But I have a feeling of unease about the matter today. If we're not in too much of a hurry, I'd like to talk to the sheriff on our way home.

Or I'll do it tomorrow.

For now, however, I stuff all those worrisome thoughts into a filing cabinet in my head to mull over later because finishing up is the most important thing on my list. That, and getting the almighty paycheck.

The other stuff can wait. As far as I know, there aren't any big emergencies going on at home.

Mr. Henderson's second crew is finishing up the landscaping. They've been here for the last two weeks. Management's already stocked the lake with trout. "Baby Beach" has a lifeguard station and imported white sand to lure families.

Five bathrooms with outside rinse-off showers and one indoor shower are strategically placed around the lake and camping areas. Covered picnic tables with barbecues are located near the dock.

It's a regular Taj Mahal.

This place has everything. A parking lot, boat launch, and even snack stand. There's an overnight campground next to the lake with spindly trees that will grow over time, more barbecues, fire pits, and even electrical hookups for travel trailers and some of those new recreational vehicles.

Imagine that. We don't even have electricity at our home yet, and this playground for jet setters has stuff we could hardly imagine, even when we lived in the city.

Palo Verde plants with bright yellow blossoms dot the desert-style landscape, and the entire resort is lined in athel evergreens, planted early on as wind breaks.

It's amazing what money can buy and water can make flourish.

The investors have considered bringing in birds of some kind. Big Bear Lake has attracted white pelicans that might be picturesque for tourists here in the high desert.

There's a rumor that Roy Rogers is going to buy the Apple Valley Inn, where movie stars have stayed, and make it even more famous.

People are beginning to discover our desert, and evidently those with a little money prioritize fun experiences into their vacations. More are buying weekend homes, complete with electricity and running water like Nick did, not at all like our little homestead cabin.

Unbidden thoughts of Claire and the family nudge their way into my mind. I've directed Claire not to contact me except in the case of a dire emergency, and I haven't heard a peep from her.

The sheriff's last update stated that he thought he had the perpetrator. Since then, however, there've been two more cases of kidnapping and foul play on the outskirts of our town.

Maybe they're just copycat crimes. A peeping Tom

Nancy Brashear

was on the loose, probably the same man who stopped the girls. Even though Nonni and Tessa are pretty smart for kids, that's what they are. Little kids, after all. Their memories are scrambled.

They only saw him face-to-face once before running out into the desert to that well where we'd almost lost Tessa. It's no wonder they can't identify him.

The sheriff sends out random patrols. Jack and Hank are keeping their eyes open for any strange doings. I haven't heard anything new. As far as I'm concerned at this moment, that's okay.

If there's anything strange going on, we'll address it when I get back home.

"Focus," I whisper under my breath.

Nothing's going to change before I get back home.

Then I can make things right. Step up to bring a sense of security to the family.

As I contemplate this, a wave of guilt washes over me. I'm the kind of guy who works best focusing on one thing at a time. I must put all my attention on this job for the final push so I can go home to my family tonight.

Like it or not, I must also trust in the sheriff's patrols, the surveillance of neighbors, and Ma's shotgun until I'm there to take things into my own hands.

With two adults, three if you count me, four children, one noisy dog, and two large chicken coops out there, what could possibly happen?

"Let's get busy here!" I open the toolbox and grab the hammer.

Chapter 47
Evil Man - The Mission Calls

I follow the voices
in my head
telling me what to do
so I can be set free...
set me me me...free...

I have watched
I have waited
I will complete the task
tonight

I will purify
I will anoint
I will reclaim
I must finish

To be free
and leave
this forsaken land
for another

Chapter 48
Nonni - Nightmares

My legs ache. Mama tells me it's growing pains, but I can't sleep. I keep thinking about my teacher's visit today. What I told everyone.

In between the beats of my heart, I hear every single sound. Taffy barks. The twins make mewling sounds, and Tessa whimpers in her sleep.

My legs are restless and ache. They won't lay still. Taffy growls outside on the porch.

I finally fall asleep, dreaming of Tessa chasing me through the sagebrush where deadly snakes strike at me.

I throw a baby bottle at one of them, and it vanishes into air.

"Snake. Red. Pouf. Dead!"

Tessa charges, locking her arms around my knees, and twirling me around and around in a circle until I beg her to set me down. She smells like cotton candy.

She sets me down, and suddenly, a man in a cowboy hat is chasing me.

A man with icy blue eyes and a scar through his eyebrow.

A man who knows my name and where I live, who threatened to hurt me and my family.

I feel his dry fingers raking across my shoulder. The clouds blur into the shapes of snapping coyotes, and I retreat into the desert, slipping out of his reach.

My father's words echo within me. "You promised! No well! No well!" I'm breaking promises, and I can't help it. I must run.

My foot catches on the cracked cement edge of the well, and I fall in, headfirst, and tumble down, down, down, just like Alice.

Down the rabbit hole.

My fingernails scratch at the rough rock walls of the well and my legs flail, ripping skin.

I hit bottom and wake up and have to pee. Again. Moonlight streams through the open window as I reach for "de pot" under "de bed."

That's when I see the unfamiliar bag jammed in between the wall and Grandma's mattress.

Without thinking, I grab a strap and yank it out of its hidden spot. I slide the zipper open enough to reach in with my fingers and pull something out.

Even before I focus on it, I know what it is.

That picture of Jack's wife.

It takes my breath away.

Actually, my voice.

For a couple of long, silent seconds.

"Mama. Help!" I dangle the photograph over her, and I shake her shoulder.

"Where'd you get that?" Mama sits up, confusion on her face.

I point to the backpack I set on the mattress. Grandma sits up, her eyes blazing at the photo.

"This child should not be looking at this filthy trash." She leans forward and snatches it away.

Mama holds her finger to her lips and points to the sleeping babies and Tessa. She balls her hands into tight fists. Her chest moves rapidly up and down under her nightie, and her jaw's clenched.

The question hangs in the air. What's that photo doing in the cabin?

Last time I'd seen it was in that man's hand. How'd it get here? My lips move but no sound comes out.

I remember every word of that man's threats. If I speak, he will harm my family, and I'll be responsible.

Responsible.

That word echoes in my mind.

This problem pierces my heart. Even though I was ready to identify him to the police, he wasn't there. And now this backpack and photo are in our cabin.

I'm confused.

Mama leaps out of bed and takes one of my hands in hers. "Nonni, let's go out to the table and talk."

She leads me into the bright moonlit-washed yard, closing the door behind us.

"Breathe." She massages the knuckles of my hand. "Take a deep breath and let it out slowly."

I inhale to steady my heart. Images flash through my mind. The photo of the naked lady. The bad man. Angry Daddy. The police.

I look up.

The dark violet sky is dominated by the Milky Way cutting a twinkling path through the stars. I spot Orion, Daddy's favorite constellation, and wish-I-may-I-wish-I-might-have-the-wish-I-wish-tonight on it with all of my heart that he were here now.

He'd know what to do.

Looking up, I am a tiny, almost invisible, speck in the Mojave Desert. We're all tiny specks. Is God looking down at us now? Has he heard our bedtime prayers? Did he just now hear my prayer-wish?

I think he's listening right now.

"Mama!" I peer at her wrinkled brow, shining in the moonlight.

"I know." She looks away and squares her shoulders before gazing into my eyes. "Nonni. You must be brave. An example to Tessa and the babies."

"What's happening, Mama? Why's that photo here?"

"I'll take the photo to the sheriff after we show it to your daddy. I promise you everything'll be okay." She looks deep into my eyes.

"I don't understand."

She gathers me into her warm embrace, and my heartbeat slows. "We're fine, sweetie. Now, go sleep so you'll be fresh for the morning even though it's a school holiday."

I hug her, and we step into the cabin.

"Shhhh. Babies, you know." She smiles at me, and I force my own small smile onto my face.

"Get some sleep. Morning's almost here."

I nestle back onto the mattress and close my eyes. I toss and turn with my mind all twisted up, like those fake trails in my Zig Zag game, thinking about that photo of the naked lady.

It's hard to let go of my worries.

I feel Mama's long, cool fingers massaging my temples. "Put it out of your mind, baby. There. It's gone."

Her words soothe me, and before I know it, I'm dreaming. The funny thing is that I know it's a dream even though I feel like I've been there before.

Tessa and I are walking home from the bus, near a river. We walk and walk down a grassy trail with me kicking a mushroom in front of me along the way.

I hear a clucking and scuffling, and a big white rabbit passes us.

"I'm late, I'm late, for a very important date!" He scurries by, pulling out a big pocket watch.

"Oh dear! I'm late!" The fluffy, white cottontail on his backside bobs as it disappears down a hollow.

As we draw alongside it, I say, "Tessa. Daddy told us not to go near wells! We promised!"

"But this isn't a well, Nonni. It's a rabbit hole, and it goes to his rabbit home!" She hurries over to it, trips, and tips over the edge.

I rush to grab her feet and pull with all of my might.

The rabbit glares up at me and yanks her hair. "Get down here right now!"

Tessa struggles to pull away.

I pull on her, and she pops out.

"Run!"

Wide awake, with cold sweat on my brow and the last nightmare hanging on, I sit straight up in bed, my heart pounding, and gasp at what I see.

Chapter 49
Gracie - Who's There?

"Wake up! Shhhhh. Listen." Claire hangs over my bed, shaking my shoulder.

I hear the regulated breathing of the children—and then Taffy's never-ending barking.

I want to smack Claire for disturbing one of the only nights I've been able to sleep for than two minutes in a row.

After all the commotion earlier tonight, after Nonni found that photo, it took a bit to get everybody back to sleep. Claire snatched it from Nonni's hand and shoved it into the pocket of her nightie.

For a fact, I don't reckon I slept much after that. Nonni tossed and turned after they returned to the cabin after their talk out at the table.

I dunno about Claire either. She ain't one much for sleeping lately. She just lays real still under the sheets, but I can tell by her breathing she's not asleep.

I'm awakened by her shaking my shoulder when she freezes still, like a stone statue.

She pulls away from me and melts up flat against the wall, right next to the window.

I open my eyes and see her point to her ear, then to the open window. I do not see anything but the sky through it until a silhouette of a head enters my view, peering in. Is my imagination fooling with my brain?

I do not reckon so, but I close my lids anyway hoping that it will vanish.

That's a coward's plan, but if I cain't see it, then mebbe it cain't see me. Or Claire. Or the girls. Or the babies.

My body freezes still, and I open my eyes. The figure's gone.

The slow step falls *crunch, crunch, crunch* in the dirt by the window.

The chickens squawk when they should be asleep. Taffy barks. Our little world is upside down.

Claire moves fast like a stealthy cat to the door. She takes the crossbar and lowers it into place, quiet like, locking the door from the inside.

I creep to the window and sneak a peek. I cain't see anything unusual. He must have moved around to the other side of the cabin. If he's planning on barging in, he has a sad surprise coming.

I remember, sudden like, the loaded shotgun stashed, for the safety of the children, in the trunk of Sally. That ain't going to do any of us any good.

Taffy's bark comes from farther away. Where is she? Where is he? The outhouse under the water tank? This makes no sense. I ferret out the sound of the bunker door opened and thrown back with a loud clang.

In the moonlight streaming through the window, Claire and I stare at each other. I point to the bag I stashed under my bed and then in the general direction of the shelter. She nods.

The man who's hidden the bag there is back hunting for it. And he won't find it where he left it. What's he gonna to do when he figures that out?

Claire reaches into a pocket in her long nightie.

She brings out the nekked lady photo. Her eyes scan the room looking for another hiding place for it, and we both spring into action.

When I'm finished with my part, that nasty empty bag is gone from sight, too.

I wish I wasn't right about that. That evil man. While everyone else, mostly the sheriff and detective—and even Sonny—was walking around moaning about that guy and how we was safe because he's in jail, I've secretly agreed with Nonni and Tessa.

They didn't get the right man. Claire don't think so either.

At least Claire and I finally talked today about everything after the teacher's visit, but did that help? We should have shared what we knew earlier. We should have done something right away like gone to talk to the sheriff.

Randall's gonna blow a gasket when he hears what happened to us. That is, if we ain't killed by that lunatic out front of our cabin. A man's gotta work, but this time his job might be the literal death of us.

For certain, I am praying right now that this ain't true. Like I always say, I ain't nobody's fool.

Claire perches on the edge of the mattress next to me drawing in ragged breaths.

Somehow, I'm still hoping this nightmare might fade away, but I know we just witnessed the truth.

But how's this truth gonna set us free? I reckon tonight's the showdown we've been dreading, and we'll find out one way or nuther.

I hear a soft gasp and see a movement from the corner of my eye. It's Nonni, sitting bolt upright in bed, her hand over her mouth, and a look of terror on her face.

We got only a few minutes to do something, and dagnabbit if I cain't figger it out.

Chapter 50
Tessa - Red!

Taffy barks outside. I rub the sleep from my eyes and see Mama. She stands next to the window.

Grandma sits up in bed and stares at it. Mama puts a finger to her lips.

What's going on? I see the color red at the window. Then it disappears. Am I awake? Am I asleep?

A picture fades from my mind of cartoon Snoopy watching a leaf fall from a tree.

Nonni had read me the words in a round bubble above the little beagle's head. "You don't know it, but your troubles are just beginning."

I didn't know what it meant then, and I dreamed about it two times this week. It feels like trouble found us tonight.

Banging shakes the door. The noise bounces off the walls inside the cabin.

Mama leaps from her spot by the wall.

Grandma jumps out of the bed like a rabbit.

Nonni sits up in bed with her mouth open.

The babies make little crying sounds in their box bed on the floor.

I'm wide-awake now.

A man shouts from the front porch. "Open up! I know you're in there!" The banging starts again.

Nonni whispers, "Mama!"

"Girls! Over here!" Grandma motions to the wall, out of sight of the window, and away from the door where we huddle together.

"He's trying to kick the door in!" Mama passes Tommy to Nonni, "Keep him quiet."

She reaches into the icebox, around the special chicken dinner Grandma had made special for Daddy's arrival this weekend.

She hands a bottle of milk to Nonni, who tickles his lips with the nipple. Tommy begins sucking on it and closes his eyes.

Fiona gives a low yelp. Mama hands her to me.

I keep her bottle tipped. She guzzles down a few mouthfuls.

Milk drips from the corners of her mouth, and her eyes do a slow blink.

"Good job, girls." Mama looks at the door. "Keep it up."

The banging starts up again. The crossbar on the inside of the door bumps up higher each time.

We all jump.

"Well, he sure 'nuff knows we're in here, so let's do something." Grandma lights the wick on the kerosene lantern sitting on the icebox.

Our shadows, tall and thin, walk on the wall.

"I'm not making it easier for that gol darn man." Grandma hurries to the open window and latches it shut.

Mama and Grandma push the dresser in front of the door. There's another loud bang.

Taffy growls outside the door.

The man yells something, but it sounds like there is more than one person yelling. Are there two men out there? More?

I hear more barking outside the door. A loud bump. A painful yelp. And then a whimper.

"Open up the door, or your dog is dead!"

I look at Mama. "Taffy!"

I hear more barking. More scuffling. The banging begins again.

"Taffy!" I wish I could see through the door.

"Tessie. Shhhhhh! Be brave." Mama touches my arm.

Tears streak down my face. Taffy. My dog. My protector. She's trying to save us. I hear her deep growl outside.

A man yells, "Open the door!" It's quiet for about five or maybe twenty seconds.

He shouts again. "Open up! Or I will break down the door and get you."

There's another loud thud. The crossbar bounces onto the floor, and he pushes it open a few inches.

His fingers curl around the inside edge of the door. He shoves against it a few more times, forces the dresser out of the way, and pushes his way into the cabin.

I gasp. I recognize the man, the bad man. He has a flashlight in his other hand.

He stares at each of us but stops when he gets to my big sister. "Oh, Nonni."

She looks down. Her arms hold Tommy tight. The baby stops sucking and tips his head like he's listening.

The man whips around, and he thrashes his arms at us.

"Do what we say!" He babbles in different voices that I can't understand. What's he saying?

He stops and points a long finger at Nonni. "Where is it?"

He steps toward her, and Mama moves in front of her in a half a second or maybe three. The man pushes Mama away and swirls around. He looks at the room.

He pulls the blanket from my bed and shakes it. Then, he turns toward Grandma's bed and does the same thing. He jerks the door open on the icebox.

The rake handle knocks into the kerosene lantern, rocking it.

"Where's it?" He is louder than before.

I press Fiona to my chest and cover her ear with my free hand. The lantern slowly stops shaking.

"We don't know what yer talkin' about. Just let us outta here." Grandma shakes her fist at him.

He pauses. "Git!" He points to the open door. "Outside!"

Tessa and I stand frozen in place.

"I said, git! Out of the cabin. Now!" He yells in our faces.

I grab Dolly. I tuck her tight up into my armpit, next to Fiona, and stumble out into the moonlight.

Grandma pulls the baby from me, and we move fast.

The bad man shoves Grandma into the doorjamb. Fiona squeals, but Grandma slows down for a minute and keeps going. We're free and out in the yard.

I look up at stars twinkling above us.

I smell wildflowers in the night air.

My chickens cackle in their coop.

The man grabs Nonni's rake from the porch and clumps behind us. He trips and lands on the dirt next to us.

Cussing, he picks himself up and fumbles with the rake.

I know Grandma wants to wash his mouth out with soap.

Then, he spins around, reaches toward me, and snatches Dolly.

My precious Dolly!

"Give her back!" I scream.

He clutches her by one leg, swings her over his head in a big circle, lets go, and she flies out into the yard.

"Shut up and keep walking!" He rams the sharp tines toward me. "Out! Out there!"

I feel a pain in my leg and scurry forward into the brush, out of his reach, sobbing. "Ouch! Dolly! Bad man! Red. Bad. Red. Dolly! Taffy!"

"Shut up! March!"

I cry for my dolly as we follow his flashlight beam into the brush.

Past the outhouse with its door banging in summer night.

Past the clothesline with its ghost shadows on the ground.

He marches us to the shelter where the door stands open like a black mouth in the dark ready to gobble us up.

"Down." He spits on the ground and then flashes the light into the dark pit.

Nonni and I stare at each other. He wants us to go down into the forbidden shelter?

And break another promise we'd made Daddy?

I look at Mama holding tight to Fiona. Grandma's on her other side with Tommy making scratchy noises in his throat.

Nonni blinks rapidly at me, her eyes brimming.

"Down! Down! Down!" He switches his light on and off. On and off. On and off.

Without warning, he twists himself around in a tight circle. His words mush together.

I can't understand what he's saying except for "save me save me savemesavemesaveme."

The beam of his flashlight bounces out into the brush. Then up toward the Milky Way.

"Down! Dammit! Down!" He flashes the light on and off, again. He points it at the opening of the shelter.

Mama speaks to us calmly. "Nonni, you and Tessa. Go down the ladder, one step at a time. Hang onto the handrail. Nice and steady."

We look at her with questions in our faces.

"You can do it."

Chapter 51
Nonni - The Bunker

"You, Nonni. First."

I need to do this even though I've never been inside the forbidden fallout shelter with its flat door padlocked.

I've never even looked down into it.

It's hidden out beyond the water tank where it's always been forbidden territory for Tessa and me.

My hand grasps one baby bottle, and the other one is tucked away safe.

I wrap my fingers around the handrail of the metal ladder and awkwardly stretch my toes to feel my way.

I search with bare toes for the next lower rung.

Then the next.

And the next.

Above me on the ladder, Tessa blocks the moonlight. Her swinging feet barely miss my head. She almost does the splits as she lowers herself to the next rung.

I lower myself again and again until I finally feel the cool cement floor. I back away as Tessa drops to the floor.

Mama slowly moves awkwardly down with the baby tucked against her chest. She clutches the handrail with her free hand until she's on the bottom rung.

"Mama. Gimme Fee." I tap her knee. "I'm right

271

here."

"Thanks, honey." She twists and hands the baby to me.

Fiona wriggles and makes small noises as I swoop her into my arms and hold her tight.

"I have to help your grandmother with Tommy." Mama lets herself down to the cool floor.

The man shouts, "I said, old woman, tell me where the bag is. Or I'm locking all you down there. Where is it?" His voice echoes in the metal bunker.

"Don't know what yer yapping 'bout." Grandma has an extra layer of southern in her words tonight.

The man leans way over and jabs Grandma in the head with the prongs. She doesn't make a sound but continues to back down, one slippery rung at a time. She's clutching my baby brother, who's remarkably quiet.

When she's out of his reach, she lets out a grunt.

Mama's shoe taps against the floor. Her hand nudges me to the right. "Back over that way. Careful."

I move slowly, prodding Tessa along the wall in front of me.

"Mama. Can't see nothing!" Tessa's voice echoes in the dark room.

I reach toward the wall. My hand lands against a glass jar. It wobbles but doesn't fall.

"Stand here." I pinch Tessa's sleeping shirt and pull her to me. Next to the canning shelf where I stand holding Fiona.

"Mother Grace. Hand me Thomas." Mama reaches for the baby. There's a rustling sound as the transfer takes place.

"Got him." Mama shuffles her feet away from the

ladder.

"Git back up here, old woman!" The man jabs the rake at Grandma again, but she's on the bottom rung now. He can't reach her.

Grandma doesn't say anything, but I hear her foot scrape against the floor.

"I am going to shut you in! All of you!" His voice changes mid-sentence to a dangerous-sounding, shrill high tone. "That will teach you!"

He screeches something about searching the cabin. From somewhere nearby, Taffy yips and growls. The man yelps in pain.

I hear Taffy's sharp squeal of pain. A scuffle above is followed by another loud yell and series of cussing words.

"Damn dog. Bite me? You're dead meat!" Without warning, he throws a furry mass, scrabbling paws over tail, down on us.

Taffy digs a frantic claw into my arm before landing on the floor, knocking the milk bottle from my grasp. It clangs on the other side of the small room and rolls out of sight.

The man slams the door shut leaving us in complete, total darkness.

Tommy breaks the long moment of silence with a shrill cry that expresses the desperation I feel.

The dog whimpers in pain, and Tessa calls to her, "Taffy! I'm coming."

Mama's directions ring out in the dark. "Don't touch the dog! If she's injured, she might bite you, too!"

"Mama!" Tessa sobs. "I have to help her!"

My arm throbs. I touch it, feeling a wet spot. Is it

blood? Mine or Taffy's?

"Save us, Jesus!" Mama murmurs, and I add my own prayer.

"And Taffy." Tess cries out. "She's right here. I found her!"

We huddle together on the cold floor.

Tommy howls, and Fiona adds her own displeasure.

Taffy moans.

Tessa sobs.

"Hush, dog!" Grandma's no-nonsense approach demands obedience. The injured dog, and even the twins, momentarily stop their yowling.

Tessa hiccoughs and there's a brief silence before she speaks in her miniature teacher voice. "Taffy, baby. Lie still. Good girl."

I pull the other bottle from my underpants and stuff the nipple into Tommy's mouth. Thankfully, he grabs onto it with his mouth, and I hear him slurp from the half-filled bottle of goat milk.

With a sense of déjà vu, I relive Tessa's and my frightening race out to the well. How I'd made weapons with these very bottles and rocks to throw at the "bad man." This bad man.

This very terrible bad man who has marched us down into this underground prison. Where did that other bottle roll? Did it break?

I touch Tessa to quiet my panic. Taffy moans again, and, injured or not, that sound brings me comfort. She's alive. She's not biting. She defended us.

"I'm pretty sure there's matches down here near the preserves." This statement follows the sound of systematic tapping along the shelf with the canned goods. The sound of glass breaking makes us jump.

"Dagnabbit!" Grandma says. "Dropped it!"

"Don't move, any of you." Mama directs us. "Bare feet and glass don't mix."

There's more soft tapping sounds along the shelf.

"Found it!" Grandma's speaks with triumph. "Well, I found the matches and the crowbar!"

I hear a different sound, this time like a stick scratched against sandpaper. I smell burning sulfur.

A flame flickers at the top of a tall wooden match in Grandma's hand.

Her face lights up with strange shadows, and I'm amazed how one small flame has erased some of my fear of being trapped in this hidden room.

Yes, we're underground where no one will find us.

I blink. In this light, we all wear that tell-a-ghost-story-around-a-campfire-look, including the babies.

"Lookin' for a candle." Grandma hands me the burning match. "Nonni, hold this. Don't move."

Its flame wavers, and I grasp the bottom of the small wooden stick tightly.

Grandma crams the crowbar into the wooden packing crate to loosen the lid. "Knew it was here!"

The heat of the flame licks my fingertips. Right as I'm about to drop it, Grandma steps toward me, a thick, short candle in hand.

"Quick, child! Light the wick!"

The fire jumps from the matchstick to the candle, and the wick comes to life. I drop the smoking match stub, sticking my pinky in my mouth. The flame wavers and then flares.

Mama points to it, weaving itself around in an invisible current. "Air! There's air down here! Look!"

"Sears and Roebuck says we're good for a bomb long as we stay underground. We mustn't have sealed it all the way." Shadows from the flame flicker across Grandma's face. "At least we cain't suffocate."

I hadn't thought about suffocating before she said that, but I'm glad it's not going to happen to us.

I spot the dull gleam of the crowbar leaning against the wall where Grandma left it. I work my way around the glass, praying I don't step on a shard, and pick up the crowbar.

As I reach the ladder, Taffy moans, and one of the twins squeaks. I'm already on the bottom rung.

Through the metal door above, we hear the man scream, and it sounds like a bunch of people arguing. Those sounds fade as he moves farther away.

"Whatcha doing, chile? You get yerself right down here." Grandma speaks to me.

I ignore her, knowing I'm going to be in big trouble, maybe spanking trouble, later.

When I've gotten myself up two rungs, I look down and see everyone, except the babies, staring at me with their mouths open and shadows flickering upward on their faces.

Fear uncurls its claws and slinks into the dark corner. A spark of hope warms my belly.

I shake my head. "We gotta do something!" I point the heavy crowbar at the trap door above us.

"Nonni! Get back down here. Right now." Mama pleads.

I pause, not sure of my next action.

"No. Wait a little minute." Grandma's voice breaks through the gloom. "Mebbe she has a point. Lookee up there."

Craning my neck, I see a faint crack of light coming through the trapdoor. It isn't closed all of the way. That's where the air's coming from.

"What if she gets up there, jams the crowbar in so the door does not flatten and seal us in, and we use some other things to prop it open wider?"

I'm not sure what Grandma Grace means for me to do, but I'm ready to take action before that man comes back.

I've been waiting, helpless, for almost six months to do something that would make a difference.

The time is now. I'm ready.

"Okay," I answer. "Like what?"

Mama says, "Everyone but Mother Grace stay still. Don't move an inch."

Grandma moves around the small room, candle in hand, opening a box. Soon, she's at the bottom of the ladder, something long in her arms. She moves toward me.

"Here. Gimme the crowbar and take this two by four." We complete the exchange with a fair amount of awkwardness, and then I'm holding the board in my arms.

It takes all my concentration to climb the ladder and not drop it on Grandma's head. I scoot up the ladder and see a piece of the night sky through the crack. A whiff of desert night fills my nostrils.

I squeeze the board under my arm and position myself on the ladder. A tickle has crept up inside my nose. There've been occasions in my life when I've sneezed as many as ten times in a row, making myself weak as a baby.

This better not happen now when we need to stay

quiet. And I need my every bit of my strength to hang on up here.

I pinch the top of my nose and tuck the tail of my nightie into my mouth to muffle the sound. The board begins to slip, but Grandma already has her hand on it and stops its fall.

When my silent sneezing fit is finished, thankfully only a three-sniffer this time, I take stock of my position.

Grandma says, "It's not locked, and it's not too heavy. Jam that dabnabbit board in the crack and let's see what happens."

With her pushing me up, and me jamming the board into the break, we make a larger gap.

I give the board an extra shove and jimmy it into place.

She nudges me and slips me the crowbar.

I'm able to create a little more space, and now I can see Orion through the widening space. I feel safer with the hunter on guard, looking down from the sky at us. At least that's what Daddy says he's doing.

I pass the crowbar to Grandma.

"I can squeeze out there." I'm scrawny, but strong. I believe I can do it.

"Try," said Mama. "But if it's too tight, stop."

Grandma pushes her way up closer to me. "Step up on my shoulders. Then push off and up. And scoot through."

That's exactly what I do, imagining myself as thin and slinky as one of those snakes I detest. I wriggle out through the crack and lay stretched out on the ground for a short minute. Then I hear the man's rants coming from the cabin, and they push me into action.

Grandma whispers directions about how to swing the door open. Within a few minutes, all of us are topside.

Mama climbs out and gives me a hug. "You did it!"

I allow myself one small moment to silently celebrate my victory. Finally, I've done something real to save my family. A small wisp of guilt untwines itself from my soul and floats up to the stars.

I hug myself, and my hand comes away slick. There must still be blood on my nightie.

"We do not have all night." Grandma grabs the edge of the bunker door and quietly closes it. "If he comes back, mebbe he'll think we are still down there."

"Shhhhhh. Hurry!" Mama beckons us forward, holding Fiona. "It's okay. We're just taking a little night walk out into this beautiful desert."

I can tell that she's trying to reassure us, and it works. Suddenly, it feels like we're just doing something normal, and I can almost put the horror of the last half hour from my mind.

Tommy wrestles to free himself from Grandma Grace's grip, and, unsuccessful, he yips.

"Hush, baby." Grandma repositions him on her hip.

"Hurry, chil'n." Grandma turns around to look at us. "Follow me." She forges ahead through the sagebrush.

A stray cloud flits in front of the full moon. Darkness slithers on the dirt around us. We stop, like a row of freight cars on the tracks at the base of the mountain a mile away, bumping into the person in front of us.

The moon pokes its shining face out and once

again lights up the sand.

We hear the voice again, ringing through the still air from the cabin. "Where is it?"

I hear crashing noises and twist around in time to see him pitch our frying pan through the open cabin door.

It bounces across the porch and out into the dirt next to Dolly.

Chapter 52
Randall - Wrapping Up

It's been a hard finish on the job. Although the project began a couple of years ago, some of us came aboard during this final six months. I'd like to think that my work, and Nick's, contributed in a substantial way to the crew catching up with its schedule.

Even so, our departure has been delayed by a couple of long, hot days. I feel an inner tic-tick-ticking as we address specific issues and tasks.

He and I tackle the broken water pipes that service the public bathroom with its outdoor shower and that flooded the pump house. We've drained the pooling water, digging the pipe out of the dirt to replace and repack it. By the time we finish, we've worked up a mighty sweat.

Everyone hurries. We'd installed a couple of pond aerators to correct the oxygen level in the water in time for the delivery of the trout and bass last week. The lake's ready for fishing. Another crew focuses on parking lot paving detail.

We've thrown our construction debris into the back of two trucks waiting to haul it away the final trip to the dump. The acreage was originally planted with rows of athel trees, fast-growing drought-resistant evergreens, to serve as windbreaks, even before the digging began.

In this final stage, we've also planted poplars next

to campsites close to the water's edge. We've installed fire rings out of big black and gray river rocks we've hauled in. It's starting to look like a real place you'd pay to go to for a vacation.

"I'll put the final layer of waterproofing on the picnic tables if you want to work on the benches." I pry the lid off the can with a screwdriver.

"Whatever we need to do to be released from this work camp!" His smile softens his words, but I know exactly what he means.

We've been racing against the clock so we can return home for two days. Then, we'll be back there for the final touches before the grand opening. There isn't a man among us who isn't thoroughly exhausted.

We're all itching to get home if only for a few days before the celebration. A more formal grand opening will happen later.

Tessa and Nonni and the entire family are looking forward to the barbeque. I've told them all about the roped-off portion of the lake, "Baby Beach," with its gold-flecked sand brought in from Carlsbad.

There's a small playground with swings and a tetherball, just like the one I promised Tessa. I haven't installed hers yet, but I will soon. I've promised her.

It's just one of many items on my deferred home "to do" list.

Heck. Claire and Ma might even want to wade into the water to cool down. This is going to be a mini-vacation for us. I'll show the twins off to everyone, well, show off my entire family.

Time's slid by so quickly. I hardly remember that Thomas and Fiona were born at about the time I began working on this job. Here it is, five months later.

We finish our list in the twilight. By the time Mr. Henderson waves us on, the garage in town has been closed for a couple of hours. Nick'll have to make arrangements to retrieve his truck when Di arrives with her kids for the barbeque.

We pack the back of the truck. It'll be another couple of hours before we're home.

"Put your stuff on this side, and I'll aim for the other." I point to the truck bed.

He and I stack up our sleeping bags and backpacks along with our toolboxes and tool belts, work gloves, lunch boxes, thermoses, and dirty laundry.

I roll my wheelbarrow over, heft it up, and turn it upside down on top of the pile. After I tie it down securely, I crawl into the driver's seat, exhaustion hitting me between my shoulder blades.

"You okay, man?" He's already settled in.

"Yep. This truck could get us home by itself. Hope it doesn't come down to that."

I crank the ignition, and the engine turns over with a slow growl before it roars to life. I drove us here the other day. Nick's truck's in the shop, and mine isn't acting so good either.

I feel my heart swell at the thought of surprising my family tonight. Most likely, they'll be asleep by the time I get there, but it's gonna be worth it to see the smile on Claire's face when I arrive.

I've missed her more than I imagined and can't wait to get our lives back on track. Maybe I'll convince Ma to go home. Then, we'll settle down into some kind of routine after I find a new job and I'm there at night with the family.

Nick dozes with his head banging against the

window, protected only by a rolled T-shirt.

My thoughts drift to my favorite dream. We're ready to build the big coop model that'll house 13,000 chickens, maybe even more later, and that plan's already been approved.

The supplier's ready to send me the baby chicks on consignment as soon as we're ready to begin with a smaller batch. I'm counting on this for part of our income.

The full moon skitters behind clouds giving the terrain ahead a ghostly look one minute and a full-out appearance of nighttime in paradise the next.

In what seems like no time at all, I pull into his neighborhood. It looks crowded with houses on one-acre lots with electric lines connecting them. I'm used to the open spaces of our land.

He opens his eyes when I turn off the ignition. He stretches, hops out of the cab, and rubs his eyes. "Thanks, man. We survived. At least I think we did!"

"To be determined!" I quip.

I scoot from the driver's seat and meet him at the tailgate. I help him pull his stuff out of the bed. In the flickering moonlight, everything looks alike, all piled up.

He grabs his sleeping bag and backpack. I pick up his heavy tool kit and some other stuff. I follow him to his front door where I drop them.

"We'll straighten it all out at later if we mixed it up."

"See you Sunday!" He gives me a mock salute, swings his front door open, and flicks the switch for his porch light on.

"Show off." I push the tailgate back up and hear it

latch. "It won't be long until we have electricity, too. Don't gloat."

I scoot into the truck, tap the horn once, and reverse my way out of his gravel driveway onto the street leading to the main road. With any luck, I'll be home in about thirty minutes.

In my rearview mirror, I see his porch light go dark. I stick my head out of my open driver's window to shake off my weariness and press my boot onto the gas pedal. The truck picks up speed.

We've worked eighteen-hour days during this last long stretch. It'll have been worth it when I get my paycheck at the gala event.

I'm the man of the family, my family, and I'm eager to be back there with them.

It's been hell being away with all the drama about the girls' encounter, but everything's under control. Patrols are in place with neighbors and the police. I don't think that guy is even around anymore.

I'm ready to get this all behind us even if Nonni hasn't identified him.

I'm tired of being away from home so much. And away from Claire and the kids. Although Claire and I hit a rough patch the last time we were together, I know it's time for me to step up alongside her as a partner. She's shouldered a heavy load with me gone. It's about time for me to take some of it back.

Ma's returning home soon, and we're ready to move ahead as our not-so-little O'Brien family unit. Speaking of which, she promised me the deed to the homestead cabin, and I intend to claim it from her. Yeah. She can come visit.

But Claire, the kids, and I are about to re-enter

modern American living. Neighbors will move into our community, ready to share the costs of bringing amenities in. We'll be heading back into the land of modern living, and she'll love that. I feel it coming in my bones.

Nick and some of the other guys have agreed to help me with construction in trade for me helping them out on their projects. I've traded a portion of my labor for some of Mr. Henderson's leftover lumber. Those boards, bags of cement, and pipes are rattling around in the bottom of the truck bed now.

My thoughts drift back to Claire. She and I need time to spread our wings, too. When I met her in high school, she was shy but had big plans for the future.

She'd wanted to see the world, but we didn't even get a honeymoon because I began working at the automotive company that week. She'd also wanted a family of her own and that we have in spades.

"Family is everything," she's said, more than once.

Yep, I agree. But this year has brought us closer while driving a wedge between us in different ways.

So much happened. Babies born. Girls accosted. The investigation. Strife between her and Ma. Me gone all the time.

We've been in survival mode since we moved here. I see a light at the end of the tunnel. We just need to hang on a few hours longer.

Nothing is impossible. Working together, we'll build our lives here. When things settle down and the twins are a little older, maybe we'll take the kids to Ma's. I'll surprise Claire with a road trip somewhere fancy. She'll love that.

Whistling, I pull off the main drag by the Colony

onto the dirt road. Imagine the surprise she'll feel when I arrive home, tonight—a day early. I'll wrap her up in my arms.

This is the beginning of my re-commitment to our new lives.

I squint toward the cabin at the end of the road where a strange light flickers. I'm not sure what I'm seeing. The truck rattles down the washboard road, and my view grows clearer.

"No!" I jam my boot down to the floorboard, and the truck fishtails. I ease up on the accelerator and turn in the direction of the skid.

I wrangle the truck off the berm and onto the road.

In the distance, I see flames licking their way out of the cabin door. Adrenaline pumps through my body.

Fire?

My family?

To hell with it. I stomp on the gas pedal and hang onto the steering wheel.

Chapter 53
Nonni - Escape

"Hurry!" Mama points out our path, and my magical sense of safety disappears.

We pick our way through the sagebrush in our bare feet with Grandma leading, Mama following, Tessa in front of me, and me taking up the rear.

I peer up at the sky, orienting myself to Pleiades, the Seven Daughters, one of my favorite constellations, before another drifting cloud hides it from my sight.

As long as I can see it, I feel safe. When it disappears, I feel lost in a sandy sea of danger.

While I'm looking up, Tessa trips, righting herself at the last minute, and a whimper escapes from her. I skid onto the back of her heel.

"Ouch!" She grabs her foot and glares at me. Mama stretches a hand toward her.

Tessa cries, "I'm okay. Nonni stepped on me. I need Taffy! We need to get her!"

I hear Grandma. "Taffy's injured. She needs to stay put."

The cloud drifts by. Moonbeams paint the dirt white as snow. It's hard to believe we were in that dark dungeon a few minutes ago.

"Taffy bit him, like she did Nonni. That time she chased me." Tessa stares at me.

My memory flashes back to Tessa and me racing

around the corner of the cabin, my sister shrieking behind me, grabbing at my shirt, and Taffy lunging out of nowhere to defend her.

I have a purple, triangle-shaped mark above my knee where her tooth sank below the skin. In the short time Taffy's been at our cabin, she's been totally loyal to Tessa.

Although Mama always tells us to hope for the best for people, I hope Taffy chomped a big, fat, deep chunk out of the bad, bad man.

I know that dog's a biter.

I wind my way around the long-dead creosote stump that almost felled Tessa and across the undulating terrain even though the ground looks flat as a piece of paper.

Walking in the night air, under these conditions, has thrown off my sense of distance and progress.

Like that Joshua tree ahead. It seems to stay in the same place, just as far away, no matter how long we trudge toward it.

The best I can do is to follow my family and stay vigilant on this night of terrifying events.

Vigilant for things that will trip me.

Vigilant for things like missiles, bombs, serpents, and strangers.

Vigilant for his screams and ranting.

His voice pierces the still night air. "Where is it?"

Turning back, I see him in the doorway where he's still pitching things out into the yard.

Grandma narrows her eyes at the cabin and puts her finger to her chin. "That fool man better not knock the kerosene lantern over and burn down our home! Like he almost did earlier."

The man appears on the stoop, flashlight in hand, and waves it around, down toward the ground, up toward the sky, over toward the water tower.

This reminds me of searchlights I'd seen down by the beach, before we'd moved out here, with beams piercing up into the sky. Only he's the one searching for us.

He steps away from the cabin and marches toward the shelter.

"Mama!" I whisper. "He's out! He's gonna get us now!"

Fiona's head rests against her shoulder, so Mama turns her body around to peer. "Quick! Duck down behind these bushes!"

We all hunker down while he stalks his way around the cabin. My heart pounds in my throat, which is so dry I can't even work up a swallow of spit.

He disappears around the backside of the cabin and reappears out in the brush, moving the beam erratically.

Grandma signals for us to continue. "This way. The crick bed is down there, where he cain't see us."

The ground slopes under our feet. We scramble and slide to the wash.

Mama and Grandma set the babies down in the sand. Fiona makes kitten-like sounds. Tommy smacks with his lips, and Tessa hurries over, sticking her finger in his mouth to quiet him.

Mama shakes her arms. "Fee's sure growing! Wouldn't think that baby would be so heavy."

Not to be outdone, Grandma snorts. "Well, young Tommy's sprouting muscles overnight. My big boy."

"Where're we going?" I'm tired and want to rest for a minute.

Grandma bends over and picks up Tommy. "We're heading to the Ritchies' for help."

Mama's brow wrinkles. "I hope they're back from their trip. Haven't seen them on patrol this week."

Grandma gives Mama a stern look.

Mama takes a breath and lets it out slowly. "Kiddos, it's time to move-on."

I hear the man in the distance but can't make out the words. Good. He's not getting closer.

I imagine him climbing down into the shelter, ready to teach us a lesson in some evil way. He'd threatened us before, and I know he means business.

Is he tearing the shelter apart like he did the cabin? What's he looking for? What I'd found tonight?

Could he track us down?

Grandma must have read my mind.

She turns to me, her face half hidden by a moon shadow. "If'n he's looking for that old backpack, he's not going to find it. No, siree! I figure we have about ten minutes before he comes after us."

"We better get the move on." Mama nudges us up and settles the babies into arms.

We creep forward, weaving our way around the creosote bushes and Joshua trees that raise their arms to the night sky in defiance. I swear they look almost human, and I can't figure out if they are friend or foe.

We follow with Grandma in the lead. Tessa's mostly silent, once in a while muttering "Taffy" and "red."

The babies are surprisingly quiet. Mama breathes with her mouth open, hanging onto Fiona.

Suddenly, Grandma stumbles and falls. Both she and Tommy smack onto the ground at the same time.

He squawks as Grandma struggles to get to her feet.

Mama hurries to them, setting Fiona down and picking him up from the soft sand of the wash.

She runs her hands over his head, shoulders, down his spine, and pats his chubby short legs. He reaches, pats her face, and his bottom lip trembles.

"Tommy's fine."

Mama sets him down and turns to Grandma. "You okay, Mother Grace?"

Grandma pushes herself upright and puts her weight onto her left foot. She winces and shifts back to her other foot.

She presses her lips together. "Dabnabbit. Twisted my ankle."

I'm shocked because I've never heard Grandma admit to being hurt.

She points at me. "Nonni. Get me a branch about this high." She holds her hand up above the ground at about the height of my shoulders. "Quick, girl! Follow the gully."

Grandma turns to Mama. "A walking stick."

Mama nods, her forehead wrinkled, and I hurry down the gully looking for the right shape.

Up ahead, I see a dark form lying in the sand, and I know it's a snake lying stretched across the gully.

I come to a dead stop. I can't take another step.

"Hurry!" Grandma's voice wafts through the warm night air to me.

"Mama. I see a snake."

"Snakes don't come out at night." Mama reassures me. "Probably a stick. Get closer.

I creep closer, ever on guard, expecting it to slither toward me or coil up to strike. It remains in place.

When I'm close enough to reach for it, I see a few stiff twigs attached to it.

Yes. It appears to be a stick. I stare at it, making absolutely sure it doesn't move before I pick it up.

Yes. It's a branch. Probably ripped from one of the pine trees in the foothills and washed down here in a storm.

I scamper to Grandma and hand the stick to her. "This okay?"

She turns it over in her hands and breaks the remaining tuft off the top. She tests it against her weight.

"This'll have to do." Grandma sighs and looks at Mama. "Girl. You're gonna hafta hold Thomas 'cuz I cain't do it without using both my arms. I need one to hang onto this dang stick."

Mama nods her head and turns to me. "Nonni, take your baby sister."

Fiona sits on the ground, her small fists pounding against the dirt as if she understands the unfairness of the situation.

"Dust off her hands, sweetie. We don't want her eating dirt."

I pick her up, pat off her diaper-padded backside, and hike her up onto my hip.

After nestling her against my shoulder, I place one hand around her back and the other under her bottom. Her chubby legs clamp around my waist like she's a Christmas nutcracker.

Tessa whines. "Mama, I'm strong. Gimmee Fee!"

Mama turns to me. "Take her until you're tired. Then Tessa can carry her."

Tessa smiles at me, eyes gleaming. This time, I

don't mind. Not only is she the tetherball champion of the school playground, but even though she's a head shorter than me, she's strong.

If she can swing me around, she can carry our chubby little sister across the desert.

Yep. She'll be a good substitute for me on this trek, I'm sure, if I wear myself out lugging my baby sister through the still, warm autumn night.

Chapter 54
Claire - Back in the Jesus Bus

We stumble up to the Ritchies' cabin, which is dark inside. I don't see Annie and Hank's truck out front where they usually park it. They're not here.

Rand had told me they'd be out of town for a family reunion, but I thought they'd be back by now.

The sheriff's been making rounds, but last time I saw the cruiser was yesterday, late afternoon.

Now that I think about it, I haven't seen Jack in the last couple of days either. Rand's not due back home until tomorrow if we're lucky.

No one knows what's happened. We're out here alone and on our own. It's up to me to save all of us.

There's been a divided opinion in town as to whether the perpetrator has been captured or not. The newspaper reported the peeping Tom had been caught.

Jack and Nonni, and even Tessa, say they didn't see him in any of the lineups.

The women who were attacked and left in the gunnysacks are still in the hospital. One is in a coma, and two others badly injured. There might have been a fourth.

But after tonight, we know the girls and I have been right all along. That does nothing to appease the dread flooding through my stomach.

As we approach the front door, I flash back to the

trek Rand and I took here what seemed a hundred years ago.

Gracie'd just arrived that afternoon before I met the Ritchies. My back ached with the soon-to-be-born birth.

Rand and I'd had an argument on the way there after we'd run out of gas. I'd fainted out front of this cabin and ended up in the Jesus bus.

Now we're back here, again, with a life-and-death emergency.

I hand Tommy to Tessa, whose eyes glint with confidence. I pound on the door, but to no avail. I bang on it again.

Gracie trails behind us, hanging onto her makeshift cane.

I can tell she's in pain just by the fact that she's silent with her chin set like it's in cement.

I try the handle. It's locked. That in itself's unusual because, until lately, none of us even thought about locking our doors.

Delaware's not in there barking, either. Silence looms, broken by the howl of a coyote in the distance.

I look over at Gracie, whose slitted eyes reflect the moonlight like a cat's. Maybe like a cat about to pounce. I shake my head.

Tessa coos at her brother in a soft, musical lilt. "What a big boy you are, aren't you?" and gives him a little jiggle. Amazingly, he's almost asleep.

That boy can sleep, too, just like his daddy, almost anywhere. Tessa dips her head and plants a kiss on his forehead. He smiles in his sleep.

"Follow me." I head around the side of the cabin to the bus. With moonlight reflecting off it, it's as surreal as when I'd seen it before with its unexpected paisley patterns and the face of the bearded man painted above the windshield.

Tessa points with excitement. "Look, Mama! His eyes are following us! He can see us!"

"It's okay, honey. It's Jesus, and he's watching out for us here."

I hope she believes me because this I believe with all my heart, and we need all the help we can get.

Nonni looks up and nods, a small smile creeping across her face.

Mother Grace forges ahead with her stick and leans against the front of the bus.

I give the closed door a strong shove, and it slowly folds in on itself like an accordion. Hanging onto the metal rails, I hitch myself up its three steep steps.

I walk all the way down the aisle between the sets of double seats to the bench seat where I'd rested that night, and then I return to the front of the bus.

Gracie peers up at me as I step back out onto the dirt.

I turn to Tessa. "Hand me the baby."

She gives him to me and then bounds up the steps, scissoring her short, sturdy legs to their maximum stretch.

I climb up onto the step behind her and pass him back to her.

She grabs him with her small, strong hands.

"Find a seat on the bus for you and Tommy, sweetie."

"Your turn, Nonni!" I take Fiona from her arms, and Nonni dances up the steps, repeating the procedure, and I return the baby to her. "Find a comfy place to sit, honey."

Gracie peers up into the bus and hands me the stick. "I'm gonna have to think about the best way to do this."

She puts her weight on her injured ankle to hoist herself up with her good one, but it gives way, and she crumples to the ground.

I rush down to her. She's reluctant to take my hand, but she lets me pull her upright. She's in worse shape than I realized. Even though she's a small woman, smaller than me, I don't think I can manage pulling her up the stairs, and she wouldn't let me, anyway.

I step down onto the dirt, and, together, we stand there, staring at those steep steps.

She sighs, turns away, and hikes her bottom up onto the lowest step. With some struggle, the use of her wiry arms, and pushing with her uninjured ankle, she hitches herself upward.

Her progress is slow, but she conquers each stair with determination and reaches the top.

Alone on the dirt, I turn in a circle, checking my surroundings. Looking up, I stare at the Milky Way, its path strewn across the sky. A falling star fizzles out of the heavens above.

I suddenly feel insignificant, lost in the sky, and close my eyes to say a prayer of thanks that we've made it here safely, even if the Ritchies aren't at home.

That's when I hear a sound, something I don't readily identify. I peek around the front of the cabin. In the distance, I make out the dull shine of a truck, no headlights on, traveling toward us from the direction of our cabin.

Beyond it, I see a red glow streaming from our cabin. What is that? And that crazy man must be out looking for us.

There are a number of abandoned cabins around, but this is the closest place that looks lived in. If he's been hanging around here, spying on us, he'll know this.

My heart does a pitter-pat, and I duck back behind the cabin formulating a plan.

Looking around, I take note of a discarded bus tire propped up beside the wall.

That might do, I consider, and awkwardly roll its bulky girth to lean it against the front wheel.

I stick my head into the bus. "Nonni! Give the baby to your grandmother and come over here to help me drag this up into the bus."

"Coming, Mama!"

I wrap my arms around the dusty tire and position it in front of the open door.

She stands above me at the top of the steps.

"Honey. I'm going to try to get this tire up there, and I need your help."

She doesn't question what I've asked her to do, or why. Bless that child.

Grabbing it by the inner rim with its dirty rubber, I grunt and heave it up onto the bottom stair.

I push against it and hope it won't mow me down.

"Grab the tire." I can just see the top of Nonni's crown above the rim. "Put your hands into the middle. I'll push and you pull. On the count of three. You ready?"

"Yes, Mama." Nonni stands on the second step, seriousness written all over her face.

"One. Two. Three!" I push hard, and she pulls up with all her might.

Together, we slowly move the tire up into the bus. Gravity threatens to bring it down on me like a giant bowling ball.

I wedge my shoulder against it and fill my lungs with air. "Keep hanging on."

Nonni huffs. "Trying. Trying to get away from me." She refers to it as a living entity with a mind of its own.

"Okay, honey. You can do it! We'll push it up another stair. On the count of three."

Nonni grabs at the outside edge of it with both hands.

I grunt as I push, and she pulls it up another stair. Thump. It lands on the target.

Only one more to go, but I'm not sure we have enough strength between us to do it again.

It's time for reinforcements.

"Tessie." I lean against the dirty rubber. "Give the baby to your grandma and come help your sister. Hurry!"

Within a minute, both girls are at the top, pulling on the tire.

I'm pushing with my body and arms and knees. Through sheer willpower, I prod it until it comes to rest between the driver's seat and the top of the stairs.

Nonni's leaning over from the driver's seat and still hanging onto it with Tessa in the aisle, her arms clutching it from the side.

"Girls. I'm gonna jam the tire in there so it stays put. Hang on. Don't pull." I push hard against tire until it angles itself enough to fill the space. I take some of my weight off it, and it doesn't move.

"That's going to have to do." I step away, wiping my dirty hands on my nightgown. "Nonni, climb over the back of the driver's seat into the aisle, and I'll climb around the tire onto the passenger seat by this window."

I squeeze onto the second step where I grab the handrail that separates the passenger seat from the stairs and attempt to swing my body over it.

I can't make it and tumble onto the bottom step. I stand up, shake my arms, take a deep breath, and try again.

This time my balancing act works, and I launch myself over the rail and land upside down with my legs on the seat. My head comes within an inch of the floor.

At least I'm over the rail and in the main part of the bus with my family. That's what counts.

"Hah. Didn't know I still had it in me!" I choke on a mouthful of dust, and my eyes water.

Nonni backs up, her eyes big.

I right myself and climb across the aisle close to the driver's seat as I can get. I drape my leg over the rail and hitch myself into the driver's seat to peer down at the bulky tire.

"You're a goner, sucker." I taunt it and catch my breath.

"Girls, come back here, and help me shove the tire. Again." I have a plan.

The girls return and push against the tire from the aisle while I shove from above.

Suddenly, it breaks loose from its perch and tumbles down the stairs to wedge itself against the door, which slams shut with a whoosh of air.

"We're safe!" I whisper and remember that only I

know about the menace traveling down the road toward us.

Thank God we're safely cordoned off in this bus. But that also means we can't get out either. Well, unless we exit through a window or the back hatch, and I'm not sure how that works.

As I walk down the aisle, out of the corner of my eye, I catch the dusty sheen of the truck pulling in front of the cabin.

"Duck! Get down on the floor! Don't make a sound!"

Silence surrounds us.

"He's here," I whisper.

Chapter 55
Randall - Missing

"No!" I stomp on the brakes, and the truck slides in next to the burning cabin. Too close.

I immediately realize my mistake, and with shaking hands, put the truck into reverse to back it away from danger.

Ma's car is close to the cabin, too, but that's not my priority.

Where's my family? I leap out of the truck onto the dirt, scanning the area around me, but my eyes haven't adjusted from the brightness of my headlights.

I see the outline of our cabin against the darkness of the desert.

Oh, and the tongues of flame licking out of the door. I taste the fire, and my eyes burn.

I sprint to the stoop. "Claire! Ma! Girls!" No answer.

I race around the cabin to locate the tin washtub. It's under the water tower at the back of the outhouse. I twist the faucet to the open position, and water flows into the container.

When it's half full, I grip it by the handles and slosh my way to the front of the cabin.

I throw the water on the blaze by the door and hear a snapping sizzle. I choke on the acrid smoke. I stagger back and forth to get more water. The flames sputter.

After five trips, I've put them out.

"Claire!" Still no answer.

I grab my flashlight from the truck and shine it around the area between the cabin and me. I move the beam from side to side, looking for my family.

Where are they?

The beam catches on something on the dirt near the porch. It's Ma's cast-iron frying pan, lying upside down. Next to it is Tessa's dolly and our constellation book.

I pick Dolly up, my heart skipping beats. Tessa would never leave Dolly out here in the dirt. She won't even sleep without her. What's happened out here? Where is she? Where are they?

If I could spit fire out my nose, I would. My anger battles with adrenaline, and anger's winning. I take a breath of clean air to clear my head before I stumble up to the door where the smoke is beginning to clear.

Holding my damp handkerchief up to my nose and mouth, I stand in the charred doorway and flash the light around. No one's in here.

"Claire!" I call out. "Answer me! Ma!

There's silence except for a moaning sound. I force myself to listen for it over the erratic beating of my heart and hear it again. Realizing it's coming from the direction of the shelter, I sprint in that direction.

My heart skips a beat when see its big, metal door thrown wide open.

I left it locked. No one's supposed to be out here. And it's the middle of the night. Why's it open? Are they down there? Who's groaning?

I shine my flashlight down into the dark pit.

"Claire!" I try to shout but my voice catches in my

throat.

I hear another moan. "Claire, that you? Honey? You okay?"

There's a muffled bark. "Taffy?"

That seems like a stupid thing to say, but I repeat it, and hear another moan. And a weak bark.

"Taffy?" I shout again.

I hear a whine, leading me to the answer. I swing myself around and down, skipping every two steps.

"Claire?" A sob catches in my throat. "Claire! You here?"

I drop to the floor and feel the crunch of glass under one of my heavy work boots. I flash my light around and look around in horror.

Taffy's on the far side in a lump, whimpering. She lifts her head and her eyes glow back at me. She whimpers again.

I step toward her, over broken jars of fruit and tomatoes, over a ripped bag of cement.

"That's a good girl." Her tail wags, and she turns her trusting face up at me before barking again.

"Where are they?" If only she could talk and tell me what had happened.

I swing the flashlight at the walls, the floor, even the ceiling. The contents of the place have been turned upside down. They aren't here.

Something terrible has happened.

My blood runs cold. Frozen, in fact. A shiver of fear hits me.

What happened? Where are they?

I bolt up the ladder and pull myself out. My feet hit the dirt. I turn slowly in a circle like I'm back in the Army again doing reconnaissance.

The moon plays peek-a-boo with clouds.

They're not in the cabin or the shelter. There're only a few other places to look.

I race to the outhouse where the door's already open and banging in the breeze. Not here.

I flash the light over the foundation of the new house addition. Nothing here.

Ma's car? I run to Sally and fling the driver's door open. I flash my light around inside. Nothing here, either.

I throw Tessa's dolly onto the seat. I pull the release lever and hurry around to the trunk. I hold my breath before I lift the lid with one hand.

I shine my flashlight into the dark cavernous space.

All I see are Ma's emergency supplies—water and a box of odds and ends.

"Thank God," I whisper, realizing that I've half expected to see them all crowded into this small space. They aren't here.

My light catches on something shiny. I look closer. Ma's shotgun. I pull it out and check to see if it's loaded. Yes, five shells are in the magazine. I don't know where the extra ammunition is, and I suddenly realize that my deer-hunting rifle is at Nick's for safekeeping.

This'll have to do. In our diligence about keeping dangerous things away from the kids, we should have protected ourselves better.

I lay it onto the front seat of the cab and take stock of my surroundings. I catch the flash of brake lights of a vehicle in the distance. It's almost a mile away, on the road under the power lines. Traveling without lights.

As soon as the moon ducks behind clouds again,

it's gone from my vision.

This is my only clue. Is my family in that truck or whatever it is? Kidnapped? My mouth goes dry.

That man. If he isn't in jail now, wouldn't the sheriff or detective have told me?

I grind the gearshift into reverse and gas the car to back away from the cabin. I stomp on the brake, yank the gearshift into drive, and crank the wheel, barely missing Ma's car.

I turn on my headlights and bounce down the dirt road. I flash my lights at the vehicle, which has just pulled in front of the Ritchie's house.

I figure I'm about three minutes out and mash the gas pedal to the floor.

"Damn!" I hit my head on the headliner on one of the rougher bumps.

Squinting, I see a man pound on the front door. He moves over to the window and smashes the glass with his fist and reaches in to unlock the door.

Within seconds, he pushes his way into the cabin and his flashlight beam plays on the walls inside. He stumbles out, not noticing me.

I'm almost at the cabin. I crank down my window.

That's when I hear him. "Nonni! Ohhhhh, Nonni."

Why's he shouting my daughter's name? He disappears around the side of the cabin.

I slide my truck in behind his, blocking his.

"Nonni! Oh, Nonni! I'm gonna get you!"

I can't see him, but I hear him.

"Nonni! Get out here. Now! I'm looking for you!"

Chapter 56
Gracie - Hunkered Down

Of all the gol darn times in my life to hurt myself.
And now I'm not sure I can drag myself up into the bus.
But I do it, one rump bump at a time.

Claire needs the girls to help her up front, so
Tommy's back in my arms. He gnaws on my fist, and I
sure pray to Jesus he stays quiet. And I'm dead serious
about this praying stuff.

Tessie hands me Fiona. I set here with the twins in
my arms, and they are one double armload of baby.

With the windows up, the air is hotter and stinkier
than a coyote den in summer. Even though it's fall.

After a short bit, Claire sends the girls back to me.

"Duck down between the seats and stay quiet."
Claire's peeking out through the windshield of the bus.

Nonni takes Fiona and sits with her on the floor
across from me.

It's kinda hard with my ankle and all, but I scootch
myself onto the dirty floor. I drag Tommy down next to
me. I stick my thumb in his mouth, and he sucks on it.

Only Claire's up front, peeking over the railing to
the bus door. Which she's wedged shut with that big
tire.

I don't want to give her a big head, but that was a
right smart move. I'd rather be trapped in here than out
in the open like a chicken about to get its neck wrung.

That girl's shown more gumption that I would've given her credit for.

Mebbe I've been wrong about her.

If'n I get out of this alive, I'm gonna change some things. For one thing, I'm fixing to return home to my ocean and garden and enjoy myself a little. I'll can me some goods, prune me some roses, and enjoy being there alone. I'll take a hot bath in fog.

I'll miss the kids and Sonny. Mebbe even Claire. But they can come visit. I've been the fly in their ointment for too long, and they'll do fine without me. Well, maybe not as good, but passable.

I'll turn the land deed over to Sonny like I promised. Pops might like that, too. Or maybe he's rolling over in his grave at the idea of letting loose of anything that is, or was, his. I no longer care.

There's things more important than that. I realize this now. In this bus. In this moment. When everything is about to change for better or worse.

Claire kneels down at the front of the aisle, facing us. She puts her finger to her lips and whispers. "He's here. Not a sound."

We could be kilt by that maniac who's only a stone's throw away now. My heart beats in a double-step, right up in my neck.

In this moment, I recollect how it felt to hobble past those Jesus eyes on the front of the bus up above the windshield. Those glowing eyes that followed and comforted me. He might just scare the everlasting bejeezus out of that guy if he comes around the corner.

All of a sudden like, I want to burst into mad, loud cackles that burble up from my belly. There's nothing, and I mean nothing, funny about what we're going through. But I cain't help it. It's like laughing is the true opposite of screaming, or mebbe the same as screaming.

All's I know in my heart of hearts is that we need be as quiet as church mice, and I'm about to explode, which might be the worst thing I ever done in my life. And could end us up all dead.

Everyone's quiet now. Even the babies. I need to keep myself still. Give directions to my body.

Breathe. Don't think about it. Keep that shriek inside.

It hurts, hurts so bad, to keep these sounds trapped inside. The pain of it makes me want to climb out a window up to the top the bus and shout, "Help!" at the top of my lungs. I purse my lips tight.

Even through the closed windows, I hear the sound of glass breaking in the cabin. After a few minutes, I hear him shouting Nonni's name.

I look over to the child, my brave grandchild, crouched across from me, her face wet and her nose dripping.

Chapter 57
Randall - Battling Evil

The man bursts from the cabin and shouts, "Nonni!"

He stomps across the broken glass and disappears around the side of the cabin. His flashlight beam bobs on the dirt.

He's disappeared from my view. Where's he now?

I swing my driver's door open and lunge out. Around the corner. The Jesus Bus where my pregnant Claire rested that night of what seems a million years ago.

One hand on the shotgun, I'm operating on pure instinct, ready to battle, even if I'm not sure who exactly my enemy is. My gut screams this is the psychopath who tortured my family. He's not going to get another shot at them.

This is the guy who went after my family! Who set the cabin on fire! Who wrecked the bomb shelter and injured Taffy. Who fled in the truck I've followed.

I can't figure out what to do with what little I know. Or don't know. But I have a feeling I'm about to learn. And I have to do something. Right now. Follow my gut.

The cowboy slinks through the shadows, circles the bus, and chants "free, free, free." He stops at the door and pushes against it with his shoulder. It doesn't budge. He drops the flashlight and pushes against the door, this time with both hands. It still doesn't give.

I'm hot on his heels, almost close enough to grab him, when he notices me.

I get a good look at his face in the moonlight. He sure doesn't match the description of the guy the woman identified as the peeping Tom. He's not a short and round man with a bushy mustache. He's tall and lanky. Confusion crosses his face, and he turns away from me.

"Hey! Put your hands up, or I'll shoot!" I aim the shotgun at him, but he ignores me and goes back to pounding on the door. I can't shoot him in the back, but it's taking every fiber in my body not to pull the trigger.

He shouts Nonni's name. "I'm going to get you!" He growls. "Where's it at?"

Is Nonni in there? And the rest of the family?

I grab his wiry arm with my free hand. I'm still clutching the shotgun in my other. "Where's my family? What have you done with them?"

He spins around and throws me off with surprising strength, propelling me back a couple of steps. He squints and focuses on me as if seeing me for the first time. He spits at me. A big, wet glob lands on my face.

"What. Have. You. Done. With. My. Family?" I wipe the goo off with my arm and wave the shotgun in his direction.

He jabs his pointer finger at me. A wrinkle bunches up on his forehead. "What have you done with my stuff?"

When I don't answer, he dismisses me. He turns back to the bus where he pounds and pushes the bus door.

The moon peeks out from behind a cloud, and I see a dark handprint on the bus door. His bloody handprint from breaking the window? Or could it be blood from someone in my family?

He screeches. "I know you're in there! Open up!"

"Hey!" I shift my stance so he's in my sight. I point the shotgun at him. I'm close enough to blow a hole of buckshot through him. "Step away from the bus. Hands up! Now!"

He leans toward me and spits in my face. Again.

As I glare at him, Nonni's small face pops up and peers at me from the bus window. She frowns and points at the man. Her lips move, saying something I can't hear. If I can see her, he can, too. If he turns around.

As much as I want to empty this gun into him or bash his head in against the side of the bus, I can't kill him in front of my family. And I don't want him to see them in the window.

I speak slowly through clenched teeth, buying time as I figure out my next move. "Why'd you pick my girls? You did, didn't you?"

He pauses, mid-movement, and quirks one eyebrow. "Nice of you to ask." He blinks rapidly. "Followed the voices. To purify them."

"Like you did the others?"

"What others?"

"The ones in the gunnysacks you left around the desert."

"Voices told me to purify them, too."

I want to hurt him. Make him scream. Finish him off. Right here on the spot. I don't know what his idea of purification is, but he's a sick man. He's tormented his victims. Physically. Mentally. And he would have done that to my girls if he'd had a few more minutes. He's pure evil.

I take a breath. *Stay in control.* If I shoot, I'd probably kill him at this range. I'd probably injure my family in the bus. I'd go to jail, and they'd be without me. He'd win. I must rein my emotions in.

"Why'd you come back?" My brain frantically searches for what to do next. Let him live? Get him locked up with the key thrown away for a long, long time? Or give into my instincts, lunge in?

"Didn't purify them. Interrupted. Voices told me to go. Need my stuff."

"What stuff?" The shotgun shakes in my grip.

"Backpack. Other stuff. Where's it?"

"Don't know what you're talking about." I level the gun at his neck.

Tessa's face is now pressed against the glass confirming they're all hiding in there.

I force myself to look away from her and focus on the man before me.

He grimaces. He swipes at me with lightning speed, knocking me and the shotgun to the ground. His cowboy hat flies off into the brush.

I scramble onto my hands and knees to grab the shotgun before he gets it. But he's right on top of me. Flattening me to the dirt. He's so close I taste his moist, rancid nicotine breath.

Suddenly, I remember Coach Preston, from my high school wrestling days. He taught us every move had an escape.

I dip my shoulder. Reach back with my right hand to grab the inseam of his torn jeans. I pull him closer.

Pivot my hips. Pull off the sit-out switch, my best defensive move. I force him to the ground with a spiral ride and snatch the shotgun.

I stand on both feet now and point it at his chest. "Get up. Hands up. Don't give me an excuse to shoot you."

I motion him with the barrel and feel my self-control begin to slip. "Over there."

He gets to his feet. Hands in the air. Slowly, he walks toward me, a blank expression on his face.

I catch another glimpse of Nonni's face, popping up. Then she's gone like Ma or Claire yanked her down.

"Turn around, hands up. March!" I give him a sharp jab in the back, and he flinches.

We move around the corner of the cabin, out of sight of the bus.

I jab him again, hard enough that it probably drew blood, toward my truck. "Untie the wheelbarrow. Pull it out."

His feet shuffle dust.

"Or I'll shoot you in a hot minute. You'll hurt all over and then die a slow, painful death. Better than you deserve."

He fumbles with the rope and yanks the wheelbarrow to the ground.

I watch his every move. "Climb in."

He stops, and I shove his back, hard, and then aim the gun at his head. He climbs in. I reach around to pull out a roll of black electrical tape and a length of rope from the truck bed.

"On your side. Hands behind you." I bend over and shout into his face. "Do it."

He rolls onto his side, hands clasped behind him. His neck rests at an awkward angle against the inside of the barrow.

I lay down the weapon and quickly bind his hands with tape. He groans as his face scrapes against the aluminum. I tape his ankles together and hog-tie them to his wrists. My hands are slippery from handling him. His blood?

I grab him by the hair. He bites me, and I curse under my breath so the kids don't hear me. I drop his head, which lands with a solid *thwack* against the metal, and slap a piece of electrical tape onto his mouth.

I secure the end of the rope all the way around the body of wheel barrel and across the handles, finishing it off with a secure knot to bind him in place. That creep's not going anywhere.

He struggles, and I hear muffled sounds. His jerking movements are useless in loosening my handiwork and knots I learned in the Army.

I reach into the truck bed and grab a tarp. Snapping it wide open with a single shake, I toss it over him. "Sleep tight, sucker, and never wake up!"

I pick up the shotgun and race back to the bus.

"Tessa! Claire! Anyone!" I pound and push on the bus door. It's jammed shut with something big and heavy. A cacophony of muffled voices call my name.

Daddy! Randy! Sonny!

I look up to see Claire leaning over the railing by the door.

She points to a window and struggles to open it. Finally, she pushes it partially open, creating just enough room to stick her head out. My heart tings.

"Honey!" The tears in her eyes spill down her

cheeks making silver tracks in the starlight. "Watch out for that guy!"

"I know. I tied him up like a hog. He won't be bothering us."

A whimper from inside is followed by one howl, and then another. I let out a sigh of relief. The twins are alive and well inside the bus. The sound of their crying is music to my soul.

Nonni pushes in beside her mom and sticks her head out the window. "Daddy, you saved us! Mama saved us, too!"

Tessa pokes her head under Claire's other arm and speaks with authority. "He's the guy, the red guy I saw that day. Bad man! Daddy, good job!"

Claire points behind her. "Mother Grace's here, too, holding the babies. She hurt her ankle, but she'll be okay."

I hear Ma voice from deeper inside the bus. "Sonny. Got a lot to tell you. But before that, make sure that evil man cain't get us."

"I wedged the door with a tire so we'd be safe." Claire motions to the steps behind the glass bus door. "Don't think we're gonna get out the same way we got in."

"Wait there," I say.

Her short laugh is followed by a fit of coughing. "Darn dust! Where else would we be?"

Claire wipes the back of her hand across her wet cheeks. Our gazes lock for a long moment, and in the light of the moon, she shines like an angel with a streaked face.

Pride swells in my heart for this woman, my woman, so strong, intelligent, and beautiful. My helpmate. Mother of my children. Keeper of the key to my heart. Strong warrior woman.

With a lighter step, I circle to the emergency exit at the back and shove the gun under the bus where the kids won't get it.

I jump onto the back bumper, press down on both release handles, and pull the big window toward me. I realize if I could do that, he could have, too. My arrival broke that destiny.

I pull Tessa out, followed by Nonni. Claire passes the babies to me, and I hand them over to the girls. Claire's next. Ma peers at me through the exit.

"Throw your legs over the window frame, Ma. I'll help you down."

Ma stretches her toes out to touch the ground and winces. I put my arms around her and set her gently on the ground next to Claire.

"Nonni, Tessa." I turn to the girls. "Follow me."

I see Ma give Claire's hand a quick squeeze. They stand close together, tears glistening on their faces. Claire wraps her arms around Grandma Grace, and our shaken family is joined in one big family huddle.

My eyes prickle, and I brush my sleeve across them. The night isn't over yet. I need every bit of my remaining strength to get my family to a safe place. "Follow me to the front of the cabin."

I grab the shotgun and stride out ahead of them to make sure the way is clear. Looking back, I see Claire tip her head to look up at Jesus' face as she walks by the front of the bus, and her lips move. A saintly smile flits across her face.

I lead the group by the front of the cabin, past the wheelbarrow with bumping and moaning sounds coming from it. They look at it with suspicion.

"Ignore it. He's not going to bother us anymore."

I peek into the man's truck. Sure enough, his keys are in the ignition. I motion to Ma and Nonni, still holding Thomas. "I'll drive his truck. We'll fit on the bench seat."

I wave to Claire and point to my truck. "Follow with Tessa and Fiona, okay?"

After some juggling around, we settle everyone into the trucks.

I hold up my hand. "Wait here. I'll be right back." I return to the front of the cabin and peer through the open door. The broken glass reflects in the flashlight beam. "There's no one in here. I'm sure the sheriff'll come back and tear it apart for fingerprints and other evidence. Let's go."

After everyone's settled into the trucks, I crank the window down and pull alongside Claire.

"Follow me. We're going to the sheriff after we drop by the cabin to make sure the fire is all the way out."

"Fire? What fire?" Claire cries out with alarm.

"From the kerosene lantern, I think. I want to be sure I got it all out. Then, they can get someone to lock this guy up. "

As we bounce along the road, I remember the frantic ride to town half a year ago. Right after he had stopped the girls. That's when the ripcord was yanked, and all hell broke out in our lives.

This ride tonight feels like déjà vu, but I finally have a sense of control. I've made sure that man isn't going anywhere.

Except jail.

Chapter 58
Nonni - Déjà Vu

I feel like I'm on a roller coaster with Daddy driving the bad man's truck over the bumpy road and jostling Tommy and me around.

Daddy left that man in the wheelbarrow. He told us he'd tied him up like a turkey about to be roasted on Thanksgiving Day. We're bouncing our way back to the cabin. It feels like we left there days, not hours, ago.

"Nonni. Stay here. Gotta make sure the fire's completely out." Daddy throws open the truck door and races for the cabin.

Mama lugs herself out of the other truck to follow.

Grandma hobbles behind, leaning on the stick I'd found for her.

From where I sit, I see Tessa with her arms wrapped around Fiona.

Her voice wafts through the open window as she looks down at Fiona. "Fee, fi, fo, fum." This sometimes makes Fee giggle. Tonight, the baby doesn't make a peep.

Tessa raises her chin, and I look her in the eye. I mouth, "Be he alive or be he dead, I'll grind his bones to make my bread."

She reads my lips. We know every word of this story by memory. She stretches her mouth wide, and her teeth gleam. We stare across the expanse at each other, her eyes shadowed like they're in a sunken skull.

I'm too tired to blink. I grimace and file this gruesome image away in my mind for later use in one of my stories.

The grownups disappear into the cabin. Even with the truck window closed, I smell the smoke. In only a few minutes, Mama returns with two bags filled and tied at the top. Grandma trails behind, limping, with one of her own.

They dump them into the truck bed behind me. I recognize those bags as the ones from Trina's mom when we'd brought the baby clothes home from school that day.

"Got stuff for the babies." Grandma says. "Thank the Lord most of their diapers and clothes weren't burnt. This here goat's milk was in the icebox, ready to go, and not too warm." Grandma coughs and rubs at her mouth with her fingers.

"We're lucky the fire burnt mostly by the door." Mama rubs her face with her hands. "If he was really trying to burn down the cabin, he would have done a better job of it."

"I made sure the embers are out, one hundred percent." Daddy aims the flashlight beam down near his feet. "I'll take a quick trip around the property. That man's not going anywhere for a long time."

From where I sit, I have a good view of him examining the area around the door after he checks the inside of the cabin.

He works his way out back and disappears. Reappearing by the new foundation, he heads to the chickens where he steps inside the coop. In the distance, I imagine I hear him shoveling their feed.

I don't know where we're going after the sheriff, but I don't think we can stay here tonight.

A coyote howls in the distance, and goose bumps run down my arms.

As I wait with Tommy, a sad, dark feeling settles on me. Here I am, sitting in the truck, the same one that stopped Tessa and me six months ago.

I replay in my mind exactly what happened and how the man had sat there with his cowboy hat covering part of his face. Then he'd sprung across the seat, where I'm sitting right now, and flung the passenger door open waving the photograph, the same one I'd found in the backpack tonight by Grandma's bed, in my face.

I look up, and the stars swirl around like they're looking for a drain. My stomach lurches, my eardrums burn, and my mouth waters.

Against my father's explicit instruction to stay in the truck, I shove the door open and step out onto the dirt, with Tommy protesting in my arms. I stumble to the closest bush where I vomit.

"Sorry," I swipe at the gooey mess with my grimy hand but only succeed in smearing it into a crease on the back of his chubby neck.

Daddy marches over to the truck, a stern expression on his face. "What in the Sam Hill are you doing out here? I told you to stay in the truck."

"Sorry, Daddy." I gulp uncontrollably, still clutching the baby. My mouth waters again, and I gag.

Daddy's at my side in three long strides, taking Tommy from my arms and pushing my long sticky hair away from my face.

"Sorry, baby." He dabs at my face and hair with

the handkerchief he keeps in his shirt pocket.

"It's the truck, Daddy." I gulp again. "Makes me feel bad, real bad, to be in it."

Understanding dawns on Daddy's face. "Ah. The truck. This truck." Concern clouds his face, and I can't make myself meet his eyes.

"Let's get you to your grandmother's car." Once I'm in, he hands me the baby.

"You okay to wait here with Thomas?"

I nod and hear the crunch of his work boots on the gravel as he hurries back to the cabin. I lay Tommy down on the crack of the seat next to me, keeping one hand on his belly, and listen to him gurgle.

That's when I notice Dolly on the seat. I pick her up, waving her at Tessa who claps her hands at me through the window.

She waves at Mama, who's rounding the front of Daddy's truck, and points at me.

Mama hurries over to me. "Honey. I saw your dad bending over you by the bush. You okay?"

"I'm okay." I don't want to worry her, and I know everyone's in a hurry to leave the cabin for the sheriff's office.

But what if that guy somehow gets out of the wheelbarrow and comes after us again? As far as I'm concerned, that bad man is more dangerous than a serpent and could probably escape from anything.

"Lookee here." I hand Dolly to her, and Mama squeezes my shoulder before hurrying back to hand her to Tessa. Through the window, I see my sister bury her nose in her hair, sniffing her. She may have lost Taffy, but she still has her beloved dolly.

Daddy disappears through the brush and returns

with a bundle wrapped in that red-and-black checkered blanket that I'd seen hanging on the clothesline the other day.

As he walks by the open window, I hear a whine.

"Daddy, is that Taffy? Is she okay?"

My mind goes back to the blanket. It looks like the one that fell out of the man's water truck at our home the day he'd spotted me. Even though it had been a different truck then. A shiver snakes down my spine as I remember how he'd called me by name, telling me that he would hurt my family if I said anything.

Well, I hadn't actually said anything aloud. I'd only written my story for Mr. Parra but, somehow, that bad man must have found out because all of this had happened. Hadn't it? But I'd already decided to speak up, and I'd helped my family get out of the bomb shelter.

No.

This isn't my fault.

It's *his* fault. He's the bad guy.

Not me.

Tessa looks over with excitement. "Taffy? Taffy! Daddy, bring her over here to me!"

Daddy handles the bundle gently as he turns to Tessa.

She reaches out to touch Taffy's head and croons softly. "That's my good doggy that bit the bad man!" The yellow dog touches her hand with the tip of her pink tongue and moans.

Even though she'd also bitten me, I'm extra glad that she'd chomped into that bad man, too. She was a hero in her own way tonight.

Daddy says, "She needs to rest. We'll have to hope

for the best." He walks to the back of his truck and gently lowers the dog.

He looks around. "Claire! Ma! Move it! Gotta go!"

They return with more bags, which they place in Grandma's trunk.

"Ma! Can you drive? With your ankle?" Daddy shouts in the dark.

Grandma snaps at him. "I am not an invalid!" The look she gives him would shrivel grapes into raisins.

"Okay, then." Daddy climbs into the man's truck, and I'm grateful to be out of that nasty truck. "Follow me!"

Grandma Grace slides in behind the wheel on the special pillow she keeps there "so's they don't mistake me for a child driving in this here vehicle."

She slams her door shut. "Child, hold that baby tight. Don't want nothing more happening tonight."

Mama climbs into Daddy's truck. Tessa's smiling face peers at me from the cab where she holds Dolly high and makes her wave her little cloth hand at me. Dolly disappears from sight to be replaced with Fiona, whom Tessa also makes wave at me with her help.

I feel a tiny smile tingle across my lips.

Daddy rolls down his window. "Claire. I hafta deliver this truck to the sheriff office as evidence, and we have to report what happened now. Follow me."

She flashes her lights to let him know she's ready.

He guns the engine, his tires spitting up a rooster tail of pebbles onto my Zig Zag, practically invisible in the moonlight, but I know it's there. It seems like a million years ago that I was working on it, and yet, just this afternoon life was normal. Most of the rake marks have been erased by tire marks from the chaos of tonight.

There's no Safe Zone left in the dirt, I think. Not in this game.

Not in my life.

Chapter 59
Claire - Showdown

The clouds flit by, and the night sky is clear once again. The moon shines her full, white face down on us, and it's like someone flipped a switch on the outside lights again.

We caravan in both trucks and Gracie's car. Once on the road, Gracie follows Rand, while I trail behind in Rand's truck.

Randall slams on his brakes and skids into a parking space in front of the Sheriff's Station. We sail into the parking lot behind him, parking at odd angles. The night officer runs outside to see what's going on.

It's almost ten at night although it feels closer to sunrise. I can hardly keep my eyes open, and I know Rand's been baking out in the hot sun all week. We're all peaked. Except for Rand, we're all in our nighties, streaked with dirt.

The officer writes down a brief report. "I'll send someone to get that man out of the wheelbarrow tonight, and we'll get formal statements from all of you in the morning."

Each of us had witnessed that man in different scenarios. Nonni, our best witness to the encounter, first saw him that day on the way home, then at our cabin, and later at the Ritchie's bus. Gracie and Nonni—when he filled the water tower. Gracie and me, last night.

Tessa, a bit, in some of those places. And Randall, last night.

As of tonight, his troubles with us have multiplied. I'm guessing we could add stalking, attempted kidnapping, setting fire to our home, and other unsavory illegal acts.

"Leave that truck for evidence."

"Let me check that we didn't leave anything in it." Rand heads toward the door.

"I'll come out with you." The deputy accompanies us out to the parking lot and watches Randall as he takes Tommy's blanket from the truck. He reassures us that someone will retrieve the man and bring him back to the station.

I sigh. We are finally safe tonight, and we'll go to bed knowing that he's been caught. I won't be setting my thread traps and listening for the crunching sound of feet outside the window. I'm pretty sure I'll be asleep before my head hits a pillow.

Gracie juts her chin at him. "You'll find him trussed up like a pig for the luau in the wheelbarrow. I don't mind if you keep him there a bit longer. Suffering would be right good for his soul."

Rand, his face set in hard lines, hands the keys over to the deputy.

We stumble in a pack to our vehicles and divide into those of us who'll be in Rand's truck and the rest who'll be in Sally. He pokes his head into his truck and holds up Tommy's blanket and bottle, which he gives to Gracie.

"I'm going back in with you." Rand turns to the officer. "I have something else to say to you, without the kids." The muscle in his jaw flexes.

I straighten my back. "I'm going in with you."

As we re-enter the building, Rand jiggles the keys in his hand. As soon as the door closes behind us, he leans forward with his hands bunched up, face-to-face with the officer. "You should've checked up on the family tonight!"

Defensiveness registers in the officer's eyes, and he takes a step back. "We had the guy in jail, so we weren't concerned about him bothering you. I had one of my men patrol yesterday afternoon. We thought a neighbor was making the rounds later. You should've been safe."

"You thought! But they weren't. You should've checked up on my family last night anyway!" Rand flexes his hands and then tucks them back into his pockets. His breath comes hard and fast.

The officer shakes his head. "Calm down and get a good night's sleep. Come back tomorrow morning around ten. We'll wrap up this paperwork then."

Rand takes a deep breath. He shakes his head as if to clear it. Finally, he nods his head in agreement. "Tomorrow morning, then."

Despite their differences, the men shake hands. I am pretty sure that Rand's grip probably hurt some, and I don't blame him. The taint of that evil man will stay with us for a while.

A tsunami of rage floods my body. That predator stopped my children with plans to harm them. And even though his plans were thwarted, he did harm them because they've become frightened little kittens too frightened to go outside unless they can see us at all times.

And we've been too traumatized to let them out of

our sight. I feel guilty that I'm so angry and protective—and don't want to show it in front of the children.

Just thinking about him makes my brain boil. I don't understand how I had missed his evil spirit the day he filled our water tank and threatened Nonni. Aren't *I* supposed to be the intuitive one?

No one messes with my family.

I hope they hang him from the highest, spikiest Joshua tree they can find and leave him there for the coyotes.

And then we'll reclaim peace for ourselves.

Chapter 60
Randall - Aftermath

We're back in the parking lot where Claire retrieves Thomas and joins me in my truck. I tell her my immediate plan. "We can't stay at our cabin tonight. I called Nick from the station to say we're coming."

Claire's expression is grim, and I'm worried about her. "You okay to follow me there in Ma's car?"

She nods. I give her a hug and her shoulders relax. She's had a tough time, and I'm proud of her strength and ingenuity in barricading the family into the bus.

I try to squeeze a little smile out of her, but it doesn't work. Her eyebrows form a furrow across her forehead.

We juggle ourselves into the vehicles. With Claire driving Sally, even though Ma protests, I lead the way. Once we arrive, I jump out of the truck and bang on his door.

He opens it in a bathrobe, his hair sticking up on end and concern on his face.

"Thanks, bud, for taking us in. Good thing you have a phone, or this'd be a surprise visit." I point to my truck and the car. In a couple of sentences, I fill him in on what's transpired in the last couple of hours.

His eyes open wide, and he smacks his head with an open palm.

"Hope we only have to bunk here for a night or

so."

"Sure, man. You guys okay?"

I wince. "Considering. I'll check out the cabin tomorrow and go from there."

I can practically see the wheels in his brain churn. "Sis isn't due 'til tomorrow night, but I'll ask her to drive out on Sunday for the picnic so you guys can stay here if you need to."

I shrug my shoulders. "I hate to disrupt your family reunion, but we're up a creek here."

"Let's go check the place out early tomorrow morning. I got your back, man." He gives me a punch on the shoulder to prove his point.

I call to Claire and Ma. "Bring the gang in. We're spending the night here."

Nick vanishes into the house, turning on lights, and I hustle to help the family.

"Grab the bags." Gracie points to the back of my truck, lines of pain etched onto her face.

If I wasn't exhausted before this nightmare evening began, I'm one of the walking dead now. I make a couple of trips to the truck. The family straggles behind.

On the last trip in, Tessa is close on my heels. "Daddy, we gotta bring Taffy in with us. I'll sleep with her and make sure she is okay."

The easiest thing to do is to ask him. He may not want a bloody dog in his fancy house. The seven of us here may have already reached his bachelor limit. I drag myself back inside and explain the problem.

He responds by pointing to the laundry room. "Just put her here. I'll get out an old paint blanket for her to lay on."

Ma catches the end of his sentence and snaps. "We don't need no dirty dog sleeping in here. She might nip at the kids, with her being injured and all."

Tessa follows me, keeping her eyes on Taffy. "I'll sleep with my doggy. She needs me. She's my hero. She saved us!"

I'm too tired to argue, so I give in to my daughter and ignore Ma, who looks shocked. I check Taffy for obvious injuries. She doesn't have any broken bones but appears to be bruised and sore. She has a cut on her side from either being kicked or thrown into the bunker. Nick helps me swab it with hydrogen peroxide.

"See how it fizzes? It's cleaning out the germs. She'll be okay." He finishes and leaves the room.

Tessa hugs Taffy and speaks to her in a low voice.

He returns with an armload of blankets, sheets, and towels and gives one to Tessa to sleep on.

I give Tessa a hug. "Tessie, come get me if you need help."

She smiles and curls up next to Taffy. I hear her whisper, "I'm here, sweetie. You can go to sleep now."

We spread ourselves out among the different rooms.

Ma mutters under her breath as she hobbles to the couch to sleep. She leans her walking stick against the wall. Nonni's already asleep on the adjoining love seat. It's been a long day and night for all of us.

I sigh and turn off the lights in that room before I enter the guest room where Claire and the twins are already bunked.

I'm relieved my family is safe. And that we have somewhere to stay tonight that's not a bomb shelter, a burnt cabin, or dirty school bus. And if I have to stay awake one more minute, I'm going to keel right over on the linoleum floor.

At the crack of dawn, Nick, Claire, and I leave to take stock of the situation at our cabin. There's all kind of stuff out in the yard.

I pick up Ma's cast iron frying pan, my work pants, and a broken glass. The Star book is there along with my dress shoes. I pick up the dictionary where it's flung out in the dirt with a partly torn page sticking out with the word "perpetrator" circled in pencil. My heart races.

Part of the doorjamb is charred, but the door itself appears to be okay. Considering what happened, the actual fire damage is minimal but the smell of smoke is pervasive.

I step around pieces of the broken kerosene lantern and shards of dinner plates over the threshold into the room. The room's been torn apart, mattresses upended, boxes emptied, the babies' sleeping drawer turned over, and most of the contents of the icebox strewn across the floor.

The floor near the door and one of the mattresses are drenched from my dumping water onto the fire. Acrid smoke lingers in the air, and my throat itches. It's a miracle the log cabin didn't go up in blazes.

Claire grabs two intact baby bottles from the bottom shelf and a box of Gerber's rice cereal. Then she scrabbles around under the table and pulls out an item wrapped in a tea towel.

Gently pulling away the cloth, she reveals her unbroken relish dish. "My inheritance!" Her back is to me, and her shoulders shake. I put my arm around her. When I turn her around, her face is damp. I'm glad this piece of her childhood is in one piece.

As for the other damages to the cabin, I know that they're just things, and things can be fixed. I'm good at fixing things, but the feelings part is harder.

But I have plans, and whatever the future brings, it's all uphill from here.

We're going to be okay. I have to believe that. I do believe that.

Chapter 61
Nonni - Breaking Out

As soon as Daddy, Mama, and Uncle Nick return from checking the damage at the cabin, we get ready to drive to the sheriff's office.

Mama sighs. "I couldn't find something to wear at the cabin last night." She's still wearing the nightgown she had on last night, and it's streaked with dirt.

Even though she took a shower last night, she had to put it back on because she didn't have anything else to wear, and she's wearing one of Uncle Nick's shirts over it.

Mama says, "I'm so embarrassed. When we get back to his home, I'll wash something I scooped up from the mess at the cabin."

Daddy said, "Yeah, he has that washing machine he's always bragging about."

"And the house comes with hot water. What a thought. I just hope they don't judge me for how I look."

Daddy puts his arm around Mama's shoulders. "Well, they've seen you before during better days. Or were they better? Maybe not. Let's just get this over with."

We split our family into two vehicles and drive to the sheriff's office. We've all bathed in that indoor bathtub at this fancy-pants house, and I'm wearing some clean clothes Grandma packed up last night. Things are looking up.

The detective's ready to talk to us when we arrive. The man Daddy threw in the wheelbarrow spent the night behind bars, and he's now in a lineup waiting for us to identify him. His clothes look they've seen better days, too.

"I can point to the right man this time. I'm sure!" This morning I am strong. "He told me if I said anything, he'd hurt our family. He can't do that now, can he, Mama?"

Mama pats me on the shoulder. "No, honey. He can't do anything to us, ever again."

I stand tall. "I can do it this time."

The wrinkle between Mama's brows clears. "Honey, they'll tell us what to do next."

The detective motions. "Come with me, little lady. Then, Tessa's up next."

Tessa beams with importance.

Mama turns toward him with her jaw clinched. "She's too young to be put through this again. Even Nonni's too young!"

We've all heard this argument before, but this time, we're going to do it—and do it right.

Tessa protests. "I'm a big girl, Mama. I wanna help!

"Ma'am. We need to get this done so we can move ahead. Please."

Mama's eyes flash. "Don't ma'am me!"

Daddy moves to Mama, his lips tight. "I know, hon. I agree with you. But let's get this behind us."

The sheriff nods at my parents and points toward the doorway of the room with the one-way window.

It'll be the same routine as before except that we're all there.

He seats everyone on the bench outside the room except for me, and I follow him into the room. As he closes the door, I hear Tommy and Fee making their baby talk sounds, and I smile.

It's easy this time. The man is there. Second from the right.

"It's him!" I point without hesitation. "He's never been in one of the lineups before."

Even though that man stares at the window, like he's looking straight through it, I know he can't see me. But even if he could, I'd be safe. We *are* all safe from him. After all, we're here, together, in the sheriff's office.

"I know, little missy. Thanks for your help. Go sit with your family."

I join them feeling as if a load of those gray cinder blocks stacked up beside our new cement foundation has been lifted off my shoulders.

Tessa's next, and she hums as she skips into the room. When she emerges, she's beaming from ear to ear. "I did it, too! I told them, showed them, the red line around him. He's a bad, bad, very bad man." She takes a seat beside me on the bench.

Daddy follows Grandma Grace, and then finally it's Mama's turn. After she returns, she asks the detective, "Can you check the shoe tracing I left the other day against his?"

He steps into room nearby and returns with a paper, which he unfolds. "Be right back."

When he emerges from the room, he has a determined look on his face. "It's a match." He points to the slash on the outline of the shoe on the tracing. "Identical to the bottom of his sole."

Mama and Grandma give each other a long look.

The detective signals Daddy, Mama, and Grandma to him, but they're still close enough that I can hear.

"Your neighbor, Jack, and the victims of the gunnysack crimes are also coming in to identify this man in the lineup. I think we've got the right person nailed this time. He's not going anywhere."

Grandma huffs. "It's about time."

The big man shifts his weight and scratches his ear. "We've been looking for the man but didn't realize that there were two men committing crimes. Ironically, another man *was* identified as a peeping Tom, but that was for different crimes. Your little girl was right. She couldn't recognize him earlier because he wasn't there."

However, I know that even if I'd recognized that man, the perpetrator, in the first lineup, I would've protected my family with silence. Or at least I would have thought I was doing the right thing.

The man they'd arrested, the second time we were here, the one that someone identified as a peeping Tom, is completely unrelated to Donald Fricker, the man who's terrorized us for the last six months.

But things have changed now. Not only did I get my family out of the bomb shelter and away from him last night, but today, he is in this lineup.

By identifying him and speaking up, I've finally released myself from that stifling prison of silence, and I am free.

It's a miracle. Like Mama always says, the truth will set you free.

And she's right.
It has.

Chapter 62
Tessa - De Pot

I'm so happy I'm hopping on one foot. Finally, they called me, and I did point to the man.

I don't think they understand why I told them he was "Red, red, red." But they know he is bad. And I helped get him into trouble. That's the best thing of all.

I look at each face of my family. One at a time. Mama. Daddy. Nonni. Even the twins look happy as they gnaw on their fists.

Mama puts her hand into the pocket in her nightie. I see it moving around as she feels for something. "Detective?"

He turns to her with a puzzled look on his face.

She takes out her hand with something small and square in it. "Here you go." She hands it to him.

"Ah. The photo." He squints at it. "Where'd you get this?"

Mama's mouth turns down at the corners. "Nonni found it last night in the backpack and showed it to me right before the man broke into our cabin."

I look from Mama to Nonni. I must have slept through this because I don't remember it.

Mama bites her lip. "I shoved it under 'de pot' just as he burst into the cabin. When we returned last night, that was about the only thing that he hadn't turned upside down, so I grabbed it and stuffed it into my pocket. I forgot about it until now."

He wrinkles his forehead. "What's 'de pot' "?

"The porcelain chamber pot under the bed so the girls don't have to make a trip out to the outhouse in the middle of the night."

When I hear Mama say "de pot," I chant along. "Put de pot under de bed and put out de light."

Mama looks at me, and one corner of her mouth puckers a little bit.

The detective looks back down at the photo, nods, and calls Nonni over. "Little lady, I need you to do something for me. Can you be brave again?"

I look at my sister as she nods her head. She replies with a big grin on her face. "Yes. I can."

"It's okay, honey. We have to do this, and I'm right here by your side." Mama sighs and gives her a soft squeeze around the shoulders.

He shows my sister the photo, but not before I see it. "Tell me what you know about this photo."

Nonni straightens her shoulders. She opens her mouth and speaks. "It's the picture that man showed us the day he stopped us. Said it was a picture of Jack's wife. He wanted me to point to where she lived, but I didn't."

I tap my toes on the floor. Maybe they'll listen to me now that I've identified that man. "She didn't point to it. I didn't point either!"

"You sure this is the same photo?" He looks from my sister to me.

She nods. "Yes. I am. And it's the photo I found last night in the cabin."

I jump up and down. "Yes! I saw it, too. When the man showed it to us."

Mama looks at me with her mouth stretched straight and her eyebrows lowered. "Tessie! You saw it, too?"

I pat her on her hand. "It's okay, Mama. That's what I keep trying to tell everyone, but they don't want to listen to me. That lady is about to take a bath."

Mama looks from me to Daddy, who has his arms crossed so tight his fingers are turning white.

Mama turns to us. "Girls. I'm sad you had to see this again, and I want you to forget all about it. We're putting all this behind us. Okay?"

She opens her arms, and we scamper into them.

The detective slides the photo into a plastic envelope and sets it on the desk behind him. "This is an excellent piece of evidence to tie him to the girls. And it matches Nonni's story exactly."

"And mine!" I don't want them to forget that I helped catch that man, too.

I'm so happy I jump up and down a few times. I want to grab the detective by the knees and twirl him around. I bet I could do it, too!

He looks at Nonni and me. "Thank you, little ladies. You're all safe now. We're moving him back into the locked cell where he's not going to be bothering you, or anyone else."

He takes Nonni's hand in his big paw-like grasp. "Thank you for identifying him and the photo. You're a brave girl."

Then he turns to me and takes my hand. "Thank you, Tessa, for collaborating."

I look at Daddy, who says, "He means you did a good job helping your sister. You both helped solve the mystery."

"Oh!" I feel a smile creep from my lips to my eyes.

That's a word I want to mark in the dictionary just like Nonni and Daddy do. *Collaborating*. That's me.

I've been collaborating and didn't even know it. "We did it together."

Mama pulls both of us into another group hug. "You did good, my little honey buns. I'm proud of you!"

And we squeeze her back.

Chapter 63
Gracie - Revelations

I motion to the detective. "Need to talk with you, too. Sonny, keep your eyes on the youngsters."

I hand Thomas to Rand and motion Tessa to sit with Fiona on the bench. "Follow me, Claire."

"I ain't told you something." I wrinkle my brow. "There's more evidence. Gotta fetch it."

I try my doggonist not to limp as I head toward my car with that stick. I root around and return with what I need to show them.

"Take a look." I hold the rag doll in one hand and tug her oversized bloomers down with the other.

Three fat rolls of hundred-dollar bills drop onto the floor. Before the sheriff can scoop them up, I reach into the pocket of my flannel nightgown, hand him a small bag with a couple of rings, necklaces, and ladies' wristwatches in it.

"That's not all. I found his blue rucksack in the shelter with this stuff in it and hid it in the cabin. Down in the bunker are a couple of those big nasty gunnysacks folded into square bundles. That's what he was coming back for. That—and us'n."

Rand sits with the girls, his head tipped toward us, listening, his mouth open like a fly catcher. None of this is news to me, but mebbe we should have told the Sheriff or Detective Hunter or Rand about it sooner.

I see Nonni tip her head toward us to eavesdrop. That girl's sharp ears will get her in trouble someday.

"I washed up that checkered blanket, too. It's wrapped around Taffy in the truck out front. That was in his backpack, too."

"Ma'am. That's certainly helpful evidence. Where's the backpack now?"

"I threw it out the window when he barged in on us."

It's 'bout time we got this off our chests. I'm feeling relief even as I'm confessing. Carrying secrets around is a burden I don't need.

When we're finished up here, we split up to head to either Randall's truck or Sally to leave. On my way through the parking lot, I kick the tire of that wretched, evil man's truck with my good foot and almost fall down.

"Good riddance!"

Chapter 64
Nonni - The Safe Zone

I'm ready to begin my new life now that we've survived everything. Mama was like Wonder Woman from the comic books. And Grandma Grace is my hero, too.

They got us from the shelter and to the bus. They kept the man from finding us, and they kept us safe.

Then Daddy found us, captured the man, and rescued us. He's my hero.

Even Tessie helped a little. And Taffy was a big hero when she bit him and defended us even though she's still healing up.

And I did my part, too, in getting us out of the shelter with that board and crowbar. Oh, and I identified him and the photo for the sheriff.

It was a family project.

Daddy puts his hands in his pockets. "Sorry, kiddos, about the grand opening. We have to fix the cabin up so we can go back. That's more important."

I've been looking forward to the barbecue at Daddy's work tomorrow.

I swallow my disappointment along with my dream of biting into a juicy cheeseburger with lettuce, tomatoes, and pickles—and a little mustard. No mayo. Just like the day we bought our school shoes and Mama took us out for lunch at the diner.

And my vision of jumping into the lake for a swim has evaporated in a split second. That would have been the treat of a lifetime, and now it's not going to happen.

But being alive is even better, so I guess I can't complain.

Uncle Nick's home is way bigger than our cabin and has two bedrooms, a living room, and a kitchen. It has light switches and water faucets and an inside toilet. And a bathtub.

Last night I fell asleep immediately and didn't wake up until morning. And now we're back at his house. I wouldn't mind getting used to all of this. It's a luxury taking a hot bath, watching cartoons, and nestling down onto blankets spread out on the living room floor.

Grandma warns us, "Don't get to expectin' that you're gonna lay around gawking at the television. No siree! We aim to be home in a shake of a rooster tail."

Taffy limps away from the washing machine as Mama takes a load of clothes out of it to hang up out back.

"You girls'll go back to school next week, just like regular."

On Monday, after a quick breakfast, Tessa and I return to school. Mama talks to Tessa and my teachers. I'm not close enough to hear, and she doesn't tell us what she said.

At lunch, Mr. Parra stops by the lunch table and speaks to me in a low voice. "Nonni. I'm proud of you for being brave and telling what you knew."

I flush with pride, and my heart is lighter than it's been in a long time.

"When we get back inside, everyone's going to

write in their journals. This might be a good thing for you to write about. You know, get it out of your head and onto paper." He winks at me.

I consider his words. Writing down what happened this weekend, well, this year, would help. Although I don't want something like this to happen to anyone else, it has given me lots to think about. Someday, it might even make a good story for someone to read.

Writing settles me down. It lets me figure out what's happening. To me. And to our family. Maybe I'll even be an author when I grow up, if that's something people actually do.

After school, Grandma picks us up in Sally instead of Tessie and me riding the bus, and she drives us home to our cabin. Mama's there with the babies napping. Grandma shushes us with her finger on her lips.

I stare out the window, glad to be back at our little home even if we don't have a proper inside bathroom and it's not all modern like Uncle Nick's. I've missed our nightly ritual of putting "de pot under de bed." What's the matter with me?

It feels good and right to be back home. I'm not afraid anymore, and my heart finally feels free.

Tonight, the babies sit propped up in their makeshift baby chairs, gnawing on their fists. My parents are next to them at the picnic table, and Daddy's arm is around Mama's shoulders, smiling down at her. Grandma rustles around in the cabin, humming under her breath.

After darkness falls on us, we lay on the still warm ground on our mattresses in sleeping bags with Taffy by our side while the cabin airs out so the smoke smell can fade.

I look up at the sky and spot Orion looking down and guarding us. My eyes scan for the Little Dipper and Pleiades. All my favorite constellations. As my lids droop, the Milky Way blurs, and my soul sighs with contentment.

That bad man, Donald Fricker, is locked up now, and the sheriff says he's going to stay that way for a long time.

I'm ready to make another Zig Zag. It won't be long before Tommy and Fiona will be walking, and I'll teach them how to play it, too.

Imagine the four of us running and laughing free through my mazes. I can do that in front of our home in this big and beautiful desert.

We'll have a brand new Safe Zone that can't be erased by car tires or predators or anything else that life may bring our way.

Chapter 65
Claire - The New Normal

We've been back home a couple of days. In comparison, Nick's house was civilized with its modern amenities, but I was ready to head back to our own humble home.

The damage isn't as extensive as I thought it would be. Rand and Nick have taken the door off its hinges so they can repair the doorjamb. We've moved most of the items out front to dry although that maniac had already tossed quite a few of them out in his tirade. The wet mattresses have mostly dried in the sun.

On the day of the barbeque, Rand asked Nick to pick up his paycheck and tell the boss he'd be in to see him early the next week. We all, especially Tessie and Nonni, were disappointed we didn't get to go to the grand opening, but I admit it feels good to be back at the cabin. And it's even better to have Rand around.

We have lots to do and a short amount of time to get it done. We're working hard to clean and organize everything, but it's gonna take us some time to get that lingering odor of smoke out of the cabin and our belongings and our heads.

Tonight, after the girls and the twins are tucked in and sleeping under the stars, and Randall's sitting at the table outside by the kerosene lamp working something out on graph paper, I motion to Gracie. I grab my flashlight, and we walk around the perimeter of the house to where I'd set the thread traps.

They're still there and still tangled. "Hmmmm. I wasn't imagining this." It reassures me to know that my fears were based on fact and not on hormones or wild flights of imagination. Maybe I'll just leave them there for a bit longer as proof for myself that I didn't dream all of this up. That I wasn't on the verge of losing my mind.

My scalp prickles. I'd seen the man for just a few minutes on the day when he'd come to fill the water tank. That's the last time he threatened Nonni alone.

Although I'd been in the cabin with the kids most of the time, nursing one of the babies, I'd missed this entire interaction, and it still shakes me up to realize that *he* had been on our land, looking at us, and checking out our home.

Because we always kept the girls in the cabin when the water truck came, I hadn't even considered that he'd seen Nonni. Why didn't I catch the unease in the air that day?

But already things are changing, and I'm grateful that Nonni could finally point him out on the other side of the glass. In the days since, she's transformed before our eyes from a timid cottontail bunny, ready to bolt, into a new child, full of confidence.

Tessie's been humming and drawing and reading to the babies. And everywhere she goes, that yellow dog limps along behind her.

We're all breathing easier even though it's going to take time for us to get things running smoothly.

"Let's go make sure that door to the durn bomb shelter is shut tight. Last thing we need is for one of 'em girls to fall in and break their necks after all we been through." Gracie maneuvers ahead, leaning on her stick.

"Yes, let's check this out, too." I point to the water tower. Everything looks the same except for one of the missing tubs Rand used to extinguish the flames and then we filled with soapy water to clean the ashy cabin. It's on the front porch. And he's put a new latch on the outhouse door so it won't bang in the wind.

I follow Gracie past the wooden structure out into the brush, aiming my beam ahead of her to the new lock Rand attached to the shelter door. A bright band of yellow crime tape is curled up on the dirt next to it.

While I'm filled with conflicting feelings that have grooved their way into my being, and I know that letting go of fear is at the top of the list, hope pokes her head out just a little.

Maybe once Gracie goes home, after all we've been through, our family will mend, and Rand and I'll rekindle our love. With a little softening on my part, I could give up my stubbornness, which I've been clinging to. I realize I want, no, I need, some peace. And romance. Sweet talking and hugs would go a long way with me nowadays.

We'll be the happy family I'd longed for as a child, a dream to which I've always clung.

I'm nothing if not a realist, however. Even with that nasty Donald Fricker behind bars, it'll be a while before we adjust to our new normal, as Rand calls it.

And for that blessing, I dip my head and say, "Thank you, Jesus." As if in agreement, a wave of soft cackles drift out into the calm desert air from the chicken coop.

Yes, we can pick up where we left off—and move ahead into a bright, new beginning, but it will take time. And we have a lot of that ahead of us.

Chapter 66
Nonni - Epilogue

All these things happened more than twenty years ago.

Exactly one week after we returned to our cabin and while we were shaking off the terror leading to the capture of this evil man, President Kennedy announced that the Russians had missiles in Cuba pointed at us, ready to strike.

Those thirteen days in October of 1962 will be remembered in American history forever. During that same month, my own family had been under attack, again, by Fricker, and those dates are just as much a part of our family history, too.

I hadn't quite given up scanning for nuclear bombs on the horizon, and now I added vigilance for missiles from Cuba that might be streaking through the sky toward us.

Daddy and Mama swept up the glass and restocked the fallout shelter with food, supplies, and a new flashlight in case we had to hunker down there.

Finally, on November 20, President Kennedy declared the crisis with Cuban leader Fidel Castro and Soviet Premier Khrushchev almost over.

We cheered, and slowly our sense of danger faded. Our president had kept us safe. But never could we have imagined that he'd be gone in a year from an assassin's bullet.

Eventually, however, I switched my worry about missiles and bombs to searching for satellites in the heavens. After all, we were in the space race against the Soviet Union, too, and that didn't seem as dangerous as them trying to blow us up.

By then, I no longer worried about Donald Fricker, who was in jail awaiting trial. Daddy found a job near home and spent every night with us, and Mama quit laying her thread traps. Our unease slowly dissipated as we established our new lives.

Grandma Grace signed the deed of the cabin over to Daddy before she returned to her home at the beach. I think Mama missed her a little when she left. I know we kids did. A lot.

Fifteen months later, I was ten and a half years old. As the key witness to the encounter my sister and I had lived through, I testified at the trial and heard the tail end of the testimony of one of the "gunnysack" women.

When it was my turn to take the stand, I publicly pointed out the perpetrator and described what had happened to Tessa and me.

As my final act of courage, I had ripped out any vestige of guilt from my heart by its roots. I knew I had saved my family by proving his guilt in court where it counted most.

With testimony and evidence connecting him to the gunnysack crimes, a jury found Fricker guilty on multiple counts including the violent physical and mental damage he'd inflicted on his gunnysack victims.

It wasn't until I was a teenager that I understood the enormity of his lewd request and what might have happened to my sister and me had Jack not driven by at that exact time. Now as an adult, I realize how God protected us.

According to the newspaper, Fricker's been granted parole this week, twenty years later. My heart has been doing a nervous time-step ever since I read that this morning.

I take a deep breath and turn my mind to remembering how a couple of years after his arrest, we'd celebrated a grand opening for our new home Daddy'd built, located directly next to our log cabin.

Grandma Grace returned for the week, bringing a carload of her preserves, fresh baked honey wheat bread, and her no-bake oatmeal cookies.

I'll never forget that day. We turned on the faucets. Water flowed. We flipped the switches. Lights lit. We flushed the indoor toilet over and over until Mama ordered us to stop.

After we added a refrigerator, we ate fancy Jello salad with every dinner. And Mama baked angel food cake for us, happy that we still had a family chicken coop that could provide the thirteen egg whites the recipe called for.

We'd re-entered modern civilization and no longer lived off the grid. It had been a community effort as people moved into the empty miles around us, seeking their own dreams. A family bought the farmhouse across from the Lone Wolf Colony, and another family built a new home next to the abandoned well where Tessa lost her shoe. I'm pretty sure that they filled that deathtrap in with dirt.

Sometimes after we were put to bed, we kids crawled down the hall on our hands and knees to spy on Mama and Daddy sitting side by side on the couch, holding hands, and watching reruns of *I Love Lucy*. Our black-and-white television with its three stations seemed like a miracle.

When the twins were old enough to toddle around in the yard, one of their favorite activities was to grab rocks from the perimeter of the Zig Zag game and throw them at Tessa and me. Surprisingly, Fiona Grace had the stronger pitch, and, later, softball became her sport. Taffy limped closely behind Tessa like Peter Pan's shadow through the remainder of her life.

During Easter week of my seventh grade, Daddy took Mama on a surprise trip to San Francisco for the honeymoon they'd never had. They sipped on hot chocolate at Ghirardelli Square and rode a cable car. They took a tour of the harbor and Alcatraz, and they searched in little gift shops in China Town for toy dragons to bring back to us.

We kids stayed with Grandma Grace and went to the beach three times. The twins loved being knocked down by waves, and we ate tuna sandwiches sprinkled with sand. Tessa got pulled underwater by an undertow, but I saved her. Again.

By then, Daddy and Uncle Nick's chicken enterprise had fallen on hard times. It's a tough business to maintain out in the desert.

It turns out that chickens are fairly stupid. Whenever coyotes howled, they would crush themselves against the outer fences in a panic. They'd deliberately stand in the free-range yards of the high-tech coops and tip their open beaks to drink in the occasional thunderstorm downpour, resulting in their having speckled gizzards.

After they did that a couple of times, making them

impossible to sell, Daddy traded in his chicken business for one in construction where Uncle Nick was, and still is, his partner.

Year by year, our apple tree grew along with seasonal vegetables. Mama took it as a testament that there was life in the desert that would sustain us. The flying red ants deleted our home from their migration route once we took down the water tower.

And, unbelievably, no snakes slithered across our five acres after Fricker's arrest. It was like an invisible wall surrounded our property, protecting us in our own Garden of Eden. Our personal Safe Zone. One that didn't include serpents.

We kids grew up fairly isolated from issues gripping much of our country during those years, but as I learned about the Civil Rights Movement, the death of Martin Luther King Jr., and Vietnam protests, my heart was tender for the struggles of our world.

I knew I was born to be a writer from a young age beginning with stories about sand fairies for Tessa to Mr. Parra encouraging me to journal about my experiences in 1962. I wrote continuously but didn't win my first award until my favorite high-school English teacher, Mr. Stalcup, entered one of my survival stories into a contest.

That's where *Gunnysack Hell* comes in. I'm now finishing my degree in creative writing, and I've documented my childhood ordeal through the eyes of my family members in this novel. I hope I did them justice.

It's taken me decades to realize that the lasting story wasn't so much about Fricker but more how we couldn't be beaten down by evil. About how love and courage prevailed in the most unlikely of settings. About how when I could finally speak out, I felt redeemed and empowered.

And it's true. The truth does set you free. Even with him out now, he'll have no hold on my life.

I make three conscious decisions every day, life lessons I learned from Mama. To dwell on the positive, to accept life as an adventure, and to keep the faith. Things work out, and love is doled out in small bites of daily living.

The memory of Mama praying at my childhood picnic table brings a smile to my soul that no one, even Fricker, can cloud.

I can still hear her soft voice saying, "Thank you, Jesus. And pass the Kraft Dinner Ring. Amen."

Yes, this is my story.

Our story.

A word about the author...

Nancy Brashear lives in Orange County, California, with her husband, Patrick, and their rescue dog, Goldie, where her grown children and seven grandgirls have supported her writing adventures. A professor emeritus in English, she has published short stories, poems, academic articles, and textbook chapters. *Gunnysack Hell* is her debut fiction novel and was inspired by a true-crime event. And, yes, she did live off-grid with her family in a homestead cabin in the Mojave Desert when she was a child.

Learn more at:

nancybrashear.com